Praise for Michelle Diener's *The Emperor's Conspiracy*,
a *Publishers Weekly* "Best Book" of the Year

"Diener delivers a rousing read."

—*Publishers Weekly*

"An exciting historical romance perfect for fans of *The Tudors*!
What an amazing plot . . . with a twist of intrigue. It was so difficult
to put this book down."

—*Fresh Fiction*

"If you love historical novels with a touch of suspense and a hint of
mystery, Michelle Diener's latest novel, *The Emperor's Conspiracy*, is
sure to please. The author has a knack for writing snappy, action
packed novels . . . pure delight for those who love to escape into a
page-turner."

—*Historical Novel Review*

"A fantastic novel! Michelle Diener has a way of bringing the past
alive. . . . I was entranced."

—*Peeking Between the Pages*

"Ripe with passion. . . . If you're a fan of historical fiction that incor-
porates specific events from the past, then I highly recommend this
book."

—*Girls in the Stacks*

"Packed with unexpected twists and turns, solid prose, always-fascinating court intrigue, and a unique story."

—*Diary of a Book Addict*

"Dramatically original with imaginative scenes of suspense and one mystery after another."

—*Single Titles*

"One fast-paced historical fiction novel! It reads like a thriller."

—*Girls Just Reading*

"The characters in this book are wonderful and believable. . . . An interesting, emotional, and dramatic story."

—*Romance Reviews Today*

"An action-adventure-mystery-historical that grabs the reader on page one and doesn't let go."

—Kate Emerson, author of *The King's Damsel*

"An enormous talent! I was absolutely enthralled and thoroughly enjoyed every last page of this story!"

—*Affaire de Coeur*

"Diener has set a standard for what good historical fiction ought to be."

—*Luxury Reading*

Also by Michelle Diener

The Emperor's Conspiracy

Keeper of the King's Secrets

In a Treacherous Court

BANQUET
OF
LIES

a novel

MICHELLE DIENER

GALLERY BOOKS

NEW YORK   LONDON   TORONTO   SYDNEY   NEW DELHI

Gallery Books
A Division of Simon & Schuster, Inc.
1230 Avenue of the Americas
New York, NY 10020

First Gallery Books trade paperback edition October 2013

GALLERY BOOKS and colophon are trademarks of Simon & Schuster, Inc.

For information about special discounts for bulk purchases, please contact Simon & Schuster Special Sales at 1-866-506-1949 or business@simonandschuster.com.

The Simon & Schuster Speakers Bureau can bring authors to your live event. For more information or to book an event, contact the Simon & Schuster Speakers Bureau at 1-866-248-3049 or visit our website at www.simonspeakers.com.

Library of Congress Cataloging-in-Publication Data

Diener, Michelle.
   Banquet of lies / Michelle Diener. — 1st Gallery Books trade paperback edition.
      p. cm.
   1. Courts and courtiers—Fiction. 2. Great Britain—History—Henry VIII, 1509–1547—Fiction. I. Title. PR9619.4.D54B36 2013
823'.92—dc23

Designed by Jaime Putorti

Manufactured in the United States of America

10 9 8 7 6 5 4 3 2 1

ISBN 978-1-4516-8445-2
ISBN 978-1-4516-8446-9 (ebook)

ACKNOWLEDGMENTS

Thanks to the real Madame and Monsieur Levéel, and Eric and Nadine, for welcoming me to their home all those years ago and giving me homemade Reine Claude jam and brioche every morning for breakfast, thus spoiling me for life. Thanks also to Edie, as always, and to my beta reader, Jo. Much thanks to my agent, Marlene Stringer, as well as my editor, Micki Nuding, and all the amazing people at Simon & Schuster who helped send this book out into the world in its best possible form.

1

STOCKHOLM
LATE FEBRUARY 1812

"I hear from the Countess de Salisburg that you collect recipes, Miss Barrington?" The plump diplomat's wife standing beside Gigi on the edge of the dance floor crinkled her pretty forehead in confusion.

"I do." Gigi wished the countess had not said anything. No one in the gilt-edged circles she and her father occasionally brushed up against had ever understood her interest in recipes and cooking. "My father's work takes me to such interesting places, and while he records the fairy tales and folktales from the areas we visit, I like to ask the women what they cook and if they would be willing to share their recipes."

"What do you do with the recipes?" The woman looked genuinely interested now.

"I'm compiling a reference work of dishes from the cultures of Europe. But mainly I follow them."

"Follow them . . ." Confused, the woman looked around

the crowded room, as if the people swirling around them could help her. "How?"

Gigi smiled. "The usual way. In the kitchen."

"You *make* the dishes?" The woman tapped Gigi on the arm with her fan. "With the servants?" Her voice was a squeak.

"With the chef who has accompanied us for the last ten years."

"Ah."

A chef was different. A giant step up from a cook.

Gigi always invoked Pierre's status when the questions became too tiresome. Cooking was considered a strange passion in a young lady. And it *was* a passion.

For her, what people ate, and how they ate, was just as interesting as the stories they told.

An uncomfortable silence fell between her and the diplomat's wife, and she raised her eyes to the clock. Five more minutes had ticked by since the English ambassador to Sweden, Sir Thornton, had come looking for her father, but he had yet to return.

Her father and the ambassador had met in the early hours of this morning, but something must have happened between then and now to have Sir Thornton so on edge.

It was time to find him.

She murmured her excuses and made for the glass doors leading to the garden, slipping out without attracting any attention.

The glitter of a party in full swing at Tessin Palace lit Gigi's way, the chandeliers casting a warm glow. Behind her, the rich and titled of Sweden, along with most of the diplomats in Stockholm, laughed and danced, the sound pleasing and merry.

She took the stairs into the garden carefully, her eyes adjusting to the semi-darkness.

Cold in her thin silk gown, she shivered and felt a sudden, inexplicable dread of the darkness before her. It slowed every step she took away from the bright chatter, as if the air became more solid the farther from the light she went. She shrugged off the sensation and forced herself to run lightly down the rest of the stairs, ignoring the prickle of irrational fear at the back of her neck.

The gravel of the garden path was sharp beneath the thin soles of her shoes, although at least free of snow after the warmer weather these last few days. Low box hedges curved and dipped in an intricate pattern before her. She caught the faintest scent of lavender. It was nearing the end of winter, but come summer, she guessed this jewel of a garden would be redolent with the perfume.

No sound could be heard over the muffled merrymaking of the ball, except the murmur of the fountain directly in front of her.

She knew her father was out here somewhere. She'd seen him leave, and had watched the door for his return ever since Sir Edward Thornton had come to ask for him.

She'd never known him to keep anyone waiting this long.

She'd certainly never had to go looking for him before, and she'd been his companion at diplomatic functions since she was sixteen.

She skirted the outside of the intricate box hedge, her satin slippers soundless, moving past dark painted doors set flush against a smooth, white wall. Someone barked out a laugh, and she stopped to listen.

Voices came from the back of the garden.

She followed the sound, walking cautiously on the bruising gravel, and stepped at last onto a smooth brick path that led into an even smaller garden, tucked between two curving walls, directly behind the stables.

She hesitated. If her father was involved in a private conversation, she did not wish to intrude. The men with whom he occasionally had special business usually didn't want to be recognized or seen in his company.

But there had been something like worry on Sir Thornton's face when he'd approached her the second time to ask if she'd seen her father. And when they'd been interrupted by a Swedish nobleman, the ambassador had lied smoothly about their topic of conversation, and pretended a relaxed, indolent air that was at odds with the tight grip of his hands on the edges of his waistcoat.

"All will be well." The unmistakable sound of her father's voice was clear.

In the limited light, Gigi saw his companion touch his hat in farewell and walk toward the stables, slipping through a door.

She was holding back, waiting for the stranger to be completely gone, when a shadow detached itself from one of the trees and lunged at her father—like an evil *stallu* from Lapland's Sami folktales come to life, using the darkness to consume its prey.

Her father gave a hiss of pain, and Gigi saw the gleam of a knife. She stepped closer, ready to shout, and at that moment her father turned his head, jerking away from the blade, and caught her eye.

With a quick movement, he lifted a finger to his lips and then indicated she get down.

"What is it?" The man holding him looked sharply toward the palace, but she was down by then, crouching behind a waist-high marble block.

"Who are you?" Her father was his usual calm self.

"No one you'll need worry about after tonight. Just tell me where it is."

"Why would I, when you've just let me know that I'll die, whether I tell you or not?"

"Because you have a daughter. Giselle."

He spoke so normally, so conversationally, she had the terrifying image of him in a drawing room, speaking about the weather and the social scene, indistinguishable from any other man, completely hiding his true nature.

"In a few moments, if you don't tell me where it is, she's going to receive a note from you, in handwriting very like your own, asking her to meet you outside. My little friend managed to keep you busy for some time, and I'm sure you've been missed by now. She'll most likely be so eager to find you, she won't question it."

"I thought Frederik's concerns a little too trivial to require such an urgent meeting." Her father made no mention of the threat against her.

The man at his back noticed. "And your daughter? Nothing to say? She's a pretty thing. I might make her very *intimate* acquaintance, if you don't cooperate." He spoke with no emotion.

Fear hammered a hard, cold nail into her heart.

"My daughter isn't easy to fool." Her father's words were curt.

The shadow man was silent for a moment, as if thinking how to escalate the threat. Time was not his friend; at any moment someone else could wander out into the garden. Even Thornton might come looking.

He finally shrugged. "I have men working as staff at the ball. If she doesn't heed the note, they will find a way to get her out."

"On what signal? You're here alone, as far as I can make out." Her father was dismissive.

Gigi shrank even smaller. Her father was warning her there could be more of them in the garden.

"The signal will be my failure to return to the party by a certain time." The man spoke coldly, unwillingly.

For the first time, Gigi realized what she had been too shocked to before—he spoke in English, the perfect English of an Englishman. This was a traitor—not an enemy spy.

Her father seemed to deflate. "I don't have it, you fool. I'd have given it to you to safeguard my daughter—you're quite right. But I don't have it to give. Your intelligence is wrong. I was the red herring this time; it's already gone. Long gone."

He spoke with frustration and anger, but Gigi knew he was lying. She had never seen her father at work in the field before, had never seen this side to him.

"You must be lying." The shadow man spoke through gritted teeth, and her father gave an involuntary cry, as if he were hurt.

Giselle peered around the marble block, her legs shaking with the desperate need to run to his rescue.

"No!" Her father briefly looked her way again as if he spoke to her, not the shadow man; as if he knew what she intended. "Please," he whispered. "I would sacrifice anything for my daughter. Her safety is worth more to me than my life. I do not have it." He ground the last words out between gritted teeth. "Search me. You'll see the truth."

There was the sound of rough handling, of clothes being torn and thrown off.

"Take off your boots."

She looked again and saw her father bending, tugging off his boots. The moon found a small break in the clouds and shone, silver-bright, down on the garden for a few moments; she could make out blood at his throat, and his jacket, waistcoat and white linen shirt were ripped.

The shadow man's face was still in darkness, but she could see his arm, his hand, with the knife gripped tight, gleaming in the moonlight.

She started to rise, and her father caught her eye as he pulled off his second boot.

"Please don't," he whispered.

"Begging now, Barrington?" The shadow man forced her father to his knees, the knife still near his throat, and Gigi saw that he held a pistol to her father's back as well. No wonder he hadn't tried to escape.

She tucked herself back into her hiding place, shaking.

The boots must have been checked, for she heard them kicked over in disgust.

"You *must* have it. I saw you meet with Thornton this morning—"

"A red herring, as I told you. The real document went this afternoon. The courier's had a head start while you and your spies have watched me."

"You'll regret that, Barrington." The shadow man's voice was frighteningly devoid of emotion. "I won't be made a fool of—and your daughter might be more forthcoming than you. I'll make it a point to find out." He was breathing heavily, making a lie of his calm tone. "You can think about that while you burn in hell."

There was a shot. A terrible, final shot, and Gigi bit down on her knuckles to prevent herself from crying out.

Her father had died rather than reveal her; she would not dishonor his last wish.

She heard a low curse, and then the sound of a man walking down the path directly toward her. She curled even smaller, flush up against the marble pedestal.

He walked straight past her.

He would see her if he looked back, so she slid around the block until she was on the far side with her father.

She crawled to him on her hands and knees, her fingers reaching out to touch his face.

She had hoped. . . . But there would be no last words, no last spark of life. His eyes stared sightlessly up at clouds edged silver by the moon.

He was truly gone.

She looked back down the garden to the palace and saw a dark figure climbing the stairs to the ballroom.

He would be looking for her now, if his final words hadn't just been a cruel taunt. And he'd be looking for the document he had killed her father for.

The document her father had given to her minutes after he left the ambassador early this morning, for safekeeping. As he always did.

2

The Duke of Wittaker's grand mansion, set beside St. James's Park in London, was lit warmly despite the early morning hour.

Gigi ignored the coachman's curious look when she instructed him to take her to the back entrance, dressed in her finery as she was. Exhaustion made her light-headed, and she stumbled as she took the steps down to the gravel drive. "Please wait."

Her journey, from the coach ride from Stockholm to Gothenburg, to the ship to Dover, and the coach to London, had passed in a blur of pain, memories and rage. She couldn't remember a single thing that had happened in the last five days, and she needed to stop that.

She needed to *think*.

She left her trunks loaded on the top of the coach, since she doubted she could stay here. But perhaps Georges would be able to send her somewhere safe for a night or two, so she could sleep, and plan her way forward.

She climbed the steps to the kitchens with a smile, even though she was so tired it was an effort to put one foot in front of the other without falling. Georges always said he would never work in a home that had a subterranean kitchen. He'd never go back to a hellhole like the patisserie in Paris where he started out, with its dark, smoky cellar-kitchens, now he was a celebrated chef.

She stepped into a kitchen in the throes of preparing breakfast. She was glad she hadn't arrived just before dinner. Then, no matter how much Georges loved her, he wouldn't have given her more than a concerned glance as he got on with his job.

Eyes turned in her direction as she opened the door and stepped inside. There was a cry from the far end of the room; then Georges was making his way toward her, fierce as a hussar, trampling down those in his way.

"*Ma petite! Mon petit chou!*" He grabbed her in a tight hug, and for the first time in the five days since she'd seen her father struck down, she felt safe.

"Please speak only French," she had the wit to whisper in his ear, speaking in French herself. She was aware of every eye on them, and she wanted no one to hear her name, or anything else about her.

He gave her a strange look, pursing his lips under his thick mustache, but he nodded briefly. Then he looked around the kitchen, raising his arms and clapping his hands so suddenly that Gigi jumped, as did everyone else in the room.

"Thierry! You take over, and do not let me down. Every

plate to be *parfait, comprends?*" He scowled at a thin, diminutive man in an apron, pointing a threatening finger at him.

Then he took her arm and swept her into a room off the kitchen. Gigi didn't think she imagined the sigh of relief from every person behind her just before Georges closed the door, leaving his staff to their own devices for a while.

"What is it, Giselle?" Georges grasped her shoulders with both hands. "What has happened?"

"My father was murdered." Her voice wavered, but she had to leave again in a few short minutes to find a place to stay, so she mercilessly crushed the pain that threatened to rise up and consume her. She glanced around to compose herself. The small sitting room led into a study, and beyond, to a closed door. Georges's bedroom, she guessed.

Her body cried out for a safe bed to sleep in.

The bone-shaking journey across Sweden to Gothenburg had taken a full twenty-four hours, and she knew without doubt that if her father hadn't already arranged it, hadn't already planned that they were to leave the party at Tessin Palace and get straight into the coach, already packed with their things, the shadow man would have run her to ground before she'd left Stockholm.

"Murder?" Georges let his hands fall. "You are certain?"

"I witnessed it." She turned away and drew in a deep breath as she got herself and the threatening tears under control. "Georges, I'm afraid the people who killed my father will work out I'm in London if I send word to Pierre. He's still in Stockholm, cooking for the Countess de Salisburg. Please, find some very discreet way of letting him know I'm safe."

"Of course." Georges stroked her arm, soothing her like she was a small child. And no doubt to him she was. He and Pierre always thought of her as she'd been when she was ten, grieving for her mother, hungry for something to do and for the sound of French around her.

"Thank you." She drew in a deep breath. "I must go. Please don't let anyone know I'm back. No one. It is dangerous for you, and for me."

Georges frowned, looking so fierce Gigi wished the shadow man was here now so that Georges could tear him apart. Or chop him with his cleaver.

"You're going home to Goldfern House?" he asked.

She shook her head. "That is the first place the man who's after me will look. I have to find somewhere else. Perhaps an inn."

He smoothed his mustache. "Would you want to be hidden but still be able to move about, or do you want to hunker down like a fox in a hole?"

"Why?"

"There is a job I hear about. I remember it because it is at a house three or four down from Goldfern. Too small a job for me, or most of the chefs in London. No prestige, you understand? Just cooking for one man, Lord Aldridge. He will pay well, but that is not the only reason to take a job. There will hardly be any parties—he is a young man, and has no other family. He will dine out, be invited out. It would be a waste of talent for me, and I am happy where I am, with my fine, high kitchen." He gave a grin, transforming from a dark demon to a cheeky boy, despite the deep grooves in his face.

"But for someone like you, who can cook like an angel, but wants time to herself and a place to hide—who would look for the daughter of Sir Barrington in the kitchens of a small town house, almost next door to her family home, eh?"

To be right near Goldfern. To be able to keep watch on it, and see if the shadow man came to look for her there, invisible under her guise as cook? The rage that was both icy with hate and hot with vengeance rose up in her, and her hands became tight fists against her thighs. "That would be a very good place to hide."

"*Bon*." Georges walked through into his study and pulled out a sheet of paper with the duke's crest on the letterhead. He sat down at his desk. "I will write a reference for you so you will get the position. They will not turn you away after they read this, I promise you."

Georges's brow was raised in an arrogant arch as he scribbled an almost unintelligible list of her virtues in the kitchen, and Gigi found herself wanting to smile.

"*Voilà!*" He left it to dry and turned to her again. "Do you want to stay here until this job is settled?"

She looked around her. "I don't want anyone to know about me, or for there to be any talk."

"Bah." He flicked the air as if she spoke nonsense. "You are my niece, we will say, no? The beloved daughter of my brother. It is not a word of a lie. In my heart, you are like my family, Gigi. You stay for a short while, no problem."

She felt the walls of her self-control crumbling, and gave a nod. "My things are in the coach outside. I have to pay the driver—"

"You sit. Georges will make it right." He stormed out, as if the coachman were somehow in league with the devil and he was going to bargain for her very soul. Gigi stumbled to a sofa and sank down on it. She closed her eyes, and let exhaustion drag her under.

———

Twilight had fallen as Gigi leaned against the tree four houses down from Goldfern House and wondered what she was doing.

Her father had always said sleep was as vital as good intelligence.

She hadn't had enough, despite the four hours on Georges's sofa this morning. But at least she'd had a bath and a change of clothes, food that was fit to grace a royal table, and the first glimmer that things would get better.

A chill breeze rustled the leaves above her, and she could smell the wood smoke and the river in the cold, heavy air. The rough bark caught at her hair, pulling at the loose arrangement under her wide-brimmed hat.

She had been too exhausted to avoid a puddle earlier, and her feet were wet and cold.

She needed to get herself together. She was about to go to her first-ever job interview. Georges had sent a note around to Lord Aldridge's butler this morning, and she was expected. She had to get this job, and go to ground.

Her escape, her success in reaching London and her father's death would be for nothing if she stumbled now.

She shook her head to clear it and realized she had a headache.

Goldfern House looked empty. As it should.

But was it?

If she were ahead of the man who killed her father then it was only by a small margin.

He wouldn't have had a plan in place to get to London, as she had, but her disappearance would have tipped him off that her father had most likely lied. That she had the document for which he was prepared to kill.

So it made sense that he would come looking for her here. With her father dead, where else would she go other than her family home?

A light came on in Goldfern's hall, illuminating the fan light above the door. She held her breath.

No one came out, and the light moved on into another room.

A servant, checking the locks?

There should be at least three servants in residence, but she couldn't be sure. And she didn't know them, anyway. She couldn't trust them.

If she could give the document to the right person, the shadow man would have one less reason to look for her. And she would not let her father's sacrifice be for nothing. Thornton had wanted it delivered fast and in secret.

She'd asked Georges if the man he worked for, the Duke of Wittaker, would do something with it—could take it to the right person. But Georges had told her his employer would most likely toss it in the fire, given his long-standing fight with the Crown over taxes.

She couldn't take that risk. She had to find someone else.

The bells of a nearby church began to chime five o'clock, and she turned and started toward Lord Aldridge's town house. She had spent too long watching Goldfern, and now she would be late.

Some of the houses on the street were truly magnificent. Goldfern was solid and large, a sort of portly uncle, she'd always thought, but some were sleek, elegant rakes or serene beauties.

Aldridge House was beautifully proportioned, and something about it tugged at her memory. She had been here before, perhaps, when she was younger and her mother had still been alive. Her eyes were on the windows, not on the street, and her foot turned suddenly on a rock in the road.

She gave a hop and went straight into two girls coming out of the narrow service alley toward which she was headed.

With a cry, all three of them tumbled to the ground.

"*Je suis désolé! Pardon mille fois.*" Gigi tried to struggle to her feet and went down again with a cry on her sore foot.

One of the girls, her face rough-hewn and florid, hauled herself up and put her hands on her hips. "You the French cook, then?"

Gigi was glad she was on the ground and in pain. It hid the blood draining from her face as she realized how she could so easily have spoken English. She had been speaking French quietly with Georges since this morning, so it was the language foremost in her head, and she could only thank the stars for that.

"Of course she's the French cook, Babs, you lump." The other girl got her feet under her and stood. "I'm Iris, miss, and Babs 'n' me'll get you in the house. Fancy you coming for the job interview and getting mown down by us two on yer way in."

Iris was strong, athletically so, and her face was quite beautiful. She also had a very impressive bosom under her wool coat. She lifted Gigi in the same way she probably hauled the coal buckets in the morning.

"Yes, I come for the cook position." Gigi ladled on a French accent as thick as a glass of chilled Chartreuse.

Iris tucked an arm under Gigi's, and Babs did the same; then they began moving her toward the service alley.

"I 'ope you get the job 'n' all. We're desperate belowstairs, taking it in turns to cook for ourselves while the master eats at his club. It can't go on," Iris said cheerfully.

"His Edginess will have something to say about our mowing her down," Babs muttered under her breath.

Gigi glanced at her, but so did Iris, and Babs shut her mouth with a snap. Her cheeks flushed a dull red and Gigi didn't think it was from the exertion of half carrying her to the kitchen entrance.

She tested her foot and found she could put more weight on it.

She had a strange sense, as they helped her along, that her plight was like that of a girl in one of the folktales her father collected. The heroine loses her home and her family, fears for her life and finds a position as a servant. How many hapless girls had taken this path, in how many fairy tales?

She was the Goose Girl of London Town. All she needed was the happy ending.

Gigi smiled at her ridiculous notions. She was more tired, more distressed, than she'd realized.

The kitchen door was slightly open and Babs pushed on it, nearly tumbling them down the kitchen stairs.

Ah.

Georges had not mentioned the subterranean kitchen. To be fair, there were large windows high up along two walls, but they were ominously closed and dirty.

"Iris? What is it?" A clipped voice came from the shadowed entrance to a dark room as they hobbled down the stairs three abreast, and a man stepped out.

"Us and the French lady cook had a little collision, Mr. Edgars, just as we were leavin'. Nothing serious, I don't think, she just turned her ankle or summat. Babs 'n' me'll be off again, now she's safe 'n' sound." In a smooth movement, Iris swung her into a wooden chair near the table, and was quickly at the kitchen door again. "Come on, Babs me girl, we only got three hours off."

Babs gave Gigi a grin and Edgars a cheeky look, and scrambled out into the gloom after her.

For a moment there was no sound but the snap and crack of a large fire in the hearth, and the beginnings of the rattle of water boiling in a pot with its lid on.

Edgars ignored her. He walked to the fire and pulled the pot off the trivet, setting it on a narrow brick ledge that ran along the wall on either side of the fireplace. He was tall and thin, with gleaming chestnut hair, and she guessed him to be in his early thirties, with an earnest, edgy look about him, as if he took his duties very seriously.

His Edginess.

She smiled, realizing what Babs and Iris's exchanged look had been about earlier.

"I expect a candidate to be on time for her interview." He turned as he spoke, his manner cool and intimidating.

Gigi's smile died, and she raised a brow. Unfortunately for Edgars, she'd been her father's hostess at parties where men far more powerful than he had tried the same trick. "There was a collision, as Iris just told you. Is the position filled?" She spoke quite calmly, almost bored.

Edgars frowned. "No."

"I'm not surprised." She rolled her *r*'s with a delicious sense of playing the fool. Her mother, born and raised in the heart of Brittany, would have roared with laughter at her accent.

Gigi knew how a chef behaved, and she would be one to the hilt.

She had Edgars' attention now. He drew himself up stiffly. "And why is that, miss?"

"This kitchen, it is . . ." Gigi looked around the kitchen for the first time, seeking something objectionable. Unfortunately, she did not have to look very hard or very long. "Extremely ill-equipped. And not properly clean." She grabbed the table, pulled herself up and tested her foot on the tiled floor. "And there is no air."

"We haven't had a cook for a month." Edgars spoke as if the words were being tortured out of him at knifepoint.

"And why not?" She put the full force of French disdain into the question. "Is the master of this house so unreasonable?"

Edgars gasped, his outrage absolutely genuine, and Gigi fought to hide her smile.

"Lord Aldridge is not unreasonable in the least. Except"—Edgars looked distressed—"he can no longer tolerate English cooking. He only has a taste for French and Spanish fare."

The poor man looked as if it were not possible for both assertions to be true—for his master to be reasonable and yet not like English food—but he was clearly too loyal to say so, and Gigi allowed herself a laugh, the first in at least five days.

"You are quite right. It is good to hear of a man as reasonable as this. Who is Lord Aldridge? What family does he have?"

Edgars went a deep, dark red. "See here, miss, I don't know who you are, but your questions are quite impertinent."

Gigi shrugged. "I am a woman on her own, considering taking on a job in the house of a man I don't know. It is quite reasonable for me to ask what kind of man he is. What he does. *N'est-ce pas?*"

"Well!" Edgars' cheeks blew up as if he'd stuffed them with lemons, and then he exhaled sharply.

Gigi shrugged again and, testing her foot a last time, began to limp to the back door.

"He's a good man." Edgars finally spoke like a proper person, rather than a Butler with a capital B. "He attends diligently to his duties to his estates and in the House of Lords. He was an officer in the Peninsula Campaign until his brother, the former Lord Aldridge, died unexpectedly, and he has an impeccable war record. It was while fighting in Portugal, Spain and France that he came to love the food there, and says he can't abide overboiled anything anymore. He is unmarried, but he does not bring his title into disrepute, and he has never abused his power with his female staff in my fifteen years here, first under his brother, and now under him."

Gigi came to a stop at the foot of the stairs, her back still to Edgars. Something he'd said rang a bell in her head. Her father talking to her about someone dying unexpectedly. A neighbor. And his brother having to leave the army and return to take up the title.

She'd met them once, she suddenly remembered, when she was ten and they were much older, around twenty and seventeen. Her mother had brought her here for tea. She had no recollection of the details of the occasion, or even what the brothers looked like, and she had no fear the new Lord Aldridge would remember, either.

He was an army man, a man of action, whose life even her father followed from a distance. If only the document she carried wasn't so very secret, so sensitive that only those requesting it could ever see it, she could give it to him to see into the right hands.

It was a tempting thought, but one she couldn't afford to indulge in.

"You have convinced me, Monsieur Edgars." She turned slowly, her face a courteous mask. "I will accept the position."

Edgars started opening his mouth and she shook her finger at him.

"No, no, no. Just wait. There will be two conditions. One, my salary will be the same as a male chef's. I am better than most of them, but I will accept the average salary. And two, I will not be paraded to his lordship's guests when they insist on congratulating me for the meal. There is nothing I hate more than that."

The thought had occurred to her because her father often asked Pierre to come take his praise for whichever masterpiece he'd created. Being recognized by someone in Lord Aldridge's circle wasn't out of the bounds of probability, so best to make it a condition now.

"Miss . . ." Edgars took a step toward her and then stopped. "What is your name? I'm afraid I couldn't read Mr. Bisset's handwriting very well."

She had considered giving Pierre's name—but the shadow man would surely know it, since Pierre was someone who could have helped her if she hadn't left him behind in Stockholm. "Madame Levéel."

Her mother's mother's name. She was sure no one could know that.

"You are married?"

Gigi's head snapped up, and she used her fear as a masquer-ade for outrage. She didn't want to lie more than she had to, and inventing a husband—even if she pretended to be a widow—was more than she was prepared to do.

Edgars actually took a step back in the face of her fury.

"That is none of your business."

He wrung his hands. "I meant, do you require to live in, Madame Levéel? It would be most difficult if you did not—"

"Oh." Gigi waved a hand. "Yes, of course I will live in. How could I do otherwise?"

Edgars seemed to rally; he drew himself up. "What I have to ask, madam, is do you have references?"

Gigi blinked. He wanted more than one? She dug in her reticule and brought out Georges's letter. "References?" The glittering courts of Vienna, the grass-roofed wooden houses of Lapland, the elegant, colorful cottages of Sweden rose in re-minder of who she was, and she pulled herself straight, nar-rowing her eyes.

"I do." She handed Georges's letter to him as if the whole transaction were offensive. "However"—she drew a sharp breath in through her nose—"the only reference of any use is my cook-ing, *monsieur*. And that you will become acquainted with tomor-row evening, after I have moved in and prepared *le dîner*."

She turned on her heel and hobbled to the stairs, pulling herself up with the handrail. At the top, she turned back and stood poised above him. "Until tomorrow." She gave a firm nod, and Edgars had no choice but to nod back.

Outside it was almost completely dark, and she walked slowly back to the main road to catch a hansom cab.

She took a last look at Goldfern, sitting squat and large just four houses down, and felt a shiver of trepidation.

The shadow man would come looking for her here.

Then she straightened and, despite her foot, walked briskly away. He wanted to find her, but she wanted just as badly to find him.

3

There was something about Edgars this evening, Jonathan noticed as he descended the main stairs.

His butler stood waiting in the hall, hands behind his back, beautifully starched and brushed as usual, but there was a dazed look in his eyes, as if he'd been hit with a club.

"My lord." Edgars cleared his throat nervously. "I have found a French cook."

Jonathan paused on the last step. "Really?" He accepted his coat from Edgars and looked at him more carefully. "You don't seem very happy about it."

"No, my lord. I mean, yes, I'm extremely happy. The staff were beginning to grumble about the state of affairs, and this will solve the issue, as well as mean that you can dine in again, my lord." Edgars spoke stoically, looking at a point just beyond Jonathan's shoulder.

"But?"

"She has a few conditions, my lord."

For the first time ever, Jonathan saw his butler turn a shade of red. "And they are?" He was suddenly most fascinated. This woman had scrambled Edgars like a bowl full of eggs.

"She claims she is a better chef than most men, and demands a salary equal to the average salary for a male French chef." Edgars' voice shook a little, as if he were reliving the moment the demand had been made all over again.

"If she is as good or better than a male chef—none of whom have deigned to work for an insignificant viscount like me—then she can have their salary." Jonathan leaned back against the baluster and crossed his arms over his chest. "And the second demand?"

Edgars shrugged. "She says she hates being paraded, and refuses to be brought up to receive the congratulations and compliments of your guests after a dinner party."

Jonathan paused to think about it, then shrugged as well. "If her cooking *is* that good, I'm willing to accept that condition. When does she arrive?"

"Tomorrow." Edgars took a fortifying breath. "She will be making dinner tomorrow evening, my lord, if you wish to sample her cooking."

"I think I will, Edgars." Jonathan pulled his coat on and gave his butler a grin. "Be nice to have a functioning kitchen again, eh?"

"Yes, my lord." Edgars' voice was a trifle faint. "Very nice."

Harry and Rob, the two footmen, looked from Gigi's pile of eight trunks to her with admiration.

"Don't travel light, do ya?"

Gigi quirked her lips. "*Naturellement, non.*" She was standing in the service alley, where the hansom had dropped her, and she indicated the kitchen door with a wave of her hand. "Thank you for seeing to my luggage, gentlemen." She walked away from them and knew they were watching her. She had dressed with elaborate care this morning—not too smart, but just smart enough.

Gigi swung the portmanteau in her hand and pretended not to hear the grunts of strain coming from behind her. The trunks weren't all hers; some were her father's, full of books and papers, but she would not tell them that.

Again, the kitchen door was partly open, and she pushed it and stood on the top step, looking down into her new domain.

"*Bonjour*, Monsieur Edgars."

Edgars was standing in the same doorway she'd seen him emerge from last night, and at the sight of her, his mouth snapped shut.

She could see him taking in her smart clothes, her hair drawn up and off her face in a very French style under her hat. There was no mistaking his look of approval. And trepidation.

She started down the stairs, tugging off her gloves as she went, and looking around the kitchen in the light of day. "You can show me to my quarters?"

"Of course. This way, madam." He walked briskly across the room and opened a heavy wooden door; she followed him into a small sitting room done in dark green and white. "This will be your private room, and then your bedroom is beyond." He indicated the second door with his arm but did not follow her as she stepped through it.

It was a very large room, set below ground level, like the kitchen. There was a large window that faced out onto a wall, and she lifted the lower pane and stuck her head out, turning her neck to see where she was.

It was the back of the house, and above her stretched a short, wide bridge from the ballroom, which appeared to be directly above her rooms and the kitchen, into the garden. A kind of moat had been dug around the lower floor to let light into the kitchen, her own rooms and, she guessed, Edgars' rooms, as well as the staff dining room and general sitting room.

The brick paving and wall in front of her were very bare. She would have to get some pots and flowers.

She set her portmanteau on the large bed, took out a soft white cap, unpinned her hat and put the cap on, then took out her knives, rolled up in thick white cotton. She walked back through into the kitchen, where His Edginess waited for her.

"I would like to open the windows. And have them cleaned. Please send me the people who will do this so I may learn their names and give them their instructions. And tell me, how many for dinner tonight?" She rolled out her knives on the kitchen table as she spoke, and lifted her head when Edgars didn't answer.

He was staring at the knives.

"We have knives," he said.

She made a sound of disgust. "No chef would travel without her own knives. I use my own, thank you very much. And woe to the person who touches them without my permission." She pulled out her largest knife as she said this, and held it out to the dim light filtering through the filthy windows. When the honed blade gleamed as she turned it, she gave a nod and slid it back into its place.

Edgars was staring at her.

"Window cleaners," she said to him, just barely restraining herself from snapping her fingers in her impatience to get some decent light. "And how many for dinner?"

Edgars pulled himself together with an effort. "Just his lordship for dinner. And you'll have to wait for Harry and Rob to finish with your trunks. They'll clean the windows."

"I see you are not including the staff in the dinner plans, but I do not know how many there are. How many for dinner, including the servants?"

He flushed. "You've met all the servants but one. There's Iris, Barbara and Mavis, the scullery maid, and Harry and Rob, and myself. That's everyone."

That was why no chef would work here—Gigi finally understood. The house must be all but closed up. This was a place run for one bachelor and would simply not be enough to challenge an ambitious chef or give him any acclaim.

But it would be perfect as a place to keep a watch on Goldfern, and to hide.

She lifted a smaller, extremely sharp filleting knife out, examined it critically—and gave a smile that came straight from the spring of hot, bitter grief inside her.

This place would do very well.

4

Gigi stepped into the staff dining room and took a seat, pleased to see that silence reigned as Babs, Iris and Mavis ate their dinner.

Rob, Harry and Edgars were busy upstairs, serving his lordship his own dinner.

Her arms held a good ache, the result of whisking the *sabayon au muscat*, stirring the beef stew and straining the consommé, and she let herself rest a moment before helping herself to the bowl of onion soup in front of her.

"What's in this stew? It's lovely." Babs spoke around a mouthful of food. Her soup bowl was scraped bare and pushed to one side, and she had a piece of bread in her hand.

Gigi was sorry the bread was bought. She simply hadn't had time to make any, but tomorrow that would change.

"I think you're tasting the Burgundy in the stew. The red wine."

"Wine? Cor." Babs took another, even more appreciative bite. "Never 'ad wine before. What's it called, then?"

"*Boeuf bourguignon.*" She broke through the crust of cheese and bread on the soup bowl, dipped her spoon in and took a sip. Of course she'd tasted it many times before she allowed it to be sent up to Lord Aldridge, but she rolled the liquid over her tongue critically, testing for any imperfection.

Perhaps a little more rosemary in the bouquet garni next time. But it was a minor complaint.

Rob came in, eyes only for his own place at the table. "His lordship sends his highest compliments." He fell on his soup without even looking her way.

"Harry has taken up the sabayon?"

He made a noise that could have been a yes. His bowl was clean before she had eaten even half of hers. He leaned back with a sigh and began spooning up stew. "Tastes as good as it smells. Harry and meself had a time disguising our rumbling tums while we were servin' up. Thought His Edginess was going to have a little heart attack about it, 'til I realized he was rumblin' just as loud as we were."

Iris grinned. "His lordship happy at last?"

"As a clam at high tide."

"Thank the Lord for that," Babs muttered.

Harry came in and groaned as he sat in his chair. "Been dreaming o' this moment since all those smells started wafting about the place this afternoon. If His Edginess hadn't told me to come down while he waited for his lordship to finish the sweet course, I'd have started looking at the tablecloth as a snack to tide me over 'n' all."

There was silence for a full five minutes while they ate.

Rob ate steadily but fast, as if he were about to be separated from his meal at any moment, and sure enough, the bell rang for him before he'd finished. He stood reluctantly. The jangle came again and he left, looking back at his plate wistfully.

The moment he'd gone, Babs lifted his plate up and put it down on Edgars' chair, out of sight. Then she carried on eating again as if nothing had happened.

"Put it back." Gigi was in charge of the kitchen, and while they could play pranks on each other without her knowledge, she wasn't going to let it happen in front of her.

Babs kept eating, but Gigi could sense there was a wariness about her now.

She said nothing, waiting it out, and Babs finally put down her spoon, retrieved the plate, and set it back, then shot her an uncertain look.

"Thank you." Gigi had only served herself a small amount of stew, and she mopped up the last of it with the passable bread.

Then she stood and went into the kitchen to get the dessert she had made for the staff, a light flan with raisins and cinnamon. No sabayon for them. She hadn't even suggested it. Edgars had been almost faint with the notion they were to have the same *boeuf bourguignon* she was serving his lordship, with its healthy dose of Burgundy, as it was.

The bell rang again, and she heard Harry's chair scrape back as he left the table and came through the kitchen. He caught sight of the flan and changed direction mid-stride to have a look.

"Cor, that isn't for us, is it?"

She nodded and he smiled at her, the light, happy, genuine smile of a man with the prospect of an excellent dish in his near future.

She laughed as he jogged off to get his duties over with more quickly, and took the flan into the staff dining room.

Iris breathed in deep. "Smells wonderful."

Gigi looked at her, Babs and Mavis, and decided she wouldn't get a better chance than now to find out more about Lord Aldridge. They wouldn't talk freely with Edgars, Harry and Rob here, and she was interested in what the women in his house, the most vulnerable members, had to say about him.

It would be useful to know if she could trust him, if she had to.

"Tell me, is Lord Aldridge good to work for?" She cut a slice of flan and handed it to Babs. "Or is he *difficile?*"

"He's all right, is his lordship. Bit of an off sense o' humor, sometimes. He'll say summat and look at you as if waiting for you to laugh—only it ain't funny."

Iris laughed. "He *is* funny, Babs. You just don't get his jokes, and now he makes a point to try out new ones on you. He's determined to get you to laugh at one."

Babs took a big bite of flan. "Mad, I call it. Bet you've seen a few mad ones, 'ave you?" The maid looked at her sidelong, her mouth full.

Gigi gave a smile, thinking of the many people she'd met while touring with her father through Europe, Russia and Scandinavia. "I have."

"I've had a few meself, but not 'ere." Iris tipped back in her chair a little, the expression on her quite lovely peaches-and-cream face unreadable. "The only strange thing 'bout his lordship is 'e don't like good English cooking."

"Tonight you don't seem to have minded good French cooking, though." Gigi rolled each syllable over her tongue.

"Weren't half bad. Finally can see what the big carry-on is all about," Babs said, then took her last bite of flan.

"And you, Mavis?" The girl was young, only fourteen or fifteen, and she hadn't said a word all evening. She'd eaten with the concentration of a champion training for a big event. She was far too thin, and Gigi wondered if she was being starved here. It hardly seemed possible, and she didn't think Iris was someone who would stand for that, but the evidence couldn't be dismissed.

"I don't mind what I eat, Cook. It's all good to me." Mavis blushed at being spoken to directly, and fiddled with her straight brown hair. "Never had too much at home. Too many of us, see? Five brothers and two sisters. And me brothers, they took as much as they could grab. Never was much left for us girls."

"We've been fattening Mavis up," Iris said, and something in the way she said it made Gigi go very still.

If this was evidence of Mavis with more meat on her bones, she must have been a walking skeleton when she'd gotten here.

There'd been deep, cold anger in Iris's voice, and she looked across at her. Their eyes met, and Gigi felt a sense of connection bloom, their mutual anger and horror at Mavis's suffering binding them together.

"And his lordship?" she asked. "No complaints about him?"

Mavis blushed again and looked away, the red flush creeping up her neck and into her cheeks, hot against her too-pale skin. "No, Cook. Ever so nice to me he is." There was a flash in her eyes, an almost secret delight as she spoke, and something stuttered in Gigi's chest.

He couldn't be taking liberties with her, could he? And using her complete lack of self-confidence to make her eager for it?

There was *something* going on there.

Iris was sitting straighter, her eyes on Mavis as well, as if she had just seen what Gigi had. She turned her head to look at Gigi and an understanding flashed between them again.

They would get to the bottom of this.

Whether Mavis wanted them or not, she suddenly had two guardian angels, although Gigi would have wagered Iris had been watching out for her from the moment she arrived.

Edgars went up in her estimation as well, for taking on a starving, skeletal child. Mavis couldn't have looked strong enough for the work when she came in. She hardly looked strong enough now.

Gigi stood and went into the kitchen, and at that moment Harry and Rob came down the stairs, laden with the used dishes. They set them down and went to finish eating, calling rudely to Babs about how much flan was left for them.

Edgars came a few minutes later, a half-empty bottle of wine in one hand and the fruit plate in the other.

"His lordship is most pleased with the meal, Cook. Would you please go up and speak with him?"

She'd expected at least one meeting. And what better way to get a sense of whether he could be trusted than to speak with him herself?

"Of course," she said, and straightened her apron, then lifted a hand to her hair to make sure it was still secure under her cap.

Iris had come into the kitchen, and as Edgars set down the wine and the fruit plate, she fetched his soup, which had been sitting near the fire to keep it warm, and handed it to him. Gigi saw his eyes widen in surprise.

"Most kind. Thank you, Iris." He looked flustered, more human than usual. "Do you know the way, Cook?"

Gigi shook her head.

"I'll show you," Iris volunteered.

Gigi murmured her thanks and waited for Iris to precede her up the stairs.

And at last, the sense of playacting, of playing dress-up, left her. She had to be believable. She had to convince Lord Aldridge she was a French cook.

Her life might depend on it.

5

A woman stepped through the door into the dining room, and Jonathan was suddenly at sea.

Dark hair, beautifully coiffed under a white cap, and strangely light, hazel-green eyes fringed with thick lashes. There was a flush of color under the cream of her cheeks, and she regarded him with the same intensity with which he was watching her, her head tilted to one side on a long, slender neck.

He had the impression of someone who knew how to dress well, but he could not drag his gaze from her face.

He had no context in which to evaluate her. She was in his dining room, looking directly at him, and all he could think was that he had seen her before.

She was familiar.

Some old, long-forgotten memory stirred in him, along with a slightly guilty yearning, but although he tried to pin it down, it slipped elusively from him and left him flat-footed.

Belatedly he rose and bowed, and felt the heat of a blush steal over his cheeks at his poor manners.

"My lord." She curtsied and watched him with a cool, composed expression. Then she nodded toward the crystal cup that had held the dessert. "Mr. Edgars says you wish to speak to me?"

No.

Jonathan looked from the cup to her, but he still refused to believe it. This could not be his cook. She was supposed to be old and plump and slightly grumpy. He was sure that was compulsory for cooks.

And yet, it could not be anyone else.

"Madame Levéel?"

She nodded. And almost as if she sensed what he was thinking, her lips quirked in a quick smile.

"I don't think I've ever had a meal I've enjoyed that much. Thank you, *madame.*"

"*De rien.*" She curtsied again and then stood, hands clasped together, a growing tension about her.

"What was this called?" He lifted the crystal cup.

"*Sabayon au muscat.*"

"Well, I can never have enough of it. When in doubt as to dessert, rest assured, you can call on this as a staple."

She looked momentarily surprised, and then she laughed. It lit her expression, and the feeling of knowing her rose again.

"My lord, there are so many desserts to make, I will never be in doubt. But if you wish it again, merely say so to Edgars, and I will make sure you have it."

"You are very young, Madame Levéel, to be so accomplished a cook." He said it as a statement, but there could be no question that he wanted some response from her.

He saw her brace herself, and wondered if it were because she had heard the comment before and was used to defending herself against it, or whether she was getting ready to lie.

She paused. "Thank you."

No explanation. He admired her for her nerve.

"How did you come by your skills?"

She smiled. "The honest way, my lord. Through practice."

Enjoying the game of squeezing water from a stone, he grinned back. "Where did you work before?"

She hesitated, and her ease seemed to drain out of her. "I have not worked as a cook before."

He stared at her. "This is your first position as cook?"

She gave a nod. Then she looked about the room, and he would have thought her bored, if he hadn't noticed her hands. They were gripping her white cotton apron as if it were her lifeline.

She must have worked somewhere. How else could she have received her training?

He wanted to ask her, but she would no longer meet his eye, and he had the strong sense she would rather be anywhere but here.

He was a man who relentlessly went after answers when he needed them. A man who didn't trouble himself too much with manners and niceties if they got in his way. And here he was, absolutely unable to ask his own cook where she had learned her craft.

He shook his head in astonishment.

He wanted her to be at her ease with him more than he wanted resolution.

"Well, I won't keep you from your kitchen anymore, Cook. Thank you again for a wonderful meal."

She raised startled eyes to his and then smiled. It was a smile of such heartfelt gratitude, it was clear that she knew he could have asked more probing questions and had not. And that she was very glad of it.

A cold thought occurred to him. If he probed too much, she could simply leave and find another job.

She had held excellent references, Edgars had told him—another mystery—and she could walk into any job she chose. After eating at his club far too long, and after the meal he had just enjoyed, Jonathan didn't want to do anything to jeopardize keeping her.

She held out her hand, and for a moment, he had no idea what she wanted from him. Her hand was small, delicate. She reached forward and took the crystal cup off the table, and he felt a fool. He had almost taken it to kiss it, while all Madame Levéel had had in mind was washing the dishes.

If cooks actually washed dishes. He had a feeling the maids did the washing up.

And had he ever been this much of a lump? Who washed the dishes had never crossed his mind before tonight.

She started to turn and then changed her mind, stopping to look him boldly in the eye.

"Mavis," she said.

"Mavis?" He scrambled to keep up.

"What secret do you share with her?"

He blinked. "Secret? Oh! The bonbons."

She kept her gaze on him. Steady.

"She's too thin. And I don't really like bonbons, but my aunt sends them to me anyway. So I give them to Mavis, a few at a time. But I know Edgars wouldn't approve, so I told her it was our little secret."

"Ah." She gave a pleased nod, and there was a definite quality to it, as if she had decided on something important. "Good evening, my lord."

As she walked from the room, slim, diminutive, with the figure and bearing of a lady, he finally understood Edgars' demeanor the day he'd hired her.

Just like she'd done to his butler, his cook had picked him up like a bottle of champagne and shaken him vigorously, and now, at last back down on his feet, he could only stumble about, ready to explode.

It was a sensation he suddenly craved again.

She did remember him. Or she remembered an impression of him.

How could she forget? She had thought him the most handsome man she'd ever seen. Tall, with dark blond hair, his shoulders so wide and his eyes so blue.

He had changed enough she would never have known him out of context. He was a lot taller now, and bulkier—more muscled. A man in his late twenties, not a boy of seventeen. But at the time she had been only ten, and he had seemed like a man to her then. A man with eyes only for her mother.

Despite everything—her mother's death, her father's murder—the thought of him, that long-ago day, making calf eyes at her mother, along with his father and older brother, made her lips twitch. She had been quite invisible. Not one of the Aldridge men had even known she existed, despite her mother's attempts to draw her into the conversation.

Seeing him again brought back the memory, as clear as if it had just happened, and that was getting rarer as time moved on. She was grateful and delighted.

Her mother had claimed the limelight, as she should, but even when she'd all but placed Gigi on her lap to keep her included, the viscount and his two sons had had eyes for no one else.

Gigi and her mother had giggled like schoolgirls about it on their short walk home, about how the three men, father and sons, had vied for her mother's attention.

"One day it will be you, *ma chère*, who will have the men fighting each other to hand you cakes and give you cups of tea. One day all too soon." Her mother had stroked her hair and kissed the top of her head, holding her close with one arm.

It was the last time they went out to tea together. Her mother had fallen ill the following week, and the worst six months of Gigi's life had begun.

At least she could be sure that Lord Aldridge would have

no recollection of her. He wouldn't even remember she'd been present that day.

She sighed as she took the stairs down to the kitchens. He certainly knew she existed now. And she knew he was suspicious of her. For the time being, he'd respected the wall she'd flung up between them, but it might not last.

She would have to keep a low profile. Become invisible, hiding in her new domain.

She stepped into the kitchen to find Babs and Mavis drying and putting the dishes away while Iris washed them.

The kitchen looked much cleaner than it had this morning, and she gave a nod, rolling her shoulders to loosen the knot of tension that had settled in her upper back. "*Bien.*"

She handed the crystal cup to Babs and started making the dough for tomorrow morning's brioche, ignoring the interested looks of the girls, who were obviously desperate to know how her talk with his lordship had gone.

She was in a strange situation. Edgars had said there wasn't enough for the maids and footmen to do, with so much of the house closed up, so she could have their help as she needed it. It meant they would have two masters, herself and Edgars.

She couldn't get too friendly with them, if she had to give them orders. But she didn't want to live in isolation, a fierce dictator like Georges.

The sound of the front door closing came from the floor above—his lordship going out for the night.

And for the first time since dinner began, Gigi let herself relax. She worked the dough and then set it in a bowl near the fire for the first rise.

"You're not going to make the bread now, are you?" Iris asked, and Gigi looked up to see she was the only one left in the kitchen, putting away the last of the pots.

"No. It needs a first, quick rise in the warmth, then I'll punch it down and set it in the cold store to rise again slowly, overnight."

Iris gave a nod. She moved toward the passageway that would take her to the servants' staircase, up to her room at the very top of the house, but slowly, as if she was working up the nerve to say something before she left. "About Mavis." She stopped and bit her lip.

"It's all right." Gigi waved a floury hand in her direction. "I should have realized it involved food, the way she attacked her dinner."

"Wot?" Iris frowned.

"I questioned his lordship during our little chat." Gigi dipped her hands into the cold water in the sink, and rubbed them to get the dough off. She pronounced *little* as *leetle* and nearly snorted at herself. Really, her mother would be laughing so hard she'd be crying if she could hear this.

"You . . . asked Lord Aldridge what he was up to with Mavis?" Iris's voice was strained.

Gigi gave a nod, turning to look at her over her shoulder. "He sneaks her his bonbons. Says he can't stand them, and he can't stand to see her so thin." She finished washing her hands

and picked up a cloth to dry them with. "He's not doing anything that he shouldn't be doing."

"He just told you, straight out?"

"Yes." Gigi shrugged. "Why wouldn't he?"

"I don't know." Iris backed away. "Maybe because he's Lord
Aldridge. And he can do whatever the hell he likes."

Gigi paused. Gave another shrug. "I don't really care who
he is. If he was abusing Mavis, I wanted to know about it."

"Cor." Iris finally stood just within the passageway. "I 'eard
the French don't care for their nobs. Guess that's right."

Gigi lifted her head, startled. "I don't mean it like that."

But Iris was already gone, and Gigi was staring at the dark
shadow of the doorway.

She shook her head. It was true, anyway. The French most
certainly didn't care for their nobs.

She knew that full well, her mother being one of the nobs
they had wanted to kill.

6

"Are you humming?" Durnham looked up from the glass of whisky in his hand and waited for Jonathan to take a seat opposite him.

Jonathan grinned, making himself comfortable in the large, overstuffed armchair tucked in a quiet, dim corner of the club.

Durnham caught the smile and lifted a brow. "Bit late for dinner, too, aren't you?"

"If I play my cards right, I'll never have to eat the slop they pass off as dinner here ever again." Jonathan stretched out his legs and placed both hands on his stomach.

Durnham leaned forward. "Finally found a French chef, eh?"

"A French cook, actually. And I can't see how the meal she produced this evening could possibly be improved upon."

"She trustworthy? You know where she's from?" An edge crept into Durnham's tone.

Jonathan stilled and then straightened in his chair. "What do you mean by that?"

"I don't need to tell you we're at war with France. You're a member of the House, and it's widely known you've been looking for a French chef for months. If they could sneak a spy across—which we know they can—it's conceivable they could plant one in your house. Even if they didn't know you've started working for me and Dervish on the side, you'd still be a source of useful information, if you were careless with leaving papers about the house."

Jonathan narrowed his eyes. "I'm never careless."

Durnham shrugged. "It was just a word of caution. I can have her checked, if you like. Ask the Alien Office to take an interest."

Jonathan sat forward, his hands fisted on his knees. "Let me get this straight, Durnham. You want me to agree to subject the woman who prepared me a meal I'd be happy to get in heaven itself to the suspicious, ham-fisted idiots of the Alien Office, just in *case*, being French, she is here to spy on a viscount with barely any influence in government and who knows almost nothing?"

Durnham pursed his lips. "You don't know almost nothing. You know more than a little about certain aspects of the war, and we're grateful for your help. How old is this cook, and how good is her English?"

Jonathan hesitated. And it *wasn't* because of her distinct lack of enthusiasm for answering perfectly reasonable questions, damn it. He took a breath. "Her English is excellent. She's spent quite some time here, I'd guess. She is also hardly a day over twenty."

He thought back to his meeting with Madame Levéel an hour ago; the way her eyes had refused to meet his when he asked for her former place of work. And the first, niggling worm of doubt began to eat at him. "You can really ruin a man's mood, Durnham." He flopped back into his chair.

"She pretty?" Durnham asked, and there was something in his expression that shot a bolt of searing anger through Jonathan.

And possibly, shame.

"God damn you. Yes. She's beautiful. Stunningly beautiful. And there's something about her. I'm almost sure she's familiar to me, but I can't place her."

Durnham crossed his arms over his chest. "What were her references?"

Jonathan stood and was shocked to find his hands were shaking. "I didn't see them myself, but they were from the Duke of Wittaker's chef, Georges Bisset." He pointed a finger at Durnham.

"Whatever plans you had for me on the committee, you can strike me off the list. If assisting the Crown means I have to answer to someone every time I hire a servant, and have insinuations about my conduct and relationships with my staff leveled at me in my own club, then—"

"Jonathan, I'm sorry." Durnham leaned back and rubbed his hands over his face. For the first time, Jonathan could see he was hollow-eyed. "Sit. Please."

Very reluctantly, he complied, drumming a heel on the floor to help work off the anger.

"I'm the least diplomatic person in London, you know that. I didn't mean to insult you or ruin your mood." Durnham sighed. "My wife is the only person who seems to delight in my blunt talk, and even then, I've managed to anger her a time or two."

He looked down at his hands. "That's why I'm here right now, truth be told. I've more or less been kicked out until she cools off." He looked up again. "I'm dealing with a hell of a mess at the moment, involving the death of someone I respected very much, and I can't seem to put a brake on my mouth. I just meant, be careful. That's all. If you knew some of the things I do. . . . Well, just be careful. I don't need another friend dead while in the service of his country. Someone just doing us a favor, killed in cold blood."

Jonathan blew out a long breath. "Apology accepted. Can I help you with this matter?"

Durnham looked past him, and Jonathan turned to see Lord Dervish coming in the door. He searched the room, turning slowly, as if the walk up the stairs had exhausted him. When he saw them, he lifted his brows and walked over.

As he came closer, Jonathan could see the lines bracketing his mouth were deeper than usual, and there were dark smudges under his eyes, a match to Durnham's. He took the last chair in the grouping, almost falling into it, and Jonathan had the sense of a meeting called to order.

"Aldridge doesn't know yet," Durnham said. He lifted his whisky and tipped the last of it down his throat.

"Do you know Sir Eric Barrington?" Dervish asked, turning in his chair a little to face Jonathan. "The folklorist?"

"Barrington?" Jonathan nodded. "Yes. Lives a few houses down from me. Although he's hardly ever there."

"Does he?" Durnham sat straighter. "That might be useful."

"Useful for what?"

"We may need to watch his house."

"What the devil for?" Jonathan tried to remember Barrington. A man of medium height, with an intense intelligence burning in his eyes. It had been years since he'd seen him. He'd seen his wife only a few times as well, before she'd died suddenly and tragically. She and her husband had attended the usual balls, and his father had invited her to tea once, he remembered. One of the kindest and most beautiful women he'd ever met.

Something tugged at his memory, just like earlier when he'd spoken to his cook, but was every bit as elusive as it had been then. He put the connection down to them both being beautiful and French. "I can't believe Barrington would have done anything to warrant suspicion."

Dervish shook his head. "Barrington is—was—one of the most loyal men I've ever worked with. Although he didn't actually work for the Crown, he just lent a hand now and then, when needed. Because of his studies and the places they took him, he was often in a country where it was useful to have a man on the ground, or else he was going from one place to another when it was useful to have someone above suspicion carry a message or document." Dervish rubbed his temples with stiff fingers.

Durnham took over the story. "Six days ago he was murdered in the gardens of Tessin Palace in Stockholm, during a party to which the diplomats and nobility of Sweden were invited." The way he said it, too calmly, showed Jonathan how angry he was. "At the time, he had in his possession a document that proclaimed Russian willingness to enter into a secret agreement with us against France, signed by the tsar himself."

"What?" Jonathan almost rose out of his chair in surprise. "The Russians are in an alliance with France. Theoretically at war with us."

Dervish gave him a sharp look, and he subsided.

"They want to change that. Their relations with France have been getting progressively worse over the last two years. They're ready to start talking terms." Dervish kept his voice very low.

"What do you think happened in Stockholm?"

"At first it seemed obvious that someone had discovered what Barrington had and killed him for it. We can't proceed with a treaty unless we have a letter or some other indication from the Russians that they'd be willing to negotiate with us and sign it. With the letter gone, we're back to asking the Russians for another document, and at the very least, it makes us look incompetent."

"And at worst?" Jonathan always liked to know the worst-case scenario.

"At worst, they'll be scared off. Someone knew about that document. So we've either got a mole in the Russian camp or in the British camp—someone in French pay. Even if the Russians simply posture a bit before coming back with a new document, it's costing us time we don't have. Dragging out the war even longer."

"You said at first that you thought the document had been taken. Something made you change your mind?"

"Barrington has a daughter. Giselle Barrington. Our man in Sweden, Thornton, was waiting to have a last, quick word with Barrington before he and his daughter took the document to London, under the guise of a trip home. He spoke to Barrington's daughter during the party, and she was worried about her father's absence. Barrington had told her he was going outside for some air, but she thought he was taking too long about it. Thornton saw her walk into the gardens to look for him."

"She wasn't harmed?" Jonathan tried to think back to what he knew of the Barringtons. He didn't recall a daughter.

"We don't know," Durnham said. "She's disappeared."

"Thornton was desperate at first, thinking whoever had killed Barrington may have taken her. But it turns out Barrington had hired a coach to take them from Stockholm to Gothenburg that night. And it appears that someone took that coach."

"You think Giselle Barrington decided to complete the mission on her own?" Jonathan asked. It seemed ludicrous, but it was clearly something Dervish was considering. "How old is she, anyway?"

"She's twenty-one. Thornton now wonders if her father managed somehow to give her the document before he was killed. Although that doesn't explain why she didn't return to the palace and get Thornton's help."

"If she did have the document, then her actions only make sense under one scenario." Durnham leaned back and steepled his hands together.

"What is that?" Jonathan did the mental arithmetic and worked out that Giselle Barrington would have been ten the last time he'd been home long enough to see her. No wonder he had no recollection of her.

"The only reason she would not have returned to the ball-room and asked for help was if the man who killed her father was someone from the party—either a Swedish nobleman or a diplomat from one of the embassies present—and she witnessed it and recognized him."

"And that," Dervish said, quietly, "is a very big problem. For us, of course, but also for Giselle Barrington."

Jonathan tapped his mouth with a finger. "Because she's the only person who can identify him."

Durnham nodded. "And if our scenario is correct, she's also got something he wants very, very much."

"That's why you want to watch Barrington's house," Jonathan said, suddenly understanding.

Durnham nodded. "It's the only place Giselle Barrington has to go. And it's the first place anyone after her will look."

"Who would she contact, if she did make it here with the document?"

There was a surprised silence for a moment. "Damned if I know." Durnham shot a look at Dervish. "Unless her father told her, and I doubt he would have, knowing how sensitive this was. She wouldn't know who to contact."

"That's if she's even made it as far as London," Dervish said softly. "She'd need perfect timing to have made every connection to be here already, or even within the next few days. We only got word of Barrington's death from Thornton last night, brought by an experienced courier." He sighed. "Chances are, Thornton and the Swedish authorities will find her body floating in Lake Mälaren."

7

The house had stilled around her, and Gigi slowly became aware of the quiet, as if it were a sound itself rather than the lack of one.

She was comfortable here, she realized with surprise, setting down her father's papers and arching her neck to relieve the stiffness. Part of that was knowing that her parents had been welcome here, and had liked both the previous viscounts and the current Lord Aldridge.

Edgars, for all his posturing and rules, had taken in someone like Mavis, and had the grace to thank his staff when thanks were due. He was better than he'd first appeared, and she knew this place could have been so much worse.

Her eyes fell on the letter she'd been reading, addressed to her father, and she fought the grief that rose up. The regard the man who had written the letter had for her father was clear, but there was no address, not even a name. The writer had simply signed himself D.

It did not help her.

If she could send the document in the hidden pocket she'd sewn into her petticoat directly to him, the massive weight of responsibility would lift a little off her chest, help her breathe a little easier. But the mysterious D. had made sure there was no clue as to where he lived or who he was.

Those details had all been in her father's head. And while he'd always given her the documents he couriered for the Crown to hide in the pockets she'd sewn into all her petticoats, she'd never known anything about them. Not what was written on them, not why they were carrying them.

Her father had said it was much safer for her that way. Keeping the safekeeper safe, he'd always joked.

It wasn't so funny now.

She stood and gathered the papers together, set them neatly back into their trunk, and locked it.

She should have been exhausted. But thinking of her father, reading his papers, had brought those last few minutes in the gardens of Tessin Palace back in stark relief.

She didn't want to close her eyes, because she knew what would haunt her dreams.

She walked out of her bedroom, through her sitting room and into the kitchen, stepping quietly into her new domain.

A kitchen under her own command.

She smiled at the heady thought. In Pierre and Georges's kitchen she had been only a sous-chef, and in the beginning, only on sufferance. She'd earned the title now, but in the old days, they had merely been humoring a grief-stricken child who wanted to hear her mother's language spoken all around her.

The kitchen was large and in darkness, except for a weak light that spilled down the stairs that led to the front hallway, left on for Lord Aldridge's return.

The scent of dried herbs, lemon and a faint, lingering smell of the *boeuf bourguignon* hung in the air.

She fussed with the stove, then with the dishcloths, turning them where they hung to dry. Then she slipped into the cold store to check her brioche dough, and as she smoothed the damp cloth back over the bowl, she admitted to herself she was simply trying to stay busy.

She walked back into the kitchen and stood silent for a long moment, listening. Edgars was either in his rooms, right next to her own, or above, waiting for Aldridge to return.

She wanted to go out. And what did it matter if the new cook took the air late at night? It might even be advisable to set a precedent where that was concerned.

Before she could reconsider, she was up the back stairs, turning the big iron key in the lock and stepping out into the night.

She took the key with her and locked the door, unwilling to be locked out by mistake. She lifted her skirt and slipped it into one of her hidden petticoat pockets, and it knocked against the side of her knee as she started walking to the lane that ran along the back of the houses.

The alley wasn't as straight as Chapel Street, twisting and winding along the rear gardens like a cat weaving through legs in a crowd. It had no lights, either. The darkness was why she had chosen to go this way.

Up ahead, the bulky shape of Goldfern rose above its stone garden walls in the weak light of a half moon.

The lane was narrow, just wide enough for a single cart, and it smelled of sewage, rotting cabbage and the throat-catching odor of dead rat.

It was at least paved with cobbles, but they were slick with grime and she had to keep her wits as she walked on them.

The door to Goldfern's gardens was poorly maintained, the paint peeling off it, and it didn't sit flush with the thick stone wall into which it was set.

This was so surprising to her that she stared at it a moment. Perhaps the other side looked very different. No servant would expect either her or her father to step out of the back door into this lane. Yet she shivered, somehow disturbed.

She turned the handle, but the door was either locked or so swollen in its frame that it wouldn't budge. She hadn't expected it to be that easy, anyway.

She could turn around now and go back, but the thought of sleep was still so unwelcome, she stepped closer to the wall and ran her hands over the stones.

There were plenty of cracks and tiny ledges in the uneven stonework for her to climb up, even though she was still in her smart wool dress and leather shoes, rather than the *gákti* and boots the Sami had given her to climb with. She and her father had been taken into the mountains in Lapland near the

Norwegian border by the Sami people they had being staying with, and she had loved it.

If she hadn't been her father's companion, traveling Europe and beyond like a nomad to collect stories for his collection, she would have been forced to turn around and trudge back to Aldridge House. But she *had* been his companion. She knew she could do this.

She stretched up and caught her first hold, bracing her foot and pulling herself up, hand over hand, until she was balancing on top of the wall. It had taken less than two minutes.

She crouched on the wide ledge and turned her attention to Goldfern. She would rather see what she could from here than risk dropping to the ground inside and having difficulty getting back.

The minutes ticked by, the house lying still and silent, and the chill of the stone began to seep through the soles of her shoes and into her palms. She lifted her hands and laid them on her thighs to ease the bite.

There was nothing obviously wrong, nothing to see, but still she waited, the sight of her family home reminding her of happier times.

She was about to clamber down when a light flared behind a window, spilling out from a crack in the curtains and illuminating a small slice of garden.

She froze.

Whoever it was didn't linger, moving to the next room and then the next, all along the back of the house.

There was something purposeful about the way the light moved, as if the person holding it was conducting a search.

But a search for what?

Evidence that she was back in London? Had been to the house?

Whoever held the lamp stood in the library now, the light shining across the lawn. It took her a moment to understand that the person had drawn back the curtains to look out into the garden, and she shrank back, catching the briefest glimpse of a man.

The light went out.

Could he have seen her?

She reasoned with herself that he could not. She was crouched low and in complete darkness, and the light hadn't been strong enough to reach across to the back wall. And yet, could she take the chance?

He could simply be done with the back rooms and have moved on to search the front of the house. But her imagination conjured the shadow man, his lantern extinguished, slipping out of the house and circling around to wait for her in the alley below.

A spike of fear lanced through her. She peered carefully into the alley—though it would be impossible for him to already be there, even if she were right—before she started climbing down. She took it too fast, scraping her hands and fumbling her footing, until she dropped and landed hard on the cobbles, hands stinging, knees jolted.

She started back for Aldridge House, hobbling a little until her legs stopped aching. She wanted to run, but it would slow her down even more if she fell on the grime-slick cobbles, so she forced herself to a quick, careful walk. She looked over her shoulder, but there was nothing but darkness and silence behind her.

It didn't comfort her in the least.

At last she reached the little alleyway that led to the kitchen door, breathing hard, with perspiration beading on her forehead and between her shoulder blades.

A sheet of newspaper skittered down the alley on a sudden gust of wind, and she thought her heart would stop. Gasping, her imagination conjuring shadow men behind her, she rattled the handle for a few panicked seconds until she remembered she had the key.

She had to steel herself to extract it from her hidden pocket without dropping it, and with shaking fingers she unlocked the door and threw herself inside, slamming it shut behind her.

She needed two tries to get the key into the lock, and only relaxed when she heard the comforting clunk of the bolt engaging. Then she leaned forward, resting her forehead on the door. When she turned slowly around, she let out a soft scream.

Edgars was staring at her from the middle of the kitchen, his body tense as if ready for danger, the candle in his hand throwing leaping shadows about the room.

"All right?" he asked eventually, when they had stared at each other for almost a minute.

She let out a long breath and briefly closed her eyes. *Careful now. Very careful.* "*Oui.* I couldn't sleep. It is always so, in a strange, new place. So I take the walk, and I think there is someone following me. But it is nothing. Just nerves. I am overtired." She let the French accent clog her speech like thick cream and walked down the stairs, giving Edgars a wide berth as she went to her door.

He had turned to follow her and was still staring at her. She gave him a nod. "Good night, Mr. Edgars."

He nodded back, but as she closed her door, she saw what was in his eyes.

Suspicion.

8

Jonathan walked home deep in thought. Mention of the Barringtons had dredged up memories for him—memories of the last time he and his brother and father had been together, while he was on leave from the army. His father, already extremely ill, had died a few months after he'd gone back to his unit.

He recalled the day his father had invited Adèle Barrington for tea. Had she brought her daughter with her that day? He couldn't recall; all he could remember was vying with his brother and his father for Mrs. Barrington's smiles and laughter. She had brought sunlight into the house.

None of them could get enough of her, of her feminine warmth, in a home too long the preserve of men only.

He recalled wondering how Barrington could bear to stay away from home for such long periods of time, with a jewel like Adèle Barrington waiting for him.

He came level with Aldridge House. The Barrington place,

Goldfern, was just a little way along. He continued on toward it, unwilling to go into his own house just yet.

He hardly noticed Goldfern going about his business day to day, but it was a huge, hulking place that took up more than its fair share of the street. He couldn't ever remember seeing anyone come or go from there; Barrington had been away since Gerald died of appendicitis and he'd come home to take the title.

The house had been empty all that time.

He'd been staring at the house for less than a minute when he became aware of a light behind one of the curtains. It fluctuated, as if someone held a lantern and was moving about the room.

He walked closer.

It was nearly midnight, and with the house empty, there was no reason for a servant to be up and wandering at this time.

He stepped over the low iron railing into the narrow strip of garden that ran between the street and the house. The window was high—as at his own house, there would be a floor below with high ceilings, housing the kitchens and some of the servants' quarters. It meant the windowsill was just in line with the top of his head; he wouldn't be able to peer inside.

He walked to the path and up the stairs to the front door, and hammered with the door knocker. Then he ran back to the window to see the reaction. If it was a servant, he or she would come to the door.

The light disappeared abruptly, as if someone had blown it out, and he heard the faint sound of running footsteps.

Nothing innocent about this at all.

He thought the person had run right, and sped along the front to the right side of the house and looked down. A figure was climbing out a low-set window at the far end.

He gave a shout and started running again, but the intruder had seen him and was off, racing across the garden. A man, well built and tall. He disappeared into the shadows at the back of the garden and Jonathan heard the door onto the access lane slam open.

The garden was simply laid out, with a wide swath of lawn to the back, and he was at the garden door himself very quickly. It was ajar, the key hanging slightly out as if wrenched, and he stepped into the lane. It was pitch-dark, and there was no sound. It was as if the runner had never been.

He was either gone or crouched down, waiting for Jonathan to come to him.

Jonathan leaned down to finger the knife in his boot, but a shout from behind him made him step back into the garden, then swing the door shut and lock it. He turned to face a man coming toward him with a lantern raised high.

"Who is it?" The voice was firm and a little sharp.

"Lord Aldridge, from Aldridge House. I noticed a burglar in your house. But he's got away."

"Lord Aldridge?" The voice quavered a little. "A burglar, you say?" He lowered the lantern, and Jonathan looked into a wrinkled face that belied the sharp strength of the man's voice.

"I was passing by on my way home and saw a lantern in the window. I thought Barrington was away but knocked in case he was back. The light went out and I heard running, and then the window opened on the side. I gave chase, but he was too quick."

"I heard the knock." The man peered more closely at Jonathan. "I came to see what was what. Escape through there, did he?" He indicated the back garden door.

Jonathan nodded. "Shall we check that all is well in the house? I don't think he had anything in his hands, or if he did, it was small."

"I'm Jones, your lordship. Me wife 'n' me look after the place, with a girl to do the heavy work me wife can't do no more."

Jonathan looked up at the hulking building, at least double the size of Aldridge House. "That's a lot of house for so few."

"All closed up." Jones shrugged. "If we need something doing, we call people in, but Sir Barrington hasn't been back for near two years. Never even met him, meself. When old Simons, their butler, passed on, the other staff moved on to other jobs. Couldn't bear to stay, 'specially with the house empty. So Sir Barrington's solicitors appointed me 'n' Mary to take it on."

They were back at the front door, which stood open, and Jones went first, lantern high.

"Two rooms down to the right, I think. That's where it seemed the light was coming from," Jonathan said.

The room was a parlor or drawing room of some kind. Everything was covered in dust sheets, except for a small, delicate Sheraton writing desk. It was open, and papers were scattered around the floor.

Jones put the lantern down on top of it and stared. "There ain't nothing valuable in there; it's just the post that comes in for Sir Barrington. His solicitor picks it up once a week. I put it in this desk meself. If Mr. Greenway thinks it's not important enough to forward on to Sir Barrington or isn't summat for him to deal with, it gets left in there."

"When did Mr. Greenway last come to collect the post?"

"Yesterday mornin'. And there ain't been any new post since then."

Fortunate. Very fortunate.

"Would you like me to let the authorities know about this, Jones? Or inform Mr. Greenway, so that he can take it further?"

"If you would, your lordship." Jones didn't try to hide the relief in his tone.

They searched the ground floor for open windows. Only the one the thief had climbed out of was open, and it had clearly been jimmied with the crowbar that lay abandoned inside the room.

With no choice but to leave it for the next day, Jones locked the room behind them and led Jonathan back to the front door. "I'll have the carpenters in in th' mornin'. Have them look at all th' windows, make sure they're all sturdy."

Jonathan gave a nod and walked home. He'd thought at

first it might have been Giselle Barrington in the house, but the person running across the garden had definitely been a man.

Was someone looking through Barrington's correspondence for evidence of where she was? Or when she planned to return?

Or were they hoping Barrington or his daughter might have posted the tsar's document to Goldfern?

His front door swung open before he reached it, and Edgars was there to take his coat.

"Good evening, sir."

He gave a nod. "All well here?"

Edgars hesitated a moment. "All fine, my lord."

Jonathan turned sharply. "What is it?"

Edgars looked away, uncomfortable. "Just the new cook, acting a bit strange."

"Strange? How?"

Edgars looked down at his shoes, a red flush on his cheeks. "She went out, sir, and then came flying back in as if the devil himself were after her. Said she thought someone was following her."

Jonathan looked toward the servants' staircase. "I wonder . . . I saw a burglar over at the Goldfern place. He got away. I wonder if our cook saw him?"

"A burglar?" Edgars raised his head. "She did seem very frightened, my lord. Perhaps she was right to be." He looked at the stairway as well.

"Call her up to the library if you will, Edgars. I'm going to

Barrington's solicitor tomorrow, and I might as well have all the information I can about the matter."

"Certainly, my lord." Edgars looked as if he were being forced to swallow a frog.

"What is it?" Jonathan tried to keep the irritation from his voice.

Edgars looked down the stairs again and fidgeted in place.

He was frightened of her! Or at least nervous around her. In that respect, his new cook was like every other cook he'd ever had.

"I think she's gone to bed," Edgars said.

"Knock softly. If she doesn't answer, we'll leave it for tomorrow."

What had Madame Levéel done to his usually forceful butler to leave him as prickly as a drenched cat? Jonathan wondered if Edgars would actually knock, or pretend he had and say she hadn't responded.

He walked to the library and stood by the fire, looking into the flames and soaking up their warmth.

"You wanted to see me?"

So Edgars had found some mettle after all. Jonathan turned, a faint sense of wrongness he couldn't pin down chiming in his head. But his brain stopped working entirely when he saw her.

Madame Levéel stood in the doorway, wrapped in a silk and lace confection like a beautiful bonbon from one of the finest confectioners in London.

She had clearly been either about to go to bed or called from her bed, but she didn't seem annoyed. Her face was curiously blank, in fact, as if she were controlling some strong emotion.

"Sorry to have disturbed you," he finally managed, after she'd stared at him for half a minute, waiting. "Edgars said you thought you were followed by someone when you were out earlier, and I caught a burglar in the act at Goldfern, the house a few doors down. I just wanted to know if you had a good look at your man?"

She went white. Quite, quite white, and her eyes widened. She lifted a hand and scrabbled it against the doorway until she had herself steady. "You caught a burglar at Goldfern?" Her voice was faint.

He frowned, the spell her appearance had cast over him receding a little. He noticed now that she looked extremely tired, with dark shadows under her eyes.

"I didn't lay hands on him, if that's what you mean. I chased him down but he got away. Ran out through the door in the back garden wall, out into the alleyway behind."

"Into the shadows," she said, her voice quiet and a little strange.

He cleared his throat. "Did you see someone?"

She shook her head. "It was just a feeling, like I told Edgars. A feeling of being watched, followed. I didn't see anyone." She drew her dressing gown close around her. "I was frightened, but it was all in my imagination."

He stared her, and she eventually dropped her eyes and pulled the robe even tighter about her, pulling it taut over every line and curve in her body.

She most likely thought she was preserving her modesty. He would have laughed, but he didn't think he was capable of it at the moment.

"It's possible he had an accomplice, waiting for him, or he was waiting in the alley for you to leave before he broke in." The thought of her being so vulnerable made him a little sick.

"An accomplice?" She bowed her head completely and closed her eyes, and then she shivered. Lifted her face to his. "I'm sorry I couldn't be of any help."

Without waiting for a dismissal, she turned and stumbled away, as if the thought that there could have been a real basis for her fears had stripped her of all proper decorum.

And as he watched her go, two things occurred him. The first was to wonder how and why a cook was wearing silk and lace nightclothes, and the second was the realization of what had appeared wrong when she first addressed him.

Most servants called him "my lord" automatically.

Madame Levéel had not.

Perhaps it was because she was French, but that didn't ring true. If she'd used the equivalent French term, that would have been enough—but she'd addressed him as an equal. And now that he came to think of it, she had left him the same way.

9

She was so tired, she swayed like a drunk in the dawn light that found its way through the clouds and fell through the high kitchen windows. It was almost too late to go to the early morning market, but she'd have to take her chances and find whatever was left of the good produce.

Mavis had stoked the stove and put a kettle on, and Gigi stumbled around the kitchen looking for coffee so she'd at least be half-awake when she bargained with the traders.

A shadow man with a lantern had prowled Goldfern in her dreams. And according to Lord Aldridge, he had run straight for the gate she'd been crouched above, only minutes after she'd left.

It was possible he'd gone over the wall shortly before she had herself, and while she sat on it watching the house, he'd been breaking in. The thought of how close she'd come to running straight into him had fear holding her close with hoary, freezing hands.

And then Aldridge added terror to fear, with his mention of an accomplice. If someone had watched her climb the wall, then followed her back to Aldridge House afterward, she was as good as dead.

The shadow man had used an accomplice at Tessin Palace to draw her father out. It wasn't inconceivable he would use one here. Her hands tightened on the cupboard door she was opening, and she wanted to withdraw to her room, cover her head with the blankets and stay there until everything went away.

She could only hope the sense she'd had of malevolent eyes on her in the alley was just in her mind. Some kind of re-action to her memories of the night her father was killed.

She stared into the cupboard, blinked, and reached for a hessian sack of beans with an exclamation of delight, lifting out the coffee in triumph.

She sniffed it.

What little smell there was was moldy, and she was horri-fied to find tears suddenly in her eyes.

A headache beat a steady rhythm in her head, and she stood with the bag in hand, trying to get herself under control. She wanted a cup of coffee, *needed* one, but a bad cup was worse than no cup at all.

"What's that?" Edgars stepped out of his rooms so quietly she almost dropped the bag.

"Coffee beans." She massaged her temple with stiff fingers. Perhaps she should just get a fresh bag at the market.

"Yours?" Edgars sounded surprised.

"No. I found them in the pantry, but they're too old to use." Her voice was hoarse, as if she had a cold.

He shrugged. "His lordship doesn't take coffee at home; he gets it when he's out. No need to get any more."

Gigi lifted her head sharply, her temper flaring. "There is every need to get more." She tossed the beans on the table. "Whether his lordship takes coffee at home or not, I require it. In my cooking, at times, but also to drink. Especially if I am to get up at dawn to go to the markets." She picked up the cooling cup of tea Mavis had made her, took a sip, and shuddered.

It wasn't bad. But it wasn't coffee.

She put it back down and stepped away from it.

"I'll ask his lordship if he will allow it." Edgars pursed his lips, and she saw something in the way he did it—an edge of power, being used for its own sake.

From the corner of her eye, she noticed Iris coming down the stairs. She ignored her and stared straight at Edgars. There was too much beating at her, and coffee was the last straw. Coffee, and Edgars' attempts to put her in her place. She would show him her place, all right.

"I will get the coffee now when I'm at the market, Mr. Edgars, as part of the household shopping. And you are welcome to tell his lordship all about it. If Lord Aldridge cannot afford to let his cook drink coffee if she wants to, or if he is so petty as to not allow anyone in his house to drink something he doesn't wish to drink, even though it will not affect him in the slightest, then he has hired the wrong cook and I will give my notice immediately. You can hurry along and tell him at

your earliest convenience—or even better, I'll do it myself."
She was breathing in sharp, quick pants.

It was insupportable.

Some people had to live with this! Had to take it, too, because they couldn't simply walk away from their jobs. They
needed them.

And so did she, she remembered belatedly. Where else
would she find a place so well situated to watch Goldfern?

No matter. She forced herself to keep her rigid posture. If
she couldn't drink coffee in this house, she would rather make
another plan.

It wasn't about the coffee, anyway. It was about egos and
control.

She glared at Edgars and took up the four baskets she'd set
on the table. "Come, Iris, we're late already." She held two of
the baskets out to the maid.

Iris came past Edgars warily and took them, her eyes on her
hands, rather than on either of the fighters in the ring.

Gigi turned on her heel and marched up the stairs, fought
the key a moment before it gave.

As she held the door for Iris she looked back down on
Edgars, who stood exactly in the same spot, his face white
with a small red mark on each high cheekbone, as if he'd been
slapped twice.

Forcing herself calmer with a deep breath, Gigi closed the
door carefully and took the alley down to Chapel Street. Their
destination was in the opposite direction from Goldfern, but
she couldn't resist a quick look in its direction.

A man walked past it, his head turned to the house, his back to her, in the clothes of a well-heeled member of the nobility. In this area it was a common sight, except for the extremely early time of day.

Returning home after a night in the gaming hells or playing cards at his club?

"Have you seen that man before?" Gigi asked, and Iris, who was facing the other way, turned on her heel and squinted in the dawn light.

"Can't say I 'ave. Can only see his back, and I don't notice the nobs if I can help it."

Gigi stared after him, looking for anything familiar about him, and as if he could feel their eyes on him, he turned and stared back for a moment, then continued on his way.

She caught the flash of a cravat, blue as a duck's egg, and a black or very dark blue jacket, but that was all.

Was it her imagination or did he pick up his pace?

He could be the shadow man.

He was the same general height, with hard, sharp features, but even this very quick glimpse of his face was more than she'd seen of the shadow man at Tessin Palace.

She started down the street with Iris beside her, and only looked over her shoulder again as they turned left onto South Audley.

The man was standing at the very far end of Chapel Street, just a tiny figure in the distance. Watching them.

Fear pricked her neck and arms with cold, sharp needles, and she shivered.

Iris kept her eyes on the street as they walked, her arms folded across her chest so she could tuck her hands under her armpits to keep them warm. "You put Edgars in his place, right and proper."

She didn't say it in a way that gave Gigi the impression she approved.

Gigi narrowed her eyes. The way Edgars had spoken to her, she should have demanded an apology from him, as well as putting him in his place.

That, and trying to deny her coffee, was a declaration of war.

"You've put him in a spot now. He either has to go to Lord Aldridge and tell him about your threatening to give notice, or he has to give you your way. And as he knows his lordship wouldn't mind at all if you wanted coffee, and would love a cup at home if someone could make it properly, he looks a fool either way."

"Why did he pick a fight over it, then?" Gigi was outraged all over again.

Iris sighed. "I don't know. I think it's 'cause he loses his head sometimes. Gets so excited about where he's at, he can't help it." It was as if the thought dragged her down.

"If he's going to play the fool, he has to accept he'll some-times end up *looking* the fool." Gigi knew her voice came out hard, unbending.

"He's got away with it since Cook left. 'Cause you're younger 'n' him, and a woman, maybe he thought he could best you." She kicked a small stone out of her path. "You have to understand, he didn't grow up with much. 'Bout the same as

Mavis, or maybe worse. That's why he hired her on, I think. Aldridge House is the only place he's ever worked. Came as a stable boy, moved up to footman, and now he's butler. Pulled himself up by his bootstraps, 'e 'as."

Gigi looked at Iris, but her head was bowed and her cheeks were high with color. There was more to the story than this.

"You know a lot about him," she said, taking her gaze off Iris in the hope she would talk more easily.

"Grew up near him. We played together as children. Got a job when he was footman, as the scullery maid."

And he'd been playing high and mighty ever since, Gigi guessed, with enough flashes of the old Edgars to keep her hoping he'd change.

"You've moved up the ranks, too, then." Gigi paused. "And it hasn't gone to your head."

Iris shrugged. "He took Mavis in. He's not that far gone."

That was true. There were rarely absolutely black villains in real life, her father was fond of saying. They were found in fairy tales to illustrate evil clearly, but most villains were colored in shades of gray.

Except the shadow man.

"He took in Mavis," she conceded. "He occasionally thanks you when you do him a favor, I notice. But that doesn't excuse him, Iris. Or how he spoke to me this morning. The nonsense he made up, to pretend he had control over what I drank, for heaven's sake!"

Iris gave a nod. She opened her mouth to speak, closed it, and then finally said: "Just ease up, will ya? Give 'im a graceful way out, if you can." She hunched a little as they came closer to the market and more and more people began clogging the way. "'Twas his kitchen, all intents and purposes, 'til you came yesterday. He can't switch it off just like that."

Gigi didn't answer. It hadn't been just a territorial dispute. Edgars had tried to belittle her, as if doing so would somehow lift him up. And no matter how much she needed the safety and anonymity of Aldridge House, she could not accept that.

If she'd been born poor, been in Iris's shoes, how would she have coped? Been pragmatic about it? Or would she finally have ended up broken?

She shook off the dark, heavy feeling that tried to settle over her like a suffocating blanket, and focused on the stalls just up ahead.

"Let me show you the art of bargaining, Iris." She caught sight of the produce on display. "And what real food looks like."

10

She had found Reine Claude plums at the market. Reine Claudes!

When she'd exclaimed that it couldn't be, that Reine Claudes were only ready for harvest in July, the trader told her they were just off a ship come in from Cape Town, from the tip of Africa. Grown by the French Huguenots who had settled there.

It was lucky for Lord Aldridge she'd found them at the end of her shopping, because once she had them in her hands, she'd gone straight home and started making jam.

It didn't take long to make it, and while it was cooling she'd put in a tray of brioche to cook, ground some coffee, and taken a long, deep breath. As the scents and aromas swirled around her, she knew she had never been closer to her mother than since before she'd died.

A bell rang above the door, a signal from Rob that Lord Aldridge was down for breakfast, and Gigi put the brioche, jam and coffee on a tray for Harry to take up.

He'd only been gone a few minutes, and Gigi was busy with an omelette, when Edgars came down.

"His lordship is down for breakfast." Edgars watched her from the stairs, his lips tight and a gleam in his eye. She had the impression he was gloating.

"I know." She gave him a friendly smile as she tipped the beaten eggs into a pan. The perfume of herbs and tomato fanned her face, and she swirled the mixture around.

"Where is it, then?" Edgars asked.

Ah. He was waiting for an English breakfast. Gigi lifted a single brow, pouting her lips, giving her head an arrogant tilt. Oh, she was the epitome of an Englishman's Frenchie. "His lordship asked for a French cook, *n'est-ce pas?*" She went back to her omelette.

He was very quiet and she ignored him, folding the omelette, tipping it onto a plate, and holding it out to him. It was fragrant, tender perfection.

"My concession to English bacon and eggs," she said. "Tell his lordship *bon appétit.*"

His face twisted, temper rising hot up his neck and along his cheeks. Before he could say anything, though, there was a knock at the door, and he turned from her without taking the plate and stalked up the stairs, anger and tension riding his shoulders like two little devils.

"Fiddle dee dee," she said in exasperation, thinking of Rumplestiltskin, because Edgars looked as if he wanted to stamp his foot in rage.

"Iris, please take this to his lordship. It cannot be eaten

cold." She shuddered as she handed the plate over. "I hope whoever is at the front door does not need to speak to Lord Aldridge. It is vital that this is eaten straightaway."

Iris lifted her brows in surprise and her lips quirked a little, but she moved quickly to the servants' side stair to avoid walking up into the hallway, past Edgars and whomever he was speaking with.

Gigi set out more brioche and jam for the staff in their little dining room and then poured herself a cup of coffee, leaned back against the table, and closed her eyes, tipping her head back to catch the rays of sun angling through the high windows.

They fell warm and golden on her eyelids.

All was quiet for the moment. Everyone was busy with their jobs, the scents and sounds of a house moving through its routine a long-forgotten memory for her.

She hadn't realized she'd missed this. Missed this connection to her mother. This peace and quiet, where the day ran as smooth and sweet as a boat through calm water.

She heard the sound of someone walking down the servants' stairs and straightened, opening her eyes, unwilling to let anyone see her this way.

It was Iris, who walked slower and slower the closer she got to the bottom.

"What is it?" Gigi took a sip of her coffee.

"That man? The one down the street you pointed out this morning?"

Gigi pushed herself away from the table. "Yes?"

"He's here. Edgars brought him in to see his lordship while I was giving him his omelette. He's been invited to breakfast."

"W̶hat's wr—" The look Dervish shot him made Jonathan blink and snap his mouth closed. He leaned back easily in his chair for the sake of Edgars, hovering in the hallway.

"Morning, Aldridge." Dervish stepped into the room.

"Out a bit early, aren't you?" Jonathan spared Dervish another quick glance and cut into the omelette Iris had placed before him. He took a bite.

"You seem in the middle of a spiritual experience," Dervish said after a moment. "Perhaps I should come back later?"

"Join me in worshipping at the altar of French cuisine, Dervish. I'm sure there's plenty, though if there isn't, you'll be the one going without."

Dervish sat, a smile finally on his face.

They both waited while Rob served Dervish some brioche, jam and coffee and then withdrew. Dervish opened his mouth to speak, but Jonathan lifted a hand to silence him. If he knew his staff, Rob would be back shortly with more food.

He bent his head to his omelette and then lifted it when he realized Dervish was too quiet.

Dervish was holding up a piece of brioche covered in jam, staring at it.

"I haven't . . ." He raised his eyes to Jonathan. "I haven't had Reine Claude jam since Adèle Barrington was alive." He put a hand over his mouth and coughed, then took a sip of coffee. "Sorry. I . . ." He shook his head. "I was a little in love with her in my youth. She was older than I was, and so sophisticated, but warm and happy. An extraordinary combination. Eating this reminds me of her and Barrington, of how he was when he lost her. And now his death . . ." He raised the cup to his lips again and looked away.

Jonathan looked away himself to give Dervish a moment. He'd never seen Dervish laid so bare. The man spent his time behind a chilly, polite mask, and Durnham was the only one whose company he'd ever known Dervish to seek out. He gave him time to regain control, searching for something to say that would move things back to normal—a place where Dervish, judging by the stark expression in his eyes, desperately wanted to be. Jonathan pulled the small bowl of golden jam in front of him closer. "Reine Claude jam? What fruit is it?"

"Greengages. The French call them Reine Claudes. Adèle used to make the jam with her own hands. Go down to the kitchen, kick her chef out for a few hours, and stand over the stove with that pretty little girl of hers at her side. Used to have orchards of greengages around the château where she grew up in Brittany, she told me." He rubbed the side of his cheek, his expression no longer as raw. "Where on earth did you get Reine Claude jam?"

Rob came in at that moment with an omelette in hand.

"Rob. Where did we get Reine Claude jam?"

Rob slid the plate beside Dervish and stepped back, hands

behind his back. "Madame Levéel made it this morning, my lord. She got the fruit at the market earlier."

Jonathan gave him a nod of dismissal and waited until he heard the footman's footsteps fade down the hall before he finally came back to his original question. "What's wrong?"

"I got up early this morning. Can't seem to sleep since I learned of Barrington's death. I had the most terrible dreams of Giselle Barrington wandering the streets of London with her father's murderer stalking her."

"So you went looking for her?" Jonathan asked incredulously.

Dervish shrugged, unembarrassed. "It's better than doing nothing. My God, if she is alive, if she has that document, she's in terrible danger."

There was nothing to say to that; it was true.

"Anyway, I went past Goldfern, just in case she's desperate enough to be hanging about there, and I saw some men fixing a window at the side of the house. I didn't want to draw attention to myself by going to inquire. Would you do so?"

"I already know. I went past the house myself last night, just to check on things after our chat at the club." He cut into a brioche, eager to try jam that could bring the stony-faced Dervish to tears. "There was someone in the house. I chased him down, but he got away."

"What was he after? Did you find out?" Dervish had almost stopped breathing.

"He was rifling through Barrington's letter drawer. The caretaker tells me Barrington's lawyer had collected the important post only the day before, so there was nothing to find, but it's telling."

"It means they didn't get the document from either Barrington or his daughter, if they're breaking into Barrington's house looking for something. Either that, or Giselle Barrington is alive and she saw them, and they're trying to find some clue as to where she is."

"Or both," Jonathan pointed out.

"Or both," Dervish agreed. "In which case, they must be desperate to find her."

"I wonder where the hell she is?" Jonathan took a bite of his brioche.

11

If the shadow man was in the house, she had to know.

Gigi looked blindly down at the kitchen table, her mind racing. If it was him upstairs, he had found her. There could be no other reason for his visit.

"His lordship's guest is very taken with your jam."

Rob's voice cut through her thoughts, and she gripped the table to keep herself steady. "He is?" She took a deep breath and turned to him.

"Yes. Not that I blame him. I nearly cried myself when I had your fancy buns and jam for breakfast." Rob gave her a cheeky grin.

She went still. "He nearly cried?"

Rob shrugged. "Actually, weren't no nearly about it. He *did* cry."

That didn't sound like something the shadow man would do. "What's his name?"

Rob shrugged. "I didn't let him in, Mr. Edgars did. Never

seen 'im before." He edged closer to the staff dining room. "Any buns left?"

"Brioche," she corrected absently. "Yes, there are."

Rob disappeared and she looked down at the table again. She'd bottled the leftover Reine Claude jam, and now she lifted one of the smaller jars, weighed it in her hand.

Perhaps she could give the stranger who had a special interest in Goldfern the jam that brought him to tears.

She quickly went through to her rooms and pulled on the chef's hat Georges had given her, covering her hair entirely, and swapped her apron for a new one.

Now she looked like a cook. Not the daughter of a famous, knighted scholar.

She stepped back into the kitchen and stood at the bottom of the stairs to the hallway, listening for any sound of Lord Aldridge's guest leaving.

She didn't have to wait long.

The low murmur of male voices floated down, and she forced her suddenly shaky legs to move up the stairs.

"*Excusez moi.*" Aldridge and the mystery man had their backs to her, with Edgars slightly off to the side, his hand on the doorknob to open the door.

If it was the shadow man, this would be the perfect way to see his face, with Lord Aldridge and Edgars right there to help her if he should attack.

Lord Aldridge and his guest turned. The man from this morning, while a little older than Aldridge, was very striking.

Not handsome, but he had a fierce, brutal beauty to him. He had suffered, this one, and clawed his way out with a will of iron.

The blue cravat she remembered from the glimpse she'd had of him just after dawn was a match for his eyes, and she wondered if a woman had chosen it for him.

There was a moment of electrified silence as both men stared at her.

She frowned, confused as to why they would seem so dumbstruck, and held the jam out to the stranger. As she did, she remembered she should probably curtsy, and dipped her knees. "Rob said *mon seigneur* liked my jam. Would you like a jar to take home?"

The man took the jar, but his eyes never left her. She hoped he would speak, because then she would know for sure. She hadn't seen the shadow man's face, but she had heard him. His voice haunted her nightmares and when he opened his mouth, she would *know*.

"I . . . thank you . . . Cook." He stumbled over her title, but she didn't care—he was not the danger she'd thought him to be, his voice of a deeper, richer timbre than the one she feared.

"Which part of France are you from?"

Relief almost made her miss the question, and she stumbled over her answer, ladling her accent as thick as the jam in his hands. "My family is from Bretagne, *mon seigneur*."

"The reason I have such a fondness for this jam is because someone I knew from Brittany used to make it, years ago.

Yours tastes just as I remember it. Your family is not related to Adèle Barrington, are they? You even look a little like she did. She was the Marchioness de Morlaix before she was married."

She stared at him, the sound of the sea in her ears. Then she blinked and shook her head. "Bretagne is the home of the Reine Claude. It is traditional to make the jam if you are from there."

There was another silence, and Gigi glanced at Lord Aldridge. He was still watching her, but the look in his eye was guarded, maybe even angry.

"Thank you, Madame Levéel." Aldridge didn't sound himself. His words were thick, as if they were caught in his throat.

Taking it for the dismissal it was, she gave a quick nod of goodbye, turned, and ran down the stairs, strangely hurt by the curt way he'd dispatched her, and equally grateful to no longer be under scrutiny.

There was no pleasing her, obviously.

Except she *was* pleased. Aldridge's strange behavior was nothing compared to the relief she felt. The visitor wasn't the shadow man. She could have run out of time, but she hadn't.

Whoever he was, he'd known her mother, though. Her father, too, if he'd been around eating jam at their house.

She wondered which of her parents' many friends he could have been.

Iris was emptying a dustpan into the ash bin as she reached the bottom, and Gigi remembered she'd gone up with the omelette before Edgars had let the stranger in.

"Who is the man with Lord Aldridge? Did you hear Edgars announcing him?" She knew she sounded a little breathless, but mention of her mother had stripped her of her calm.

"Lord Dervish, Edgars said." Iris looked up, her strong, beautiful face smudged with ash. She looked like the Scandinavians of Norway, from good Viking stock. Perhaps her far-off ancestors had raided the coast of England and left more than just huts burned to the ground.

"Are you from the coast originally, Iris?" She couldn't help the question, even as she sifted the name Dervish through her memories and came up with nothing.

"Aye. From Kent." Iris straightened. "Why do you ask?"

"You look like a beautiful Viking maiden. I can see you with a raven on your shoulder, riding into battle to choose who will fall and who will be spared."

"Eh?" Iris stared at her, holding her ash-smudged hands away from her white apron.

"The Valkyries. From Norse legend. They rode horses into battle, and chose who was to fall and die."

"Not sure I'd like to have that sort o' responsibility." Iris turned and rinsed her hands at the sink. But she seemed pleased, as if the story appealed to her, gave her a new view of herself.

Above them came the sound of the front door being closed, and Gigi thought of the letters in her father's chest. The letters of a man who signed himself D.

Dervish?

If he *was* involved in the secret business her father sometimes undertook, her father wouldn't have mentioned him. He'd been fearful of telling her anything that might endanger her if she was questioned. So she never had any names, any idea what the documents said or why they were taking them. She'd trusted her father that it was better that way, but now it left her running blind.

It would be useful to know where Lord Dervish lived. If he *was* the mysterious D., she could give the document to him.

"Iris, I need something for this evening's meal. I'll just step out to see if I can get it." She was already walking into her rooms as she spoke, ripping the chef's cap off her head, throwing the apron over a chair and pulling her hat and cloak from the peg.

"You don't want me or Babs to go, Cook?" Iris asked, a little hopefully.

"*Non.* I need to find it myself." She ran up the stairs, slipped out into the alley, and raced down to Chapel Street. There was no one to the left, in the direction of Goldfern, but when she looked right, she saw Dervish just turning right onto South Audley.

Holding her skirts to one side, she ran, following him as he turned left onto Farm and then right onto John Street, keeping well back.

John Street was narrow, an exclusive enclave very close to Berkeley Square, and she watched as Dervish climbed the stairs of a thin, smart town house and tried the door. His own house, then. He was juggling the jam and the knocker when the door opened and he stepped inside.

Once the door was closed she walked down the street toward his house, fast and with her head down, as if she were in a hurry. She turned her head at the place where Dervish had gone in and noted the number.

Now all she needed was a sample of his handwriting, and she could determine if he was Mr. D.

And if he was, then, finally, the document would be safe.

12

The look Madame Levéel cast him when Jonathan had sent her scurrying down the stairs like a naughty schoolgirl had been laced with surprise and hurt. Jonathan didn't want to even think about the look Dervish had given him.

Surprise, too. And pity.

He flicked out a crinkle in the newspaper he was pretending to read, unable to get comfortable.

Madame Levéel had taken him unaware, popping up from behind them like some kind of exotic jack-in-the-box, all sweeping dark lashes and plump lips, tied up in an apron that showed all her dips and curves.

And she had no idea how she'd affected them.

He'd noticed her frown of confusion at their staring, and he knew when she'd held out her jam, Dervish had barely been able to understand what she was saying to him.

Jonathan had been hard-pressed to grasp it himself, and he hadn't been the subject of her intense scrutiny.

Because she had watched Dervish with all her concentration.

Jealousy had swept over him like a London fog, obscuring his common sense. But he could think better now, with a little distance, and he had the feeling it wasn't interest but trepidation that had had his perplexing cook watching Dervish with those huge green-gold eyes.

Dervish had hardly said a word after Jonathan had banished his cook belowstairs. He'd rubbed his face, muttered something about not enough sleep and, seeing ghosts everywhere, he left. Jonathan wondered if the small progress they'd made in their friendship this morning had been wiped out for good.

If it meant Dervish would never see Madame Levéel again, he could live with it.

Jonathan lowered his paper slowly.

Had he really just thought that?

He folded the paper and set it aside. Stood up. He needed to walk, to *do* something, rather than sit and brood over things he had never brooded over before. Like the look his cook had given an acquaintance.

He needed to see Barrington's lawyer and let him know about the burglary. It was as good a reason for a walk as any.

He went to the hall and grabbed his hat and coat. Edgars appeared as he turned the door handle.

"I'll be back in time for dinner. Tell Cook I'd like to eat early."

"I will," Edgars murmured. "When she returns."

He refused to ask where Madame Levéel was. Edgars had never seen fit to give him this sort of information before, damn it. He'd never had the slightest curiosity about where his staff were in the past, and he refused to do so now.

It was an admission he would not make.

He gave a nod of disinterest and stepped out into the crisp air.

He felt calmer, less restless, by the time he reached Barrington's solicitors, where an efficient clerk ushered him into Greenway's office.

Dervish had cautioned him this morning to say nothing of Barrington's death when he spoke to Greenway, and the need for secrecy hampered him as he watched the lawyer fidget at the news of the burglary. He wondered what Greenway would tell him if he knew Barrington had been murdered and his daughter was missing.

"Did Mr. Jones say anything was stolen?" Greenway played with the quill on his desk, his eyes on his fingers.

"No. Barrington's correspondence was rifled through, that was all. If they took anything, Jones didn't think it was important."

Greenway tapped quick fingers on the desk, and something flickered behind his eyes, as if the news of someone searching through Barrington's letters meant more to him than a strange burglary. "I'd already taken the letters the day before. Jones is right, there was nothing useful there." He looked like an English setter, about to go for a walk. He was vibrating with contained energy, but he had no reason to confide in Jonathan. And there was nothing Jonathan could think of to change that, without spilling secrets that weren't his to spill.

"Have you already sent the letters on to Barrington?"

Greenway lifted his head sharply. "Yes, I have. Why do you ask?"

Jonathan raised his brows at the suspicion in Greenway's voice. "Merely that if the burglar was after some specific correspondence, they may try your office next. And perhaps a warning to whoever takes Sir Barrington's mail for him on the Continent would be prudent, as well."

"Oh." Greenway had clearly not thought of that, and he scribbled a note on the paper before him. "Quite right to err on the side of caution, Lord Aldridge. Thank you for the advice."

There seemed no reason to extend the meeting, and it was almost painful to see how badly Greenway wanted him to go. Jonathan rose from his deep leather chair. "Do you know Miss Barrington, Mr. Greenway?" The question left his lips before he had a chance to think better of it.

Greenway rose himself, shaking his head. "No." He looked sideways at Jonathan as he walked to his door.

"Pity. I haven't seen her in many years, and being back at Goldfern last night reminded me just how long it's been. I wondered if she was well."

"Barrington's never said anything different." Greenway shrugged. "Girl's already had one paper published, on the social customs of Europe, or some such. I forwarded the payment for that on to her last year."

Jonathan raised his brows. "I didn't realize she shared her father's interests."

"Not much else for the girl to do, I suppose. It was a prestigious journal she was published in, so I've no doubt she knows what she's talking about. Writing a book as well, I think Barrington mentioned." He looked at the outer door pointedly.

He was a man who had something to do, and wanted Jonathan gone so he could do it in private.

Jonathan bade the solicitor goodbye. Perhaps he could persuade Dervish and Durnham to talk to Greenway. If Barrington had given him special instructions in the event of a burglary, or in the event of someone being interested in his correspondence, it would help to know.

Jonathan stepped out onto the street, wondering how a young woman whose interests lay in academic papers could possibly have survived the kind of people who were after her.

Dervish was probably right—the Swedish authorities would find her floating in Lake Mälaren.

It was an unpleasant thought. One Dervish clearly hoped wasn't true, or he wouldn't be walking the streets looking for her.

Jonathan turned homeward reluctantly. He had two papers to read for the next session in the House of Lords, as well as some work to do for Durnham and Dervish—if Dervish didn't decide to kick him out of the very exclusive club of three he seemed to have joined.

As he turned onto South Audley, he saw just ahead of him, going the same way and weighed down by two baskets, the cause of his rift with Dervish in the flesh.

Madame Levéel was in a dark coat and bonnet, her boots tapping on the pavement.

He lengthened his stride, even though he knew it would be awkward to escort her home, awkward to speak with her after his rudeness this morning.

But just like last night, when he had not asked her questions that he knew he should have asked, he found himself helpless to resist the urge to catch up.

At the sound of his heavier tread, she turned her head to look back at him, and he didn't think he mistook the fear in her eyes, or the way it changed to a guarded friendliness when she saw it was him.

It seemed she didn't hold a grudge for this morning's dismissal, and the relief of that almost made him forget about the fear.

Almost.

"May I help you with those?" He took the first basket and held out his hand for the other. She handed it over without a word.

"You were afraid when you heard me behind you. Did you think it was the man who followed you last night?"

She massaged her shoulder, and Jonathan, hefting baskets that were far heavier than he'd anticipated, didn't blame her.

"I did." She rubbed her hands on her arms and then shook them, as if they were numb.

"If you didn't see him, though, or if you thought it was your imagination, I can't understand why you would be so scared."

She said nothing, looking down at her feet as she walked.

"Madame Levéel, if you saw him, if he threatened you or intimidated you in any way, please tell me. There is something even more important than a robbery at stake, and if you could describe the man to me, it would be very helpful."

"I didn't see him." She turned her gaze on him, and there was such rage in her eyes he nearly stopped in surprise. "I wish I had seen him, if he was there at all. My fear is because of something that happened to me. Not in London, somewhere else. That is why I'm a little scampering mouse, my lord." Her voice was as bitter as burned coffee, and just as dark.

"You are not a mouse." His voice came out an octave lower than usual, and he cleared his throat. "You are more like a cat."

"A cat?" She looked at him sidelong, brows lifted.

He realized anything he said now would be dangerous. To him, she was unpredictable, sensual and deeply mysterious. But he could say none of that to her.

"I would like to be like *le chat botté*. Puss in Boots." Her own boots tip-tapped on the cobbles. "Wily and courageous, and not afraid to take big chances." She stopped, and he saw they were already at Aldridge House. She held out her hands for the baskets.

"I'll take them—"

"No." She said it kindly. "I will take them down the side alley and go in through the kitchen. You will go in through the front door." She put her hands on the handles, and he felt the brush of her gloves on his wrists as she tugged the baskets away. "Thank you for your help, your lordship."

She walked away, swinging the baskets and humming a little tune to herself, and he stared after her.

She'd treated him as an equal again.

She'd told him how things must be, with a firm practicality. She had not deferred to him or felt the slightest bit uncomfortable giving him orders.

But this same woman was afraid of the sound of men's footsteps behind her, of people following her in the night.

Jonathan waited until she disappeared into the kitchen and he couldn't see her anymore.

And then, as she'd told him to, he went in through the front door.

13

Gigi ground the coffee, each turn of the grinder turning something inside her: tight, pent-up, ready to burst with the need for action. She had to get a sample of Lord Dervish's handwriting to compare to the letters in her father's trunk. The only way she could see to do that, short of somehow stealing his correspondence, would be to write him a note and ask for a response. And still somehow remain anonymous—just in case she was wrong.

"His lordship wishes to convey his compliments on the almond-and-courgette soup, Cook." Rob placed the empty bowl on the table.

"*Merci.*" She tapped the ground coffee into its canister, then pulled the cherry-and-frangipani tarts from the oven. "Will you whip the cream for me, Iris?"

She handed the deep bowl with the cream and a whisk across, and turned back to the table.

Edgars was coming down the stairs, his eyes fixed on Iris as if he were in a trance.

Gigi looked over her shoulder, trying to see what he saw. While Iris looked her usual lovely self, with cheeks pink from the exertion of whipping, she couldn't understand what would catch his attention so. She looked back at Edgars, tried to follow his gaze, and then blushed.

Iris's bosom was jiggling and bouncing as she beat the cream.

With a cry of surprise, Edgars fell down the last three steps and stumbled into the kitchen, arms flailing about.

"You all right, Mr. Edgars?" Gigi asked.

He gave her a dazed look, as if he'd walked into a door, and she turned away to hide her expression.

"Here you go, Cook." Iris handed her a bowl of glossy white peaks.

"Perfect." Gigi beamed as she took the cream. "Isn't Iris perfect, Mr. Edgars?"

"What?"

Edgars stumbled across the kitchen toward his own rooms, realized halfway he had no reason to go there, and changed his path to the cellar to fetch wine.

"We getting any o' these?" Rob stood over the cherry tarts, his eyes as riveted to them as Edgars' had been to Iris's bosom.

Gigi shooed him away. "Not enough good cherries. But I made apple tart for you instead. It is very nice."

Edgars appeared with a dusty bottle and kept his gaze firmly down, his pace faster than usual.

Could it be he realized at last who Iris was? What everyone

else saw when they looked at her? And how small his chances of success were, given the way he'd treated her in the past?

Iris had disappeared into the staff dining room, none the wiser, and Gigi hoped she led him a very merry dance.

As she sent Rob up with the tarts and cream, and then the coffee, she wondered how she could word a note to Dervish that would force him to respond without giving herself away. And where she should ask him to drop the note off.

Somewhere easy for her to get to, but which wouldn't lead back to Aldridge House.

The cracks and loose bricks in the wall near Goldfern's garden door would be easy to get to unseen, and Goldfern was surely a place the mysterious D. would find a reasonable drop-off. It also had no direct connection to Aldridge.

She would need to find the courage to walk down that dark alley again.

She made the brioche dough automatically, thinking of what the note should say. When she was done and standing at the sink to wash her hands, she realized the maids had already done the dishes and gone up, and Rob and Harry were back from their serving duties and talking quietly in the dining room over coffee and apple tart.

She finished her breakfast preparations and went to her room, sinking down on the little chair by her desk with relief.

It felt almost too good to be off her feet. She didn't want to stand up again and walk to Dervish's to deliver a note without being seen.

She knew it was cold outside, and from the sigh of rain on

the high kitchen windows it was wet as well. And someone wanted her dead.

She hugged herself, trying to stop a shiver. She could see her father: body crumpled on the cold ground, open eyes staring sightlessly at the silver-rimmed clouds.

She hadn't looked at the letter he'd died for. She'd been conditioned by years with her father to leave it alone.

But if she was to have any chance of convincing Dervish to reply to her note, she needed to know what the letter contained. And if she was going to risk her life for it, she needed to understand what the stakes were.

The letter isolated her from every acquaintance her parents knew, because she could only give it to the right person. And with the shadow man circling, unknown and disguised, she had the feeling she would only have one chance to get it right.

She flipped her skirt up over her knees and then lifted the hem of her petticoats. Felt for the crackle of paper and slipped the letter out of its secret pocket.

She reached for the small silver paper knife that had been her father's gift in celebration of her first published journal article, and hesitated.

He wouldn't be happy about her doing this. She sighed and, in one smooth move, broke the wax seal and opened the letter.

Then read the contents with a buzz in her head.

The Russians were saying they were prepared to break with France and join Britain. The signature at the end of the page made her blink. No wonder men were prepared to kill for this.

She pulled out a piece of paper with shaking hands and wrote a draft to Dervish, then another and another, until at last she thought she had it right. Then she took a fresh piece and wrote the note out in simple, neutral script. She folded it, waxed it closed, and gnawed on her thumbnail for a while, considering what she should put on the front.

What would get the note brought to his attention immediately? Make him open it as a matter of priority?

If he was the mysterious D., she knew a surefire way. If he wasn't. . . . She rubbed at her brow and then wrote carefully in Russian:

A *most urgent communication for D*.

With the Russian letter safely back in its hiding place and her letter for Dervish in her coat, Gigi dug in her trunks for the heavy, fur-lined cloak her father had bought her in Finland. She fastened it around her shoulders, but left the hood down as she stepped into the kitchen.

Rob and Harry were still in the dining room, and she took the stairs to the back door quietly, unlocked it, and slipped the key in her pocket again.

She was grateful for the cloak as a sharp, rain-laden wind hit her when she stepped outside. As she pulled the hood over her head, the door slammed behind her and she winced.

She would be hard-pressed to explain a trip outside in this weather to anyone at Aldridge House, but she could always speak in French until they gave up in the face of a crazy foreigner.

The wind half blew her to where the alley opened onto Chapel Street and she hesitated, looking toward Goldfern quickly to make sure there was no one there.

Then, drawing her cloak tight about her, she faced the other way and stepped out, head bent against the rain—a Little Red Riding Hood, intent on her task.

She let the darkness swallow her up.

Jonathan swirled the last of his wine around in its glass and decided it was better to know tonight if Dervish held his behavior this morning against him or not. Rain, wind and cold notwithstanding.

The idea had bothered him all day. More than he wanted it to.

He had friends aplenty in London, but since his return from the Peninsula, very few were men he felt at ease with anymore. Dervish and Durnham were the only two he could sit with quietly, with no need for conversation, and feel comfortable.

Neither had served in the army, but now that he was in their private circle, he realized they fought the war just as fiercely from the home front.

He set the wine on his desk and stood. He would see if Dervish was at their club.

From deep within the house he heard the faint echo of a

slamming door over the sound of the rain on the window and wondered who else had decided to brave the weather.

Edgars had been distracted this evening. Even Rob and Harry had been confused by his lack of usual focus and intensity, shooting Edgars strange looks while they served dinner.

Edgars had even gone up to do his valet duties with a dazed expression, but now, as Jonathan walked into the hall to get his coat from the stand, he stepped out of Jonathan's rooms and looked down from the top of the stairs.

"I'm going to my club for a short while, Edgars. Don't worry about waiting up."

Ordinarily Edgars would have run down and fussed, but this evening he simply nodded and turned back to his work.

As Jonathan fought his way into his fitted coat, he wondered what was happening to his household.

Madame Levéel had turned them all topsy-turvy.

Another battering of rain against the door made him reach for his greatcoat as well, and a hat. He stepped outside and immediately turned his collar up against the rain, catching the door just before it slammed and easing it shut.

A movement immediately ahead caught his eye, and, compelled by a sudden sense of urgency, he ran down the steps and squinted through the downpour.

A small figure, swathed in a fur-trimmed cloak, bent against the wind and rain.

He started after her, a strange tension gripping his shoulders. There was no question in his mind who it was. And he had no reason to follow her—he was her employer, not her keeper.

But he couldn't forget her strange behavior, the risks Durnham had warned him about, and her intensity this morning with Dervish.

This was the second time she had taken a walk in the dark by herself in two days, even though she was frightened by something and, even in broad daylight, was as nervous as a mouse.

And suddenly he knew he was lying to himself.

He was not following her for any reason other than that he was far too interested in her. And something about the way she had looked at him this afternoon—with such relief—when she'd heard someone walking behind her and seen it was him, disturbed him deeply.

No woman should be that afraid.

She turned right on South Audley. His long strides had brought him close enough for her to see him if she turned around, but the wind and rain masked the sounds of his footsteps.

She kept hunched against the weather, and slowed as she turned up Farm, and then stopped at the junction with John Street.

Jonathan stepped behind a large oak growing close against the wall of a house, as deep in the shadows as he could get.

His cook peered down John Street, then back the way she'd come, her eyes passing over his tree and beyond, to where Farm met South Audley.

Hesitantly, fear in every step, she turned onto John Street. Jonathan stepped out from the tree and crossed the street, crouching behind another tree that grew on the corner.

John was narrow and short, letting out onto Audley Square

at the end. And it was also, he suddenly realized with a cold, sinking dread, the street on which Dervish lived.

He'd never visited Dervish at his home, but they had exchanged notes more than once. Number eighteen John Street, if his memory served him.

From behind the tree, he watched Madame Levéel stare up at a house halfway down the street, and then dart up the stairs and fumble with something inside her cloak, slipping it under the door. She pounded once on the knocker before she ran down the stairs and back the way she'd come, toward him. Her face showed lips tight with nerves, and when she looked over her shoulder to make sure she hadn't been seen, he saw fear in every line of her body.

He froze in astonishment.

His jealousy had come roaring back when he'd realized the address, but he had expected her to be an eager visitor, not a woman who had to work up the courage to leave a note and then run like Dervish meant her harm.

She ran past his hiding place in the shadows, and he was left with the conundrum of whether to follow her, or knock on Dervish's door himself and see if he could work out what this was all about.

Madame Levéel was already halfway down Farm, and he had decided to visit Dervish with an innocent report on his visit to Barrington's lawyer, and see if he could glean any information when a man walked past his hiding place and stood a moment on the corner, within touching distance, looking after Madame Levéel.

He must have come from the other side of Dervish's house, and wouldn't have seen Jonathan take up his position. Jonathan watched as he moved, fluid and fast, down the street after her.

He rose from his crouch and the wind took his hat, but he didn't even look to see where it had blown. With the rain plastering his hair to his head, he moved swiftly after Madame Levéel's follower.

It seemed his strange little cook was right to be afraid, after all.

14

She knew she was being followed. She'd seen a movement, furtive and quick, out the corner of her eye, and she didn't try to pretend to herself that it meant nothing.

She slowed, even though her legs quivered with the need to run, trying to think as the rain blinded her and the wind pulled and twisted her cloak around her.

She should have known the shadow man would have Dervish watched, if Dervish was D. Since the time of his terrible conversation with her father at Tessin Palace, she'd understood that the shadow man was a diplomat with the Foreign Office. He would know where Dervish lived. Know his role.

She had only realized Dervish might be D. this morning, but if she'd been thinking properly she would have taken precautions, thought through the implications.

Such as the danger of approaching Dervish directly.

She forced herself to shrug off her self-recrimination and focus.

She could not lead her follower to Aldridge House. It would be unfair to everyone there, and it was her only safe haven. She had to assume her watcher had picked up her trail at Dervish's house and didn't know where she lived.

She slowed even more as a cab rumbled down the street, throwing up water.

Just as it passed her she ran, darting around it and across the street, diving into a narrow alley between two houses.

Her follower gave himself away with a shout, and she heard the pound of his boots on the cobbles behind her, despite the rain and the whistle of the wind.

She clutched her cloak closer about her as she put on speed, turning right to race along the back of the houses lining South Audley. She turned right again, thinking to emerge from the alley onto South Audley as close to Farm as she could. To run back to Dervish and throw herself on his mercy.

But instead of coming upon the main street, she stumbled into a small square surrounded by high walls, with two doors at the far end. The rear accesses of two large town houses on South Audley.

It was a dead end.

The warm lights shining from the top floors of the houses before her illuminated a cart parked close up against the wall between the two doors, and a stack of barrels close to her on the right.

She was trapped. Suddenly the danger she was in hit her full force, and her knees almost buckled.

The sound of pounding feet snapped her out of her panic

and she ran for the barrels, crouching down and squeezing between them and the wall, her heart beating as fast as the little mouse she was.

She'd thought it unlikely the shadow man was personally watching Dervish, especially in this weather. He would have hired a lackey, just as he had in Stockholm, to draw her father out.

And surely the lackey should just want to know where she went, where she was staying, so that the shadow man could close in for the kill himself?

He should—but if so, why was he running her down?

He burst into the little square, stumbling to a stop in surprise. He was breathing hard, his hat pulled down low over his eyes and his hands clenching and unclenching.

He did a thorough sweep of the small space, his gaze lingering first on the cart and then on her hiding place, and her heartbeat picked up even more.

She couldn't bear to be cornered here and dragged out.

The thought of it snapped something inside her, and fear gave way to anger in the next breath.

She felt around on the ground for some protection, and her hand found a smooth rock the size of her palm. It felt good, heavy and comforting.

She rose up and took a step toward him, and he flinched.

Confrontation was the last thing he'd expected.

"Who are you?" She spoke sharply, letting all of her anger into her words, and the wind caused her cloak to flap around her like the wings of an angry bird.

He took a step back, then rocked on his feet, unsure, and Gigi decided the shadow man had employed someone not too good at thinking for himself.

Someone who would do as he was told and not question his orders too much.

Perhaps, like any predator, this man had acted on instinct when she ran, chasing her down and only now remembering his job was to follow and observe, not bring himself to her attention.

He looked torn, and the rain glinted off his cheeks as he tipped his head to the right. He wanted to grab her, to win. He looked over his shoulder, nervous and edgy, and she could almost see the wheels turning in his head as he realized this was the last thing his employer wanted.

Too late to be at all convincing, he put his hands up in front of him. "I didn't mean you no harm, an' all. Just thought you needed help. Can I walk you home? Make sure you're safe, like?"

She almost laughed at the open slyness in his expression. "You may not." She stood even taller, weighing the stone in her hand. "Please leave me alone."

"Dark night, bad weather. You'll be wise to let me see you safe."

She said nothing, staring at him with open hostility, and he gave an exaggerated shrug and began backing out of the little square. She had no doubt he intended to hide somewhere close by and follow her home when she tried to leave.

It was a frustrating stalemate.

She would have to find some way to lead him away from Aldridge House and then slip home, and she didn't know what he would do if this game ended the same way again. Even he would know he couldn't bluff his way out of it a second time, and she had seen those clenched fists, that compulsion to best her. She doubted he'd hold back a second time.

He disappeared down the alley, and she could hear his footsteps ringing on the cobbles. There was no place for him to hide in the twisting narrow lane into this courtyard; he'd have to take up a position somewhere beyond it. Lurking like a troll beneath his bridge.

She'd assumed the doors set in the wall were locked, but she tried them anyway. Both doorknobs rattled as she pulled on them, but didn't budge.

She looked at the cart against the wall, but even if she got into it, it wouldn't boost her high enough to climb the wall. And this wall was new brick, not the rough-hewn stone at the back garden of Goldfern House, with its many handholds.

Then her eyes fell on the barrels.

They were empty. She had noticed that when she had hidden behind them, and shifted them a little. It was possible she could lift one.

She eased one off the pile and rolled it to the cart, heaved it inside. Then she scrambled in after it and set it against the wall.

It wobbled as she climbed onto it, the thin wooden lid giving a little beneath her weight.

But it held. And she was high enough. Thank God, she was high enough.

She heaved herself up onto the wall, kicking the barrel hard enough to tip it out of the cart so that when he returned to see what had happened to her, her follower might miss how she had escaped.

Up on the wall she was easy to see, backlit by the lights from the town houses, and her vulnerability spurred her on. The drop on the other side was long, but there was plenty of ivy. She grasped wet, slippery handfuls of the vines and swung down, her feet scrabbling for purchase.

She pulled down half the vines as she fell, slower than she would have without them, but still too fast. She was grateful there was only well-tended lawn below as she landed hard, overbalanced, and fell on her back.

At least she hadn't screamed.

She stood slowly—tired, bruised and afraid. She had to get home before her pursuer came looking for her and realized how she had gotten away.

The thought put some speed into her steps as she limped across the fine garden and skirted the side of the house, walking with care so her boots made no sound on the paving.

She emerged onto a well-kept front lawn, with a low brick wall separating the garden from the pavement. Bent low, Gigi ran to the wall and looked up and down the street.

There was no one that she could see. The rain was still falling, although lighter now, sweeping over her in glittering waves.

She took a last, deep breath, rose up and ran the short distance to Chapel Street, turned onto it and raced to Aldridge House.

As she took the sharp turn into the alley to the kitchen door it felt like she had reached safety, trip-trapping over the bridge to the green, green hills on the other side.

No troll was getting her tonight.

15

Jonathan was edging down the alley, the knife from his boot in his hand, when he heard Madame Levéel ask her follower who he was.

He paused, interested in the answer. But the man did not answer, merely made a ridiculous offer to escort her home "safe."

When she refused, Jonathan pushed away from the wall and was about to intervene, when the man backed away, still facing the little courtyard but moving down the alley.

Jonathan moved back as well.

There was so much going on here that he didn't understand. And he would rather watch and observe, learn as much as possible before he waded in with demands for answers. You were lied to less if you knew almost as much as the person you were questioning.

So he slipped out into the larger alley that ran parallel to South Audley, and crouched low beneath an old door propped against the wall.

The man emerged and looked left and right. His gaze fixed on the door where Jonathan hid, but then he moved across the narrow road and hid in the dark entrance to another alley.

He was going to wait for Madame Levéel to leave, and keep following her.

Jonathan wondered how long it would take her to get up the courage to leave the tiny courtyard in which she'd trapped herself.

The rain eased off a little, less a stinging slap and more a gentle caress, but his trousers and boots were soaked, and he was starting to shiver. His legs began to cramp, and he was considering rising up and going in to get her, to hell with revealing himself to the mysterious watcher, when, with a curse, the watcher broke cover himself.

He stalked back to the alleyway and disappeared into the darkness. Jonathan crept after him, stopping just short of the light filtering down from the houses behind the wall.

The man was looking behind some barrels, kicking them aside in frustration, and then crouched down to look beneath the cart against the wall. He tried the doors, rattling the knobs in frustration.

"She's bloody gone." There was a vicious note to his exclamation, and when he did a slow, full turn, as if hoping to find some small hiding place he might have missed, Jonathan saw murder in his eyes.

He backed away, quiet and fast, and just made his former hiding place before the man burst out of the alley and disappeared to the right, in the direction of Dervish's house.

Jonathan rose and ran left, turned into the narrow lane that led back to South Audley, then right onto Chapel and down the service lane to his kitchen door.

He stood a moment, hand on the knob, gripped with the need to know that she was safe, and then forced himself to drop it. He walked around to his front door.

He wasn't prepared to let Madame Levéel know he had followed her, that he knew what had happened to her this evening.

For the first time, Durnham's warnings seemed to hold some weight. And if his cook was a spy for France, he would do well not to let her know he was watching her.

But he did want to know if she was home and safe.

He took the stairs to the front door two at a time and pushed the door open, dripping onto the black-and-white tile of the entrance hall.

"My lord?" Edgars appeared from the dining room, a cloth in hand, far more like the usual Edgars than he'd been earlier. He helped Jonathan off with his greatcoat and coat.

"I got soaked by a cab, I'm afraid. Lost my hat, too. I'll need to change before I can go on to my other appointment tonight. And could you ask Cook to make me some coffee?"

Coffee was the last thing he felt like. Brandy sounded far better, after the evening he'd had, but Edgars wouldn't need to go speak to Madame Levéel about brandy.

The butler gave a small bow and disappeared down the service stairs, while Jonathan dawdled on his way up to his room, giving Edgars time to return before he reached the top of the stairs.

"Cook will have your coffee ready in a moment." Edgars appeared in the hall again and looked at the water trail with a frown. "I hope you don't catch a chill, my lord."

"I'm sure not, Edgars." Jonathan ran the rest of the way up the stairs on a wave of relief. The mysterious Madame Levéel had made it home, then, and was calmly going about her duties.

Knowing what she'd been through, he could scarcely believe it. And he sorely wanted to know how she'd escaped. But he'd tackle her later. Unless she had a death wish, she wouldn't be going anywhere again tonight.

And he would very much like to meet up with Dervish, either at their club or at his home. He had no right to the possessiveness he felt for Madame Levéel, but he felt it nevertheless. He wanted to know what Dervish was to her.

Jonathan hoped Dervish would also be amenable to discussing any interesting letters he might recently have received. And if he wasn't, Jonathan was prepared to be as subtle as a nine-pound cannon.

She had to go back out.

Gigi sent up Lord Aldridge's coffee with a smile she didn't feel, then stepped close to the fire, letting it burn away the chill in her bones.

She couldn't risk going to Lord Dervish to warn him he was being watched. But when he came to drop off his note at Goldfern, the shadow man's watcher would surely be following him and would either take the note Dervish left or wait to see who came to collect it.

The only solution was another note, left in the place she had told Dervish to leave his reply, warning him that he was being followed, and asking him to take both notes back home with him.

She would have liked to compare his handwriting, have definite confirmation that Dervish truly was D., but it seemed more and more likely he was. Why else would he be watched?

"You done for the night, Cook?" Edgars came to stand beside her, rubbing his hands near the fire. Something in the way he stood, hunched and stiff, spoke of anger and confusion. She wondered if it was to do with his feelings for Iris, or something she had unwittingly done.

"Yes. I'm done." She stepped away from him, hoping her turning in would lead him to do the same, so she could slip out again without arousing even more suspicion.

"Good night." She went to her rooms and heard Edgars turn the lock in the kitchen door and then close the door to his own rooms.

She'd need to let him settle down before she snuck out to the alley behind Goldfern, but there was a sense of urgency riding her—a fear that Dervish would respond immediately to her request, that he might already be on his way to leave the note for her.

She rubbed her arms and shivered at the thought of the man from earlier watching from a dark corner.

She would just have to go as soon as possible.

She pulled out her stationery for the second time that evening and wrote a quick, succinct note, letting Dervish know he was being followed and to take everything back with him. That she would find some other way to contact him.

It was the best she could do.

She could still hear Edgars moving about in his rooms, but she dared not wait a moment longer.

She pulled a scarf over her head, draping it across her face to keep out the cold and hide her features, and went out into the kitchen.

She'd hung her soaked cloak on a hook near the fire to dry. She pulled it on, making sure her note was safely in her inner coat pocket, and walked quietly up the stairs to the back door.

"Going out, Madame Levéel?"

She strangled a gasp and turned, pushing herself back against the door for support and pulling the scarf down so it no longer covered her face. "Just for a moment, Mr. Edgars. The rain sounds like it has stopped. I like to get some fresh air after breathing the smoke and the heat of the kitchen all day."

It would have seemed an eminently reasonable notion, if Edgars didn't know she'd been out once this evening already.

"Want me to escort you? After your scare last night?"

Gigi smiled, hoping it didn't look like a death grimace. "That's very kind of you, but *merci, non*. The thief from last night would hardly be back twice in a row. I am not going far, just a few steps."

He gave a nod but kept watching her as she opened the door. She couldn't take the key from under his very nose, so she'd have to hope he didn't lock the door after her and make her knock to come back in.

The rain was falling so softly she could barely feel it, a fine drizzle as light as dandelion seeds.

She skirted the large puddles in the lane as she walked to the dark alley that ran behind Aldridge House. It seemed better tonight than it had yesterday. She knew where she was going, and there was more light from the houses on either side—more people were staying in tonight because of the weather.

It helped.

In some places she had to walk through puddles that stretched across the whole width of the alley, and she held her cloak close to make up for the water freezing her feet.

She saw the back door to Goldfern up ahead and slowed. There was no light from Goldfern, and the shadows were long here.

She allowed herself a few moments to listen for the sounds of someone nearby, but there was nothing.

She moved quietly and rapidly to the door, and wriggled the loose brick she'd found yesterday. There was no note tucked behind it.

She slipped her own note in.

The follower wouldn't know where to look, or even why

Dervish was coming here until it was too late. And unless he attacked Dervish and took the notes by force, he would never read them, either.

She'd have to hope this was enough.

She stood back and looked at the brick carefully. It was easy enough to spot, if you knew what to look for.

She turned and walked quickly away, ears straining for the sound of footsteps following her, for any movement at all.

She was so focused on listening to what was happening behind her, looking back every few steps to make sure she was still alone, that she didn't pay any attention to what was in front of her.

She turned the corner back into the service alley for Aldridge House, and ran straight into Edgars.

16

"I'm afraid Lord Dervish isn't in, my lord. He's left the country." Dervish's jowled and dour butler stepped back to let Jonathan in. "However, he did leave a note for you. I was going to arrange for its delivery tomorrow, but if you'll wait, I'll fetch it now."

Jonathan gaped at the man. "Left the country?"

The butler gave a nod and disappeared into a room, returning almost immediately with a note.

Jonathan took it and ripped it open, uncaring that the butler would be startled by his haste and lack of decorum.

Dervish's scrawled hand read:

Got word earlier today from a Foreign Office colleague,
Frobisher, recently returned from Stockholm, that there is
evidence Giselle Barrington is in Lapland. She may have
run to some of the Sami people she and her father know to
hide. Thornton's so weighed down with diplomatic issues

he's unable to leave his post, so I am traveling to investigate myself. Had to leave today to make a boat waiting at Dover, as the next boat leaves next week. Have left forwarding address at my house. Send any information you learn through there, not office. We still don't know who's involved in Barrington's death. D.

Jonathan had known Dervish was cut up about Barrington's death and worried for his daughter, but this instant response went beyond that. Dervish must have owed something to Barrington, if he felt so strongly that he needed to be responsible for his daughter's safety.

And of course, the girl could still have the letter. The Foreign Office would be saved a great deal of embarrassment if Dervish could get it from her.

Dervish cared more about Miss Barrington than about the letter, he didn't doubt that, but the letter might have been how Dervish justified the sudden trip to his superiors.

Jonathan raised his head and found Dervish's butler staring at him. "When did he leave?"

"Late this afternoon, my lord."

It was nearly ten in the evening, now. There was no way he would catch him. And the letter Madame Levéel had delivered was no doubt sitting on his desk, waiting to be forwarded.

"I came to discuss a note Lord Dervish would have received sometime this evening. Perhaps, as he's gone, I can deal with it for him?" Jonathan folded Dervish's note and stuffed it in his coat pocket.

"I'm afraid that's not possible, my lord." The butler didn't sound apologetic at all. "Some of Lord Dervish's correspondence is quite sensitive, and I'm not able to hand it over to anyone."

"It's urgent. Damn it, if only he'd let me know sooner that he was leaving." Jonathan looked over the butler's shoulder to the room he'd just been in, and guessed it was Dervish's study. He would have given a lot right then for five minutes alone in that room.

That thought must have shown on his face.

The butler shifted to block the door more fully, and for a moment Jonathan contemplated taking him on, pushing past him and getting into the room. But he didn't know where the letters were kept, and he would ruin any chance of communication with Dervish while he was away—of that he was sure. The butler looked the kind to hold a grudge.

He sighed. "I'll write a response and send it round tomorrow morning." He turned for the front door, and the butler held it open and then closed it behind him with insulting alacrity.

Jonathan smiled. He couldn't blame the fellow. He'd have wanted to boot himself out, too, in his position.

Standing on the top step, he looked out into the night and wondered if the watcher was still there. He'd come back this way after losing Madame Levéel, but had he known Dervish wasn't here? It seemed strange to watch a house when its owner was on his way to Sweden.

Unless they were watching to see who tried to contact Dervish.

Jonathan walked slowly down the stairs and hunched against the fine mist that fell from the sky. It almost blinded him, the drops so tiny they clung to his eyelashes and blurred his vision.

He kept his ears tuned for any sound of following footsteps, and after he turned down Farm Street he hid behind the tree he'd used earlier.

The watcher had to be employed by someone who knew Dervish was important. What he'd seen and heard made him sure the watcher was merely a paid thug—so the thug's employer was interested in . . . Dervish's sources? His spies? His lovers?

Jonathan rolled his shoulders at the last thought. Madame Levéel wasn't Dervish's lover, of that he was sure. But what *was* she? Was she giving him information? Bribing him?

There was still no sign of the watcher, and Jonathan moved carefully out from behind the tree and continued on his way.

In the few days since his new cook had entered his household, he'd taken to skulking around his neighborhood, hiding behind trees, creeping through alleys with a knife in his hand and contemplating fisticuffs with a friend's butler.

He could simply ask Madame Levéel what she was up to, but if she were a spy, she would run or lie, or both—and he'd rather get to the bottom of it.

He increased his pace, lengthening his stride.

He hadn't felt this alive since he was in the army.

Taking the title after Gerald's death had been killing him

slowly with boredom, and he knew that was a large part of Madame Levéel's charm for him. She exuded a suppressed excitement, an air of danger he simply couldn't resist.

So he wouldn't turn her over to Durnham, or his connections in the Alien Office. If she was guilty of some wrongdoing. . . . He didn't want to think about where she would end up. Something in him rebelled at the idea of her being locked away, spy or not.

Which was precisely why he should take this to Durnham. He was so far from objective, he was the wolf guarding the sheep.

And he didn't care.

As he swung back onto Chapel Street, he saw Goldfern down the road and hoped that at least Giselle Barrington was safe in Lapland.

––––––––––

The sound of the front door opening forced Edgars to rise from the kitchen table. Lord Aldridge was home.

"Good night, Monsieur Edgars." Gigi's accent had become slightly more French since they'd literally slammed into each other in the alleyway. Easier to pass off bizarre behavior if you were foreign.

"Good night, Madame Levéel." He went reluctantly, as if taking his eyes off her for even one moment would result in some catastrophe.

Gigi waited for him to disappear up the stairs to the hall, grinding her back teeth together. Then she stood and poured her tea down the sink. She hadn't wanted it, but making it had given her something to do while Edgars tried to question her. She rinsed her teacup and slammed it down a little too hard on the drainingboard. She was certain he thought he was being subtle. The man was as subtle as chillies in a soufflé.

He was probably trying to get her dismissed right now.

And she needed to stay here. It was her one safe place.

Well, she couldn't stop Edgars talking, but she could at least find out what he was accusing her of.

She walked to her door, opened it, and took her shoes off, leaving them within her little sitting room. Then, still standing in the kitchen, she closed the door loudly.

She tiptoed up the stairs in her stockings, the stone floor icy.

"No need to stay up, Edgars. I'm going to write a note to Lord Dervish and leave it in the hall. If you could see it's sent round first thing tomorrow?"

Gigi reached the top of the stairs and saw Lord Aldridge walking to his library. Edgars was hanging a dripping coat on the coatrack. He followed Aldridge, leaving the hallway empty, and she ran across, skirting the little pools of water on the floor, and slipped under the semicircular table pressed up against the wall near the library door.

A perfectly starched white linen tablecloth covered it to the floor, and she was just small enough to fit under it, her legs tucked up under her chin.

"I'm sorry, my lord, I need to speak . . ."

She heard Edgars trail off, almost miserably. She had put

him in quite the spot. And she could hardly bear a grudge about it; she *was* behaving strangely.

She closed her eyes and laid a cheek on her knees, suddenly exhausted.

"What is it, Edgars?"

"It's . . . well, it's the new cook, my lord." Edgars was quiet for a moment, and she wondered what he was doing. Fiddling with his waistcoat probably, or tugging at his hair. "I know I hired her on, and she had such excellent references, but I've found her doing strange things—"

"What things?"

Did she imagine it, or was Lord Aldridge's voice a trifle too sharp? A trifle too interested?

The now-familiar beat of fear and panic surged through her, forcing her to lift her head and pay more attention.

Edgars was silent a little longer. "If there is something . . ." His pause this time was actually painful. "If there is an . . . understanding between you and Madame Levéel . . ."

Gigi frowned. What on earth was he talking about?

"What do you mean by that, Edgars?"

Gigi didn't need to see Aldridge's face to know Edgars had made a grave, grave error; it was all in his lordship's voice. She'd have felt more sorry for Edgars, except his mistake might mean she'd get out of this without having to talk herself back into a job.

"Nothing, my lord." Edgars swallowed audibly. "You were both out at the same time tonight, both came in so wet, it crossed my mind that you may have met up . . ." He coughed, so terribly embarrassed now, Gigi was glad she couldn't see either of their faces. It was never pretty to see a grown man cringe.

"It was raining. If we were both out, it only follows we both got drenched." Aldridge's words were soft. "Now, what strange things, Edgars?"

"This . . . this morning, my lord. She left straight after Lord Dervish. Iris said she didn't even stop to explain properly what she was off to get. She grabbed her coat and ran out." He cleared his throat. "And then, this evening, she went out again"—he sounded truly aggrieved at her frequent trips— "and came back in wet as a drowned rat, and with grass stains all over her coat. Like she'd been rolling round on a lawn somewhere. . . ." His voice trailed off, and Gigi wondered why.

And then it came to her, in a sudden flash of understanding.

She bit her lip and her cheeks burned, hot and fierce, like she'd leaned straight into the oven.

Edgars thought she and Lord Aldridge had . . . that Lord Aldridge had taken her . . . in a garden?

She buried her face in her hands and shuddered.

She knew the ways of the world, from the glittering ballrooms of Europe to the small villages where she and her father were the only strangers the villagers had ever met.

But she had never been compromised, had never even been tempted to risk it.

Her father had kept her close, partly because of the double life he led, and her interests in her studies had given her a channel for her energies. She had been busy with her recipes, her book, her cooking and her adventures. She led a far more exciting life than most young women of her class and age.

It must be from the shock of the accusation that she now felt something tighten inside. Her heart was beating fast, and the burn of her cheeks wouldn't abate. She squirmed, trying to get comfortable.

She wondered what Lord Aldridge felt. His face must be quite an interesting sight, because Edgars still hadn't spoken.

Perhaps his lordship was choking him to death.

Perhaps she should leave her hiding place and lend him a hand.

"It was suspicious." Edgars plowed bravely on, still clearly alive, although his voice was an octave higher.

It suddenly occurred to her that Edgars had no room to point a finger, after nearly landing face-first on the kitchen floor, ogling Iris's breasts. Although he'd thought she and Lord Aldridge had done more than simply admire each other's . . . bits.

"Tonight, after you went out again, my lord, she went out a third time. She said it was to breathe in the night air after a day in the kitchen. Said she was just stepping a few yards from the door. But after about ten minutes, I went out to find her." He paused again and it felt like it was for effect, not out of fear this time. "She was hurrying to the kitchen door when I stepped out, coming from the back alley. And she was looking over her shoulder, frightened, like she expected someone to be following her."

There was another long silence.

"What is it that you suspect Madame Levéel of, Edgars?" Lord Aldridge's tone was mildly curious.

"I . . . I don't know, my lord. But she's up to something. I'd bet on it."

"I didn't realize you were a gambling man."

Edgars choked. "I'm not, my lord. But this time it's a sure thing. I can't believe the Duke of Wittaker's chef would have recommended her without believing her aboveboard, so she's pulled the wool over his eyes, same as mine."

Lord Aldridge made a *hmm*ing sound. "With everything that's been going on, I'd forgotten she'd been recommended by Wittaker's chef." She heard the soft clink of a crystal glass on a silver tray. "Edgars, has Madame Levéel done her job since she's been in this house?"

"Yes, my lord." Edgars sounded like he was in pain.

"And all you have against her is that she has gone out more than you obviously think is normal—is that right?"

"Yes, but . . . she's hiding something, my lord. Lying."

Poor Edgars. He was quite right.

Well, about her hiding something. Not about rolling about on the grass with Lord Aldridge.

A bolt of pure, sensual heat shot through her. The idea of being so earthy, so passionate, as to make love in a garden in the rain.

With Lord Aldridge.

She had a terrible feeling that she would imagine it the next time she saw him, and she hoped she could control her blushes.

"You have raised your concerns with me, Edgars. If any-thing occurs that concerns Madame Levéel that I don't like, the fault of it rests with me. Consider the matter in my hands."

Edgars must have made some sign of assent—bowed, per-haps—because she heard him walk toward the door.

"Oh, Edgars." Lord Aldridge's voice was still soft, but Edgars stopped short. "Your many years of loyal service in this household saved you this evening after your implication about Madame Levéel and me. But be assured, if you should ever raise it again, with me or her, I will dismiss you."

Edgars went completely still. "Yes, my lord."

His steps were fast and nervous as he walked back down to the kitchen.

She heard Aldridge draw out a chair, and then the scratch of pen on paper. Ah—the letter to Dervish.

If Dervish replied and she could see the note, it would solve one of her problems. She'd know if he was D.

She tightened her grip around her legs and wondered if Edgars had had enough time to settle in for the night, if she could sneak back down to the kitchen without running into him.

Aldridge's chair scraped again and he walked out of the li-brary, standing right next to her, in front of the little table.

She could reach out and touch his leg if she wanted to.

Then he moved off, the stairs creaking as he climbed them.

When she heard his bedroom door close, she crawled out

from her hiding place. She stood for a moment, looking at his note to Dervish, ready for Edgars to send off. She picked it up but it was sealed, and she put it down again. She didn't think the contents would concern her, anyway. It was just Dervish's handwriting she wanted to see.

There was another letter on the table. A thick, expensive, cream-colored envelope, with the flap open. She picked it up and slipped the card out. It was an invitation from a Lady Crowder to a ball the next day, and she wondered why it was lying out here.

Surely it had been received a few weeks ago, at least.

She turned the card in her hand over and over. She didn't know Lady Crowder, but she might know someone at her ball.

She'd met many English noblemen and women through the years, some in Vienna, some in Scandinavia and a few in Russia. She knew who her father had liked and trusted.

Perhaps she could spot one of them in the crowd? Ask them for help?

Time was running out, and it was worth trying. She couldn't risk going back to Dervish's.

And if she found no one at the ball, she would turn to Aldridge. She'd have no choice.

Holding tight to the stolen invitation, she walked on silent, stocking-clad feet to bed.

17

Wrapped in her black cloak, Gigi stood in the shadow of one of the many oak trees that lined Grosvenor Square, and watched the men and women spill from their carriages like sparkling gems from a velvet bag. The double doors of Lord and Lady Crowder's town house stood wide open above, welcoming them in.

She shifted her weight from one aching foot to the other. The Crowders lived only seven minutes on foot from Aldridge House, but after the first two minutes she'd realized that her pale gold slippers, which so perfectly matched her dress, hadn't been made for walking over rough cobbles.

It didn't help that she'd been on her feet all day.

She'd sidled down the alley twice to see if she could make it unseen to Goldfern to check whether the note had gone, but during the day the back lane was as busy as a highway.

Edgars had breathed down her neck the rest of the time, watching as she made a hearty lunch and then dinner for

Aldridge and his estate manager, down from Suffolk to discuss his lordship's business.

A man got out of a private carriage and laughed at something his companion said as he helped her down, drawing Gigi's focus back to her goal.

The entrance to Lord and Lady Crowder's house.

A rowdy group of young men tumbled out of the next coach, teasing the footman at the door by dropping their invitations and muddling them up. A crowd of guests began to build up at the foot of the stairs as the coaches continued their relentless stop and go.

Gigi undid the catch of her velvet cloak and took it off, rolling it up tight and pushing it into the fork of one of the branches in the tree. Then she slipped from the shadows, drew level to the carriages, and stopped on the outer edge of the growing group—close enough to look as if she were with them, but holding herself slightly aloof from the crush.

With a sharp word from one of the older men waiting in the irritated huddle, the smug, laughing youngsters finally trooped in.

The crowd began to move.

Gigi gripped her stolen invitation tightly enough to bend it.

Halfway up the stairs she saw that, in his stress and fluster, the doorman was letting everyone in en masse. She gave him a friendly nod as she passed, and he tried to smile back.

She'd deliberately arrived late, hoping the Crowders would

no longer be standing in the hallway to greet their guests but would be busy entertaining within. And there was no sign of them as she was carried along on a wave straight through into the ballroom.

She stumbled to a halt just within the door, momentarily at a loss as the people she'd come in with rushed across to friends or formed small groups.

She was suddenly on her own.

Heads turned in her direction and she wondered, for the first time, if she had made a very serious misjudgment.

This was her first ball in England. She'd left with her father when she was fourteen years old, so her experience of these things had been on the Continent.

The cut of her clothes was very similar to those worn by the other women here tonight, but the pale gold satin with its fine edging of ivory silk stood out amongst the pastels and whites.

A murmur rose up like a hot breeze on a summer day and danced its way across the crowds. She suddenly became the eye of the storm.

Desperately, she lifted the fan hanging from her wrist and gave a definite incline of her head, as if spotting an acquaintance in the crowd. Eyes continued to watch her, undaunted, and she took a step toward the refreshment table, keeping her step light and unconcerned as the weight of a room full of gazes tried to drag her down and strip her of her nerve.

Her plan would only work if she was the observer, not the observed.

Perhaps she should have come as a maid?

The thought almost made her laugh and steadied her. She was a topsy-turvy Cinderella as it was. The lady pretending to be a cook, sneaking into the ball to play herself, even though it was with a stolen invitation.

The first high, sweet note of the orchestra starting up diverted attention from her for a blissful second, and she dived into the crowd around the refreshments. She ignored the younger men and women as she squeezed her way through, searching for people around her father's age or older.

There was someone . . .

She stared at the jowl-cheeked man with pure white side-burns and a rounded stomach and tried to recall the circumstances under which she'd last seen him.

A diplomatic function in Russia. Her father shaking his hand, but with a look in his eyes . . .

Gigi turned. Not that one. Her father hadn't liked him.

She was propelled into a knot of lords and ladies sorting out who was down to dance with whom.

"It's unpardonably rude to ask for a dance without an introduction," a man said quietly into her ear as she was pressed against him in the jostle, "but in this crush, no one will notice, and I have the feeling you would not be completely insulted. I believe Lady Crowder is being old-fashioned and starting with a minuet."

She looked up and found he was in his early thirties, with a handsome face and eyes as dark as his hair. There was a spark of interest in those eyes, and a slight leer on his face. One she'd seen on a hundred different faces, at a hundred different balls.

She almost relaxed into the familiarity of it all.

It was unpardonably rude to ask a woman to dance without being introduced to her first. Unheard of, in fact.

But this man had seen something in her—that she was here under false pretenses, or had something to hide—and thought to test if she'd be interested in more than a dance. Not that it mattered. Dancing would make her blend in, and give her a way to move around the room in plain sight like nothing else.

"I accept your invitation." She held her hand out and saw his lips twitch a little at her cool tone.

He bowed and took it, and led her onto the floor with more of a flourish than was necessary. While the minuet was usually started by the couple with the highest rank and worked down, tonight was a more informal arrangement. Lady Crowder's nod to modernity, no doubt.

"Name's Harriford. Captain Reginald Harriford."

"Very pleased to meet you, Captain." She followed his lead, at home enough with the dance to let her gaze sweep the other dancers on the floor.

None of them stood out to her as familiar. Most of them were too young, anyway.

She cast her gaze to the watching crowds and as Harriford twirled her around, she looked straight at the entrance—just in time to see Lord Aldridge enter the room.

She fumbled her next step. She let Harriford spin her again so that her back was turned to her employer, her heart thumping louder than the many boots and slippers on the tiled ballroom floor.

What was he doing here? He wasn't supposed to come. She had his invitation!

She was a Cinderella who most definitely did *not* want to dance with the prince tonight.

Harriford made a sound, and she looked up to find him staring at her, eyes narrowed. "And you are?"

"I'd rather not say, to be frank." Gigi smiled at him, at the disbelief on his face. Captain Harriford had just learned two could play at his game. Her response was as outrageous as his forward approach earlier, but what could he do about it?

Just then, the dance led them to the far end of the room.

"Lovely to make your acquaintance, Captain. I have to find a family friend somewhere in this crowd, so I'll have to leave you mid-dance, I'm afraid."

Before he could answer or tighten his grip on her hand, she pulled free and slipped into the crowd, leaving Harriford openmouthed with shock.

She'd been desperate, coming this evening. She had a lot to lose, but a lot to gain if she could find someone familiar in this heaving, crushing crowd. Now that Lord Aldridge had arrived, the balance had tipped in favor of losing.

She peered through a gap in the wall of people to see if he'd moved away from the entrance, her only way out, and for a single instant, looked him directly in the eyes.

She spun away, allowing the currents in this sea of satin and starch to suck her deeper into the morass.

In her head, she repeated a number of the curses Georges and Pierre had uttered through the years.

Midnight had struck early tonight. Far, far too early.

Jonathan sorely regretted being talked into coming to the Crowder ball. He'd gone to the club hoping to find Durnham, but he hadn't been there, and for once, Jonathan had felt strangely at a loose end.

Now both Fitzgerald and McKinley, who'd nagged him into coming in the first place, had taken themselves off to the card room and left him to his own devices.

It was a crush. More so than usual, as if the poor weather that had trapped them in their houses for days had turned them all slightly mad, and this first dry evening had sent everyone leaping and shoving down the glittering cliff of social elegance.

He scanned the crowd, wondering idly if Durnham could be here with his wife, and his gaze locked with Madame Levéel's.

Though surely not?

He took a step forward but she was gone, if she'd ever been there at all, her place taken by a tight-packed rainbow of color.

His focus was entirely on the spot she'd stood in, and he began to stride across the room.

"Tallyho." A friend from his club, Craigmore, twirled past him with a giggling girl in white, almost knocking into him.

He stopped and took a step back.

The movement steadied him.

Either it was Madame Levéel or it was not. And it was easy enough to find out.

He went left, weaving through the people watching the breathless couples as they spun, dipped and turned.

Perhaps not so easy.

She—or whoever it was—had been wearing a gown in a light gold color, and he caught a flash of it up ahead; the view of a shoulder lifted to plow through the crowd, the sparkling gleam of a diamond earring, the curve of a chin.

If he hadn't known better, he'd have said it *was* her.

He caught another view, the slim line of her back, before two laughing men stepped together to shake hands and blocked her from sight.

By the time he'd reached them, moved around them, there was nothing to see.

"Looking for her, are you?" A man watched him with interest, keeping his place in the crowd with slight adjustments and side steps.

Aldridge gave him a quick look, his eyes scanning the crowd again.

"She's making for the door. She panicked when she saw you. Nearly fell, and until then, I'd have said she was a most accomplished dancer."

Jonathan spared him another look. "What's her name?"

He didn't pretend he didn't know what they were talking about.

"She wouldn't tell me." The man gave an amused laugh. "Not that I behaved all that well—I deserved a set-down. Though I feel a little better knowing you don't know her name, either."

But he might. He really might.

"Harriford." The man put out his hand, and Jonathan shook it, quick and hard.

"Aldridge. If you'll excuse me." He turned sideways so he could squeeze through any gap that presented itself, Harriford's eyes still on him.

He was about thirty feet from the door, cut off by a large group of society mamas with their newly presented daughters, laughing and making social plans, when he saw her dart across the threshold, using two dowagers as cover.

All he had was an impression—slim, lithe, golden dress shimmering in the warm light from the chandeliers—and then she was gone.

When he at last fought his way clear and ran to the front door, he found nothing but a surprised doorman and a cool breeze that smelled of more rain.

"Did a lady come by here?" he asked. "Golden dress?"

"You mean Cinderella?" the doorman asked, a smile of genuine humor on his face.

"Cinderella?"

"Aye. Ran down the steps, she did, muttering about her shoes."

"Where did she go?"

"Didn't see, my lord." He pointed to the line of carriages strung like beads down the street. "Once she was behind one o' those, she could have gone any direction."

Even straight home, to Aldridge House.

Jonathan started walking. And once he got beyond the line of carriages, he started to run.

18

These shoes.

If she could have taken them off, she would have, but she had a feeling it would be worse. The streets weren't clean and they weren't smooth. Hobbling home wouldn't get her there fast enough.

And she needed fast.

She didn't try to understand the prickle between her shoulder blades, the sure sense that Aldridge wouldn't give up but would chase her down.

She'd wasted precious minutes getting her cloak out of the tree but didn't regret them. She couldn't walk back into the kitchen in her gown; she would need the cloak to hide what she was wearing. Thinking of that, she reached up behind her neck as she walked and undid the clasp of her diamond-and-pearl necklace, then slipped it into the deep pockets of her cloak.

She was almost home. She'd taken the less direct route of

Grosvenor and then Park Street, coming out onto Chapel at the lower end.

She passed Goldfern, her steps slowing as she imagined shadows reaching long-fingered hands out to grab her.

But it was quiet. Completely dark.

Better to walk past the house than to chance South Audley and the thug from last night. She increased her pace.

Then Aldridge House loomed ahead and her hands moved up to her ears to take off the last of her finery. But before she even touched the dangling earrings she heard the sound of a man's shoes scuffing the pavement.

She went still, and in the sudden silence he stepped out of the shadow, into the weak light of the streetlamps.

It was almost a relief to see it was Aldridge.

Almost.

He crossed his arms over his chest, breathing evenly but a little hard, as if he'd been running, and she tensed.

He looked dangerous.

Not dangerous like the men she'd met in Vienna and Russia sometimes did, with that cruel, blatantly sexual interest, although there was definitely heat in his gaze.

He looked as if he could move faster than she could run, could hold her with laughable ease, and was considering doing just that.

"Who are you, really?" He spoke quite normally.

"I'm the woman who cooks for you, Lord Aldridge." She was so tempted to tell him the truth—but there was more at stake than making her life easier.

And why had he chased her down? Run all the way from the Crowders' down South Audley to make it here before her? What did it matter to him?

"You're very good at word games." His voice dipped a little lower, and he took a step toward her, lifted a hand to her ear, skimming her diamond earring before tracing higher.

At the touch of his hot fingertip on the cold curve of her ear, she drew in a quick breath.

He paused, made a sound at the back of his throat, and pulled her close.

She didn't resist. She didn't understand it—how they could be close to arguing one moment, tension thick between them, and then suddenly pressed against each other. But she had no inclination to fight it.

She leaned in, rested her head against the scratchy wool of his coat, closed her eyes and let him prop her up with his warmth and the muscled strength of his body. Breathed him in.

She had never been in such an intimate position with a man, close enough to smell the wool of his coat, the warm sandalwood of his soap.

She lifted her hands and slid them under the lapels of his coat, burrowed a little closer, and his arms came up around her to grip her tighter, so she was completely encircled.

"I'm afraid to ask you questions, and I've never been afraid to do anything before." His voice was a rumble against her temple, a vibration she felt deep in her chest.

"What are you afraid of?" she whispered.

"That you'll run, like you did tonight. But not home. Away somewhere, where I won't find you again."

She sighed. Then pulled back. "You may feel differently one day. Might wish I would disappear. But I'm not going anywhere for the moment, my lord."

"No," he said. "You're not." And then he dipped his head and touched his lips to hers.

———

J onathan deepened the kiss, ignoring the voice in his head that warned him not to do this.

He should be asking questions, trying to find out why his cook was at a ball she had no business attending—but he was honest with himself.

He didn't care if she lied her way into a thousand balls. He only cared that she stood wrapped around him, kissing him back with shy, delightful eagerness.

Durnham would say he should care. That she could be a French spy, gathering information that would harm England's cause . . .

Hell!

He jerked back, taking them both by surprise, and she stood quiet and pliant in his arms for another beat of his heart before she drew away.

At that moment, the rain started falling again. A light, steady patter on the stone cobbles around them.

"Were you at the Crowders' tonight to cause some mischief?" He blinked the raindrops from his eyes.

"*Pardon?*" She stared at him, a frown creasing her forehead.

"To disrupt something, or eavesdrop?"

"No." She gave him a look as cool and controlled as it had been surprised and hurt only a moment before.

She seemed otherworldly, a figure from a fairy tale in her deeply hooded cloak, with the sparkle of rain dancing around her, catching the light.

"You just wanted to go to the ball?" Jonathan couldn't help the amusement in his voice as he thought of the doorman, calling her Cinderella.

Her head jerked up.

He took a physical step back at the snapping anger in her eyes.

"You think this is a jest?" She tilted her head to look him directly in the eye. "This is not a jest."

"I don't know what it is. Why don't you tell me?" He didn't keep the anger at her lack of trust from his voice—all he wanted was for her to shed a little light from her hiding place in the shadows.

She stood taller. "I will. I will tell you, but not now. When I can, I promise you will be the first to know."

"What if I tell you that isn't enough?"

She gave a disgusted shake of her head and spun on her heel. She had almost reached the side alley before he had the wit to move.

"Wait." In two strides he had his hand on her shoulder.

He couldn't see her face well here, and he pushed back her hood. "Why do I keep getting the sense that I know you?"

She closed her eyes. Drew a deep breath. "You don't."

He didn't want to let her go, but she was pulling away, and he reluctantly released his hold on her though every instinct screamed at him to hang on.

He wasn't going to turn her in. He knew that. Whether she told him anything or not.

Which meant she would be with him a little longer. He had some time.

He turned and took a step away.

"Where are you going?" she asked on a sigh of exasperation, and he wanted to laugh despite the rain running down the back of his neck.

She was watching him, hands on hips and, if he wasn't mistaken, impatience in every line.

"Going in by the front door." He didn't add, *like you always tell me to*, but her lips twitched as if he had.

She moved toward him, and he went still at the look on her face. She lifted a hand to his cheek, her glove touching his skin lightly. "Thank you."

She didn't need to say for what. They both knew he could have made this a lot harder, forced her to offer some explanation.

He caught her wrist and for a moment they were standing close enough that he could feel the warmth of her breath on his lips, see the way the raindrops clung to her eyelashes.

She rose on her toes and kissed his cheek. Then she turned and walked away.

The faint scent of lamb-and-artichoke stew, overlaid by the buttery, tangy scent of the crepes spread with *crème au citron* she'd made for dessert, enveloped her as she closed the kitchen door behind her.

She fought to slot the heavy key in the lock, still thinking of Aldridge. The way the rain left his hair curling along his forehead. The touch of his lips against hers. The solid, taut strength of his body.

She went still at the scrape of a chair behind her.

"I'd appreciate it if you would let me know when you're taking the key, Cook. I am responsible for locking up in this house."

She turned to face Edgars and frowned a little at the strange way he was staring at her. "Certainly. I didn't want to be locked out, because I didn't know how late I'd be."

"Mrs. Rogers, the cook before you, never went out once in all the years she worked here. Sometimes not even on her actual days off."

Gigi kept the irritation prickling under her skin under control as she walked down the stairs. "I am not Mrs. Rogers." She gave a shrug.

"No. You most certainly are not."

Still that strange, considering look.

She couldn't let this bother her. Edgars had some fixed idea of how cooks comported themselves. Some standard according to which she was obviously failing, yet what had she really done but go about her private business?

"Mr. Edgars, is his lordship unhappy with my work?" She didn't mean for it to come out quite so sharply.

Edgars said nothing.

"Has any meal been missed, or late, or inferior in any way?"

Above her, the front door opened, and she wondered why it had taken Aldridge so long to come inside.

Could he have walked down the street to check on Goldfern first? Make sure all was well since the burglary?

Edgars' attention shifted from her to upstairs; he tipped his head back, listening.

"I'm assuming by your silence not." She raised a hand to the neck of her cloak to undo the tie, and stopped herself just in time, horror at the thought of Edgars seeing her ball gown making her momentarily light-headed.

Edgars glanced at her. "You'll know immediately if your performance of your duties isn't up to scratch, madam." He turned smartly and ran lightly up the stairs to the hallway.

The way he'd looked at her . . .

With trembling, shaking fingers, Gigi reached up to her ears, touched the earrings dangling from them. Two-carat diamonds with a lustrous pearl hanging below.

Earrings no cook would ever own.

19

Jonathan stood in the small withdrawing room off Durnham's hallway, waiting for the butler to tell him if Durnham was at home, and forced his hands to unclench.

Rocking back on his heels, he clasped his hands behind his
back and stared out the window at the rain-washed, wind-
blown street.

He was still angry with Edgars, even though two days had
passed. His anger had been just beneath the surface with every
interaction he'd had with his butler since his insinuations of a
tryst with Madame Levéel. And last night and this morning,
Edgars had behaved in a tight, affronted manner, which could
only be the result of both him and Madame Levéel coming in
within minutes of each other again after Lady Crowder's ball.

And even though it annoyed him beyond belief, edging his
anger sharper, he felt a little splinter of contrition. Because
even though Edgars was completely out of bounds regarding
his relationship with Madame Levéel, Jonathan couldn't help

the flash of white heat that must have shown in his eyes when Edgars had voiced his suspicions.

The blood had drained from Edgars' face when he'd seen it.

Now that Jonathan had had time to think of it—and he'd thought about it a little too much—how Edgars imagined that he'd tumbled his cook in a garden without getting any grass stains on himself was an interesting puzzle.

He'd spent yesterday with his estate manager, a long-standing appointment he couldn't change, and had found his thoughts turning the problem over, trying to solve it, all too often.

Those thoughts had recently been replaced by the feel of her against him, the touch of her lips. The sensation of her glove on his cheek, and the look in her eyes before she'd run to the kitchen door.

He drew in a deep, long breath. Began to move around the room to distract himself.

One thing Edgars *had* done was remind him that he did have a trail to follow where his cook was concerned. The celebrated Georges Bisset himself had written her reference letter. And if the drunk and disorderly Wittaker would let Jonathan speak with Bisset, he would see what he could find out about her.

"My lord, Lord Durnham invites you to join him in the library." Durnham's butler was at the door, and Jonathan turned away from the window and followed him down the hall.

He'd been to Durnham's house a few times before, back when Gerald was still alive and had been one of Durnham's close friends.

The place, especially the library, looked a little different. There were subtle changes, touches of elegance and taste where it had once been merely utilitarian.

Durnham was seated in one of several chairs cozily arranged around the warm, friendly glow of the fireplace, and he stood when Jonathan came in. "I should have sent you a note the day before yesterday, or yesterday at least, Aldridge. I'm sorry I didn't. There was so much happening I forgot about it."

"A note about Dervish, you mean?" Jonathan sat opposite him on an old leather armchair that was more comfortable than it looked.

Durnham nodded. "I've taken over some of the projects he's working on while he's away."

"You obviously have strong evidence that Miss Barrington is in Lapland, then?"

Durnham steepled his fingers under his chin. "Not really. Frobisher stressed it was only a rumor he'd heard, that it wasn't confirmed, but Dervish wants it to be true so badly, there was no stopping him."

"He wants the letter?"

Durnham tapped his fingers together, his eyes sharp and intelligent above them. "Dervish owes a debt to Giselle Barrington's mother. He's been uncomfortable with the favors we've called on Barrington to grant us over the years, because he's always been aware Giselle was with her father, and we were asking him to put them both in danger. Barrington's death has hit him hard. He feels guilty and responsible."

"He was walking the streets looking for Miss Barrington the day before yesterday," Jonathan said. "I expect having a destination and some hope of finding her is a relief to him."

"Dervish's butler said you paid a visit." Durnham quirked his lips.

Jonathan grinned. "Ratted on me, did he?" He leaned back and crossed his arms over his chest. "I actually considered punching him to get into that study."

"He conveyed the impression that he thought you were going to. I think he feels lucky not to have a broken nose." Durnham leaned forward. "What were you after?"

"A note I saw someone drop off at Dervish's the night before last. I was coming to see him about Barrington's lawyer and watched the note being delivered. When the messenger slipped away, a thug popped up out of nowhere and followed him."

Jonathan never knew he had such a talent for lying.

Perhaps it was because he was sufficiently motivated. And because most of his story was true. There was no way he was going to admit to knowing who the messenger had been, though.

"I followed them both but lost them in the back alleys. I returned to Dervish's house to warn him he was being watched, and to make sure he understood the note was important, only to find out he wasn't even there. Hadn't even been there when the note was delivered."

"That's very interesting." Durnham lost his amused look and frowned. "I suppose his butler has already sent the note on to him, so all we can do is wait until Dervish lets us know what it says. And I think I'll have Dervish's house watched."

"Not with Foreign Office men," Jonathan said sharply.

"No." Durnham shook his head. "I don't trust anyone there, either, not until we know who killed Barrington. My wife has connections we can use. Very discreet watchers."

"Your wife?" Jonathan looked at him in astonishment. Lady Durnham had previously been Miss Charlotte Raven, ward of Lady Howe and a great society catch.

"Yes." Durnham didn't explain any further. "Now, you wanted to see Dervish about Barrington's lawyer. Anything I can help with?"

"There is." Jonathan thought back to his meeting with Mr. Greenway. "The break-in meant something to the lawyer. He reacted immediately. But Dervish told me not to let him know Barrington was dead, and I felt that if I could have told him, he might have been more open with me. There may be some instructions in place from Barrington that could help us.

"And aside from that, Greenway sent the letters the burglar seems to have been after to Barrington's address in Stockholm, so if possible, Thornton or Dervish himself needs to fetch them, see if there is any clue amongst them as to where Miss Barrington could be."

"I'll visit Greenway myself and tell him the circumstances of Barrington's death, and the need to keep it quiet for now. If Barrington set up a safe house for his daughter, or if Greenway has any idea where she is and it's not in Lapland, we need to know."

"You don't think she *is* in Lapland, do you?" Jonathan stood, his voice soft.

Durnham hesitated. "I want to. But she's a young woman alone in a foreign country. I don't think she could have gotten far, and if *we* haven't found her, I can only imagine it's because she's nowhere to be found."

"Not all young women are helpless society misses," a woman said from the doorway. The cool, low voice definitely did not belong to a helpless society miss. Jonathan turned and bowed as Lady Durnham walked into the room. She was as beautiful, as untouchable, as an ice princess. It was how he'd always seen her before. But when she looked at Durnham, he realized he'd been mistaken. There was liquid heat in her gaze.

"Daniel told me about Giselle Barrington's upbringing, and she sounds as if she could be quite resourceful if the occasion arose."

It took Jonathan a moment to realize she was talking about Dervish, when she'd said "Daniel." He hadn't realized Dervish was on quite such intimate terms with the Durnham household.

Lady Durnham reached them and smiled at him, and it was such a warm, open smile, he wondered how he'd ever thought her cold. "Good morning, Lord Aldridge."

She cast another quick look at her husband. "There is someone from the Foreign Office waiting for you. I told Jeffreys I'd deliver the message, and that he could send him through. A Mr. Frobisher."

Jonathan recognized the name of the helpful informant who'd sent Dervish off to Sweden half-cocked. He looked expectantly at the doorway.

A man stepped through it, beautifully turned out, with a nervous tension about him. His eyes flicked a round the room, as if assessing its value.

Frobisher was also angry, although he tried to hide it. His step was a touch too stiff, and his lips tightened at the sight of Jonathan, then curled up into a sneer at Lady Durnham.

"You've just come from the consulate in Sweden, Mr. Frobisher?" Lady Durnham watched him with the cool look Jonathan was used to seeing at society balls.

"I arrived back yesterday morning." Frobisher's smile was forced. He turned to Durnham, a muscle jumping under his eye. "I have the document you asked for, my lord." He didn't offer the document up and turned his back slightly to Lady Durnham, excluding her from their circle.

Durnham's eyes narrowed and Lady Durnham stepped to his side. She smiled that summer smile at Jonathan again. "Perhaps you can walk me to the door, Lord Aldridge? I must be going, I'm afraid. I have a busy day." She gave Frobisher a nod, let her husband take her gloved hand and kiss it.

"Come straight back if you don't mind, Aldridge," Durnham said, and Jonathan noticed Frobisher tensed at that. He didn't want this interview, and he certainly didn't want it in front of an audience.

Jonathan held out his arm to Lady Durnham, and she slipped hers through it. She was elegant and as sharp as a blade. As they walked from the room, Jonathan suddenly didn't doubt she had unusual contacts who could watch houses and not be seen. He wouldn't have liked to get on the wrong side of her.

As they stepped into the hall, she gave him a sudden grin that seemed more like that of a guttersnipe than a lady of the ton. "That Frobisher is too far north for me. What about you?" She pitched her voice low.

Jonathan's jaw dropped. Then he snapped it closed. "He's a file, all right."

Her eyes lit with laughter, although the rest of her face remained as serene and calm as ever. "You know your slang, my lord."

"I was in the army." He lifted his shoulders. "Rubbed shoulders with my men long enough to pick some up."

"I meant to ask you to dinner some time ago, but the months have run away with me, and, well, we've only been married for four months." She slowed as they came to the door. "Would you like to join us one evening?"

"I would love to come to dinner." Jonathan had the sense of receiving a rare invitation, and of being offered a camaraderie that was very selectively extended.

"Would Friday suit?" Already dressed for outdoors, she took a cloak down from a rack.

"Friday does suit." He looked back at the library. "Why did you take against Frobisher so quickly?"

She looked at him in surprise. "First impressions are usually the right ones. He doesn't like women, and he definitely doesn't like having one around when business is discussed."

Her gaze followed his to the library. "Never trust a women-hater, Lord Aldridge. There is something wrong with a person who hates half the human race." She paused. "That, and he looked over the library with a thief's eyes. I've known enough thieves to recognize one when I see one."

The butler appeared and opened the door, and Jonathan gave a bow as she swept out to a coach waiting for her, too surprised to respond.

"Charlotte get off all right?" Durnham asked as Jonathan walked back into the library. He and Frobisher were still standing near his desk.

"Yes." He came toward them and wondered why Durnham hadn't invited Frobisher to sit.

His rudeness to Lady Durnham might have had something to do with it.

"Frobisher was just telling me how things stand in Stock-holm." At last Durnham motioned to the seats. Frobisher chose a hard wooden chair and sat on the very edge of it.

"Were you there when Sir Barrington's body was discovered?" Jonathan asked.

Frobisher stiffened. "Yes."

Jonathan saw Durnham frown, but kept his own face blank. "Terrible business," he said conversationally.

"Terrible." Frobisher answered, quite without emotion, but there was something Jonathan sensed—some sharp edge that played in the set of his mouth. "Always bad when a British national is killed on foreign soil."

Jonathan had the feeling he was talking about the red tape and paperwork, rather than the tragic loss of life.

Frobisher raised his head when both Jonathan and Durnham kept silent. "Your report, sir. I rather expected Lord Dervish to be the one to request it." He put a hand inside his jacket and pulled out a piece of folded paper.

Durnham took it, his eyebrows rising. "Not much to it, Frobisher."

"I told Lord Dervish there was barely anything to go on. That's all I have. Will Lord Dervish require a copy, as well?"

"Lord Dervish is on his way to Stockholm," Durnham said shortly. He unfolded the paper and read the contents. "Based on the rumor you told him you'd heard."

Frobisher's face went white. "Lord Dervish has gone to Sweden based on *this*, sir?"

It was the first genuine emotion Jonathan had seen in him since he curled his lip at the sight of Lady Durnham.

"Yes." Durnham smiled at him. "But don't worry, he knew there wasn't much hard evidence. I don't think I realized how very little there was, though." He tapped the paper against his thigh. "Tell me about this, Frobisher. This informant who told you he'd seen Miss Barrington in one of the smaller towns north of Stockholm—did he say how she was traveling?"

"By coach, he said. He saw her when the coachman stopped to feed and water the horses at an inn."

"How did he know it was her?"

"That's why I told Lord Dervish it was unconfirmed, sir. The informant *didn't* know it was her. We were asking if anyone had seen a young Englishwoman, and he said he thought the woman he saw spoke English, and that she was heading north. Because Barrington and his daughter had recently come from Lapland, it's possible it was her."

"Yes." Durnham leaned back. "It's possible. You trust this informant?"

Frobisher shrugged. "As much as I trust any of them."

There was nothing to say to that. They'd all used informants before, and Jonathan knew how untrustworthy they could be.

"Very well, thank you, Frobisher." Durnham stood, and Frobisher stumbled to his feet.

"May I ask, sir, why you wanted the report now, with Lord Dervish already gone?" He still looked shocked to his core at the consequences of his information.

"I asked for it the day before yesterday, before Dervish left. If you only received my request today, it's because the message was delayed, or you weren't in to get it."

Frobisher's eyes narrowed at that, and Jonathan wondered which poor clerk was going to suffer for it. There was a mercilessness to Frobisher. A look he'd seen countless times in the give-and-take of violence on the battlefield.

Frobisher took his leave curtly, with none of the fawning some junior Foreign Office diplomats might indulge in with Durnham. Jonathan should have liked him better for it, but he couldn't.

"What did you think?" Durnham leaned against his desk, only speaking when the front door closed.

"Cold." Jonathan looked out the window and saw Frobisher turn left, hunching against the rain, his face turned away.

"What did Charlotte have to say about him?"

"That he's too far north for her."

Durnham blinked. "What the hell does that mean?"

Jonathan laughed. "It means he's too wily by far. Completely untrustworthy. As in, akin to dealing with a Scot from the far north of Britain."

"How do *you* know that?" Durnham asked. "I bet it impressed her that you did."

"I was invited to dinner." Jonathan gave him a smug smile. "What do you make of him?"

"This is only the second time I've met him. He has a smarmy attitude but he's efficient. I don't have to like him to work with him, and he doesn't report to me." Durnham spoke evenly, reasonably; straightened and thrust his hands deep in his pockets.

Then: "I wanted to smash his face in. That sneer when he looked at Charlotte . . . like he wanted to fuck her and hit her at the same time." He drew a breath. "Some men are just pigs, Aldridge."

"Any chance he was the one who killed Barrington?"

Durnham sighed and shrugged. "He was at Tessin Palace that night and certainly had the opportunity—but so did about two hundred others. There is no evidence to suggest an English traitor. It's far more likely to have been a French sympathizer amongst the Russian camp, or a French operative making sure an Anglo-Russian alliance doesn't come off. Or even a Swede, for that matter, doing it to keep Sweden out of the alliance, or for nothing more than the gold the French would be willing to pay him."

Jonathan nodded. Everything Durnham said was true. "So why didn't Miss Barrington go to Sir Thornton?"

"Perhaps she was too afraid to return to the ball. Good God, if she witnessed her father's murder, she may have been out of her mind with shock and grief. And despite what Charlotte said earlier about her, the most likely reason we can't find her is that she's dead. Whoever killed her father chased after her and killed her somewhere in Stockholm and dumped her body, or threw it in the river."

He hoped that wasn't true. "And Frobisher's informant?"

"A dud. Or someone overeager to be helpful. Or even someone trying to muddy the waters, create a false trail."

"Whatever the reason, Frobisher was certainly not expecting Dervish to hare off on that trail." He thought again of how white Frobisher had gone. The reaction seemed extreme.

"May be worried a finger will point back at him, if Dervish finds nothing. Waste of money and time and all that." Durnham looked at the report in his hand. "Might be why he was so damn surly about handing the report over to begin with, come to think of it. Never leave a paper trail to your mistakes, if you want to get ahead in the Foreign Office."

Jonathan grimaced. That sounded all too likely. He was glad of one thing in taking Gerald's title—that he was no longer in the ugly, duplicitous game of climbing the army's promotional ladder. "Is there anything else I can do in the Barrington matter for you?"

Durnham shook his head. "I'll speak to Barrington's lawyer, and if there is anything you can do arising from that, I'll let you know."

Jonathan said his farewells and left, lifting his collar against the cold needles of rain as he waved down a cab out-side Durnham's house. He'd go home and wait for the after-noon calling hour. And then he was off to see a duke about a cook.

20

She wanted to trust Lord Aldridge, wanted to go to him and confess everything.

It was the exhaustion talking, she knew.

The idea of handing this mess over to someone else was as appealing as a glazed strawberry tart. Tears welled in her eyes and she blinked them back, angry with herself.

She was alone in the house. It was most of the staff's half day, and Lord Aldridge had gone out early and wasn't expected back until this evening.

She had dinner already prepared, lamb marinating in mint, garlic and lemon, and the crème brûlée baking gently in its bain-marie. There was nothing for her to do for the next half hour, and she went back into her room to pull on her grass-stained coat and sneak over to Goldfern to see if Dervish had come to drop off his note and take hers.

She shouldn't do it. If Dervish had come and gone and been followed by the thug from last night, the drop-off might well be watched. But she couldn't let it go. She needed to know if Dervish had responded and taken her note.

If he hadn't, she had to face the fact that he might not be D., and might have no intention of responding to her.

She slipped out the kitchen door. When she reached the alley she heard a shout from the direction of Goldfern, and then another, and then clanging and bashing, as if someone was rolling a metal bin over the cobbles.

She peered around the corner, and though it was difficult to see with the way the alley twisted and turned, she caught sight of a rag-and-bone man in a small cart, having a loud argument with someone standing on a ladder. They were outside the house just before Goldfern.

A maid came out of another back door and joined in the fray, and Gigi rested her head against the wall and closed her eyes.

There was no way she could go now.

She turned back and gave a shiver of relief when she stepped back into the warm, familiar kitchen.

She would miss this job—this place—when it was over.

She hung up her coat and then stood in her sitting room, wondering what to do. She couldn't sleep, although she desperately wanted to. She had to pull the crème brûlée out of the oven in a bit.

But . . . since the house was empty, she had a chance to see if Dervish had responded to Aldridge's note. Harry had been sent round early with it, and Edgars had received several notes this morning after Aldridge had left.

She might also learn what kind of man Aldridge was, from a quick look through his papers. Whether, as a last resort, she could trust him to take the letter to the right person and keep quiet about her identity.

She rubbed her forehead.

No.

No man in his position would allow her to continue on her current course, looking for a way to bring down the shadow man. He'd insist on putting her somewhere safe, and sooner or later, the shadow man would hear of it and he would come for her.

Gigi rejected that.

She would be coming for *him*.

But it would be good to get the letter off her hands. If Dervish's note was above and the handwriting proved he was D., she would hand it over to him immediately.

Before she could overthink it, she pulled off her boots and put on some soft slippers, then made her way up the stairs.

Even though she was alone, the creak of the house in the wind, the groan of the floorboards under her feet, set her on edge.

She didn't like this. Not at all.

The silver tray for correspondence wasn't in the hall, so Gigi tried the library first. The desk was clean of anything, gleaming from a recent polish by Babs.

She didn't know where his study was, but hoped it was on the ground floor. Climbing the stairs seemed too much

an invasion, although she knew her reasoning was totally il-
logical.

She went back into the hall, and tried the door next to the
library.

His lordship's study.

She admired it for a moment. She would have loved a
place like this for herself.

There was a massive desk, neatly ordered with piles of
papers and books, a stand with pens and ink, and a wall with
shelves of books. It looked out on the back garden, probably
directly above Edgars' rooms.

The thought made her go cold. If Edgars was in his rooms
right now, he would hear every step she took.

But he wasn't, she reminded herself. He had gone out.

He hadn't been able to look at her this morning—or at Iris
either, for that matter.

Guilty conscience on both counts.

Not that she blamed him for his feelings for Iris. She was a
gem. One a rumormongering, dirty-minded little man like him
didn't deserve.

Her thoughts went back to Edgars' imagined garden inci-
dent. She'd replayed the notion in her mind so many times,
she could almost believe it had happened, and every time she
did, something coiled inside her, hot and tight.

Although she was sure her imagination was leaving out the
bad parts. Like the cold rain, and the even colder ground.

Perhaps in the heat of passion, lovers didn't notice things
like that?

She shook her head and forced herself to concentrate on the desk in front of her.

Here were the letters Edgars must have taken in earlier. She sorted through them one by one.

None looked right. If any of them were from Dervish, then he wasn't D.

She was nowhere nearer to finding an ally than she'd been before, and her frustration and bone-deep exhaustion overwhelmed her.

She struggled against it for a moment and then let the tears filling her eyes fall silently while her body shook.

There was a small sound, a creak so tiny it was amazing she heard it at all.

She turned—and saw Lord Aldridge leaning in the doorway with his arms folded. Watching her.

———

He had walked into the house through the kitchen, not sure what he hoped to achieve by that, but giving in to the compulsion.

It was warm and smelled so wonderful, like vanilla and rich cream.

It was also empty.

Though today was the servants' half day, the fragrance of something baking was too strong for there not to be something in the oven.

He opened the oven door, and the scent of vanilla clouded around him like a puff from a perfume bottle.

Madame Levéel must be here; the dessert looked almost ready to take out.

Then he'd heard the creak of a floorboard above, and he'd followed the sound, walking silently up the stairs and into the hall on instinct.

He knew she'd been looking through his papers—he wasn't delusional enough to expect an innocent explanation. But he hadn't expected her to be crying.

Weeping, actually, as if the world had come to an end and there was no hope for her.

He must have made a sound—he was certainly startled enough—and she turned and looked at him. There was such embarrassment in her eyes, such shame at being caught looking at his things, that he had the sense that she had come here unwillingly, only under great duress.

"What is it you're looking for?" he asked.

"Something to help me," she answered, scrubbing the tears from her cheeks.

She was being used. Forced to do this by someone threatening her or her family. He made the leap in logic in an instant.

And she went from spy to victim in a heartbeat.

"I'm so sorry." Her lips trembled, and he couldn't help the step he took toward her. He couldn't take his eyes from that mouth, the memories from last night crowding his thoughts, driving him even closer.

She looked at him uncertainly when he took another step, and then another until he was right in front of her, so she had to tip up her chin to look him in the eye.

"Oh." The word left her lips on a sigh as he pulled her close and lowered his head, so the air from her exclamation brushed his skin, and the vanilla scent of her teased him.

She was delightful dips and curves, all quivering breathlessness and surprise.

He had never wanted sex so badly in his life.

His hands ran down her sides, and then behind to cup her bottom and pull her hard against him.

She made a little noise at the back of her throat and he maneuvered her backward until she was up against his desk.

He still hadn't kissed her, their lips almost touching as they breathed hard, and he breached the final distance and cupped her head with a hand, holding her in place as he slanted his lips over hers.

Below them the kitchen door slammed, and the sound of laughing and joking drifted up.

He jerked back his head and her eyes widened, all trace of desire gone.

There were footsteps on the stairs, and in a smooth motion Jonathan spun from her, moved behind his desk, and sat down.

It was the only way he could hope to hide his arousal.

Madame Levéel turned at the same time, facing him with her back to the door, and took two steps away, putting more distance between them than just the desk.

"Of course I can make you coffee, my lord," she said, and there was a stain of red across her cheeks. "And some galette, as well, perhaps? A light meal to hold you until *le dîner?*" Her accent was as thick as the sweet cream he'd smelled downstairs, and for the first time, he realized she could lay it on heavy or light, as she pleased. Or perhaps, a voice whispered in his head, as she remembered.

"Thank you, Cook, that would be very nice." He spoke just as Edgars stepped through the door, eyes narrowed at the sight of them.

He saw the way she took a surreptitious breath and blanked her face of all emotion before she turned. "Mr. Edgars." She inclined her head and stepped toward him, and he was forced to move out of her way.

Jonathan watched her swing out into the hall and then heard her light tread as she retreated to her domain. Without having to explain herself, damn it.

Explain what she was doing, rifling through his desk.

If he hadn't had to touch her, kiss her; if he'd demanded answers right away. . . . Ah, well. It had probably been worth it.

He surprised himself by grinning. "I'm afraid I'd forgotten it was the staff's half day, Edgars. I was lucky Madame Levéel was in to answer when I rang."

Jonathan watched Edgars try to keep his face from revealing what he thought of that. He truly had forgotten it was the staff's half day, but otherwise, this was a day for lies. "Please tell Cook just the coffee will be fine. I've got another appointment today."

"Certainly, my lord." Edgars turned to go, but not before Jonathan saw the flare of disapproval in his eyes.

And what could he say? This time, Edgars had him bang to rights.

21

No one had ever touched her like he did. She knew Lord Aldridge would never have taken hold of the daughter of Sir Eric Barrington and kissed her. Either last night or just now. But because she was his employee and cook, it seemed he had no compunction.

She needed time to work out whether that was a good or a bad thing.

Trying to hide her trembling, she pulled the crème brûlée from the oven, grateful to have something to do straightaway. Her hands shook as she set it down, and she moved on to the coffee, turning the grinder with quick, sharp bursts while she listened to Babs and Harry joking with each other.

Everyone was in high spirits after their morning off, and she was grateful for the laughing and teasing around her, the swirl of movement as everyone shed their coats and hats and pulled on their uniforms. It hid her confusion and fear.

Edgars came back down the stairs, and things got a little less rowdy.

"His lordship says not to worry about the ga . . ." He trailed off with a sudden fury on his face, and Gigi wondered if it was because he couldn't remember what she'd offered Aldridge, or because she'd offered it to begin with.

"The galette?" she asked.

"Yes." The word snapped like the click of a castanet. "Just the coffee will be fine. He has to go out again."

She gave a nod and tapped the last of the ground coffee into a canister.

"How long has his lordship been home?" Edgars' voice was strange, almost strangled.

She lifted her head in surprise. He was walking on very shaky ground. Aldridge had warned him last night to keep quiet about his suspicions, and by the croak in his voice, he knew he was crossing a line. He had found them fully clothed and six feet apart.

This line of questioning was a fishing expedition. One she sorely resented. "About ten or fifteen minutes, I suppose." She gave a careless shrug designed to irritate him.

"You can't worry about that," Iris spoke up, standing close to the fire and warming her hands.

"Worry?" Edgars jerked his head her way.

"If he comes home early on our day off. He's forgotten before, but he's not the type to be out of sorts when he realizes we aren't in. And Cook was here to answer the bell."

"Did he complain?" Gigi asked Edgars as she poured hot

water over the coffee. She watched him with her most guile-less expression. "He was unhappy that it was just me in the house?"

"No."

Everyone swung their gaze to him at his tone, and he cleared his throat.

"Well, then." She shrugged again, Gallic to the bone. "It is none of our concern when he comes home, whether it is the staff's half day or not."

Edgars flushed, which had the strange effect of steadying her. Pitting her will against his brought out a side to her she'd never known existed before. She almost enjoyed the game they were locked in, and she was able to place the coffee cup and saucer on a tray with a steady hand.

"I'll take it." Rob lifted it carefully and made for the stairs. As if that were the signal, the others all disappeared to do their jobs, leaving Edgars and Gigi alone.

She watched him force himself not to watch Iris as she looped her apron over her head and walked toward the stairs. Despite herself, she felt a tug of pity.

She could sympathize with him—wanting Iris but not sure she would have him.

Would Aldridge want her like he seemed to do in the study if he knew who she really was? If he knew how she had tricked him and used his house for her own convenience?

She had been brought up with impeccable manners, and she knew she was putting herself beyond the pale with her ac-tions.

Aldridge might find the notion of dallying with his cook enticing, but dallying with his neighbor and social equal was probably not on his list. It came with far too many complications.

She blushed suddenly and, to cover it, crouched down beside the oven and opened it a little, let the heat fan her cheeks. It was still a little too hot to slow roast the lamb.

As she stood, she smoothed a hand over her skirts. Aldridge's kiss had woken something in her, something that had already been stirred to life by last night's brief encounter, and the notion of an imaginary garden tryst.

The thought made her still, and she looked over at Edgars, who had taken up a glass to polish.

Had he given Aldridge the idea that she would be an easy lover? A woman at home with rolling about with men and coming home covered in grass stains?

He hadn't seen much of her since she'd started working in his house, and now that she thought of it, his actions last night and in his study had been bold. Overly bold.

Unless that was what a man did when he caught a servant rifling through his private things?

She had been lucky to escape his study without having to explain herself, and now she counted herself lucky to get out of his grasp before she made even more of a fool of herself than she had already.

If the shadow man didn't kill her, this would eventually be over. And as neighbors, she and Lord Aldridge were bound to meet.

When that happened, everything that occurred between them now would be seen in a very different light.

She busied herself with peeling the potatoes for a gratin.

Though she wanted this deadly game of hide-and-seek to be over, meeting Aldridge as Miss Giselle Barrington was something she was already dreading.

———————

There was no question which of the ten people hard at work in the Duke of Wittaker's magnificent kitchen was Georges Bisset. Jonathan spotted him immediately.

He stood whisking something in a bowl while he watched his underlings, the movement of his hands oddly hypnotic. He was tall and broad shouldered, with a barrel chest and a face that was cherub-round, topped with dark hair threaded with silver.

He murmured something to a woman in an apron, and she gave a grave nod and moved off, her demeanor serious. Everyone looked serious, come to think of it.

Bisset ran a very focused kitchen.

He'd planned to let Wittaker know he wanted to speak with his chef but on the way over had decided that this was personal business, and therefore none of Wittaker's concern.

If Wittaker ever heard of this visit, Jonathan hoped the duke took the same view, because he'd been known to call a fellow out over the slightest trifle. While he wasn't afraid to face Wittaker with pistols at dawn, he'd prefer to avoid it. Besides, Jonathan had to see him occasionally at the House of Lords.

He stepped fully into the room, and Bisset looked up from his whisking and frowned. He handed his bowl to someone else and walked toward him, and something in his stride and attitude brought to mind a charging brigade.

"*Qui?*" Bisset sized him up, and there was a tension about him.

"Monsieur Bisset?" There was no doubt, but he asked anyway for politeness's sake. "I am here about Madame Levéel."

The tension Jonathan sensed before seemed to ratchet up another notch. "What about Madame Levéel?" His eyes narrowed. "Who are you?"

"Lord Aldridge." He bowed slightly, keeping things polite and respectful from his side. There was no question Bisset knew Madame Levéel well; his reaction was too strong. "I would like to talk to you about her, if I may?"

"If you have a complaint about her, you don't deserve her." The Frenchman spoke with a sneer. "I would have her here in my kitchen in a flash. It was a sacrifice to send her to you."

He meant it, Jonathan realized. "Why did you send her to me?"

Bisset didn't answer, and his shoulders rose, tense and ready. Every instinct Jonathan had honed from ten years in the military went on alert.

"What is it about Madame Levéel that brings you to my kitchen?"

"She is afraid." He'd thought to dance around the issue, maybe not raise it at all, but Bisset's attitude made that impossible. "I think she's in fear of her life, and I have a feeling she is being coerced into spying on me."

Bisset's jaw dropped in surprise, and there was no question the emotion was genuine. "Spying on you?" He frowned; then a look came over his face that was part derision, part disgust. "I would imagine you think it is all about you, n'est-ce pas? It must be about you, because you are an important lord. But my petit chou is no spy, and I can assure you, the reason she is afraid, the troubles she may have, they are nothing to do with you, Lord Aldridge. Nothing at all. If you don't want my treasure, you can send her back to me right away." Two slaps of the back of his hand into his palm as he said the last two words punctuated his sudden fury. "You have taken enough of my time now, go away." He flicked his hands at Jonathan as if shooing off a chicken.

"I want to help her." Jonathan curled his hands into fists at his side. "Tell me how I can help her."

Half turned away, Bisset stopped. Turned slowly back to face Jonathan. "I have lived in England for twenty years, since I escaped the mobs of France with my employers, and it has been my experience that no English nobleman ever cared to help his staff over much. So I have to ask myself, why are you here? And what do you really want?"

There must have been something on his face, some memory of the feel of the curve of her waist under his hand, the soft touch of her lips, that he was helpless to hide, because Bisset took a threatening step forward.

"Mon Dieu, you want her! If you have touched a hair on ma petite's head, I will be using your testicles in a new recipe."

Jonathan had had enough of people telling him what he could do when it came to Madame Levéel. "Someone cornered her in an alley two nights ago. They threatened her. Last night she went uninvited to a ball, and this morning, I caught her going through the papers in my study. There is something going on, Bisset, and the question you should ask yourself is would you prefer the Alien Office to be looking into it, or me?"

"The Alien Office?" Bisset spoke carefully, as if Jonathan had gone mad and he didn't want to set him off. "You think . . ." He started to laugh, a real, deep laugh from the belly. "Call in your Alien Office, you *imbécile*, but before you do, I will be coming to fetch *ma petite* and bring her back to me. What was I thinking, sending her to some lecherous lord? *C'est stupide!*"

His face hardened. "Now get out of my kitchen." He picked up a knife and held it like an extension of his hand. "And believe me, I meant every word about using your testicles for a pâté."

Jonathan wanted to hit that contemptuous face so badly he shook with the desire. But this man was something to Madame Levéel. Her father, perhaps, or some other relative. He was in his fifties at least, and far too old to be her lover, and Jonathan was sure that if they were romantically involved, the Frenchman would never have sent her to work away from him.

So if he struck the man, and somehow the impossible happened, and Madame Levéel became his, he knew it would count against him. Very much against him.

He lowered the fist he didn't recall raising and clasped his hands behind his back, as if nothing of the sort had happened. "If you change your mind and care to let me help, please don't hesitate to send round a note." He kept his voice so smooth, he was impressed with himself.

Something flashed in the Frenchman's eyes, or it might have been the light reflecting off the massive blade in his hand.

"Good day to you." Jonathan gave another bow and stalked out the kitchen as if he didn't feel the sharp cut of Bisset's stare all the way to the door.

22

Edgars fidgeted at the table, the accounts ledger in front of him.

In the last hour he had managed to annoy everyone who'd come through the kitchen, interfering in their work where he usually had the good sense to let them get on with it.

Gigi wished she could leave in angry silence, like Babs and Harry just had, but she was stuck in his company as she poured the egg custard over the thinly sliced potatoes of her gratin.

"Cook, what is this?" He pointed accusingly at the open page.

Gigi lifted her gratin dish and put it in the oven before leaning over him to look.

"Comté."

"And what *is* that?" His hands tightened around the ledger, and his knuckles went white.

"It is a type of French cheese," she said gently. Edgars was far too tightly wound.

"In future, please make sure there is an English explanation beside your entries."

"*D'accord.*" She gave a nod. "Of course. I apologize."

He blinked, and she wondered if she was too hard on him, since he was that surprised by a simple apology.

Iris came down the rear stairs and, like a pointer scenting a bird in the rushes, Edgars became riveted to her. He hung on to the ledger like it was the only thing keeping him anchored to the earth.

This was why he'd sat in her kitchen and subjected her to his ill temper and nerves all afternoon. A chance to speak to Iris!

And then he ruined it.

"Iris, do you need any help in the bedrooms?" he asked, quick and nervous, almost snapping, the moment she stepped into the room.

She looked over at him in surprise, tipping the ash from Lord Aldridge's bedroom grate into the ash bin. "Since when have I ever?" There was a thread of indignation in her tone.

"I'm simply asking." He made the crucial mistake of going cold.

A smile and a bit of humor would have undone the damage, but Edgars seemed to have a knack for making things hard on himself.

"Well, the answer is no." Iris sniffed. "Thank you."

Rob shouldered open the kitchen door and came in with a tray of eggs from the deliveryman. As he kicked the door closed with the back of his heel, Iris caught his eye and they shared a look.

Edgars went stiff, then stood with a scrape of his chair and walked into the wine cellar without a word.

With another sniff, Iris went up the service stairs, coal bucket under her arm.

Gigi shook her head. His Edginess was an idiot.

Rob set the eggs down carefully on the shelf and came to stand beside her at the table. She handed him a brioche left over from breakfast, smothered in Reine Claude jam. He took a bite and groaned in appreciation, then cast a quick look at the wine cellar.

"I reckon the nob you gave this jam to t'other day ran off to find some more." His tone was teasing, an attempt to lighten the mood.

"Ran off?" She regretted she wasn't able to keep her voice as light. Perhaps she had more in common with Edgars than she thought.

"Yeah." Rob took another bite. "Went round to his place this morning to drop off a note for his lordship. Maid at the back, she told me he ain't even there. Took off for foreign parts day before yesterday. Unexpected, like."

The world seemed to whirl around her for a moment. She'd pinned all her hopes on Dervish. Had risked everything the other night to drop off her note. "The same day he was here for breakfast?"

"Yeah, just after lunchtime, th' maid said. Fancy just decid-ing to go off like that, without any preparation? Had 'em all running round like a flock of hens, packing his things an' all. Came back from his office when the carriage was packed, hopped on and waved 'em goodbye."

Dervish hadn't even been there when she'd delivered her note. If she'd known, she never would have gone into Aldridge's study. Would never have been caught.

A cold chill washed over her.

There was nothing that led back to Aldridge House in the note she'd left behind the loose brick at Goldfern for Dervish, but if the shadow man found it on one of his midnight forays over the wall, he would know for sure she was in London.

Dervish wouldn't be coming for it, so she'd better get it back. "Did Lord Dervish's maid say where he was going?"

"Aye. Sweden." Rob laughed. "Not sure I even know exactly where that is."

"Well, he won't get any Reine Claude jam there." Gigi forced her voice to hold the hint of a laugh. It was one of the hardest things she'd ever done.

Dervish *had* been D. He'd stood right in front of her.

And now he was off to Stockholm. To look for her, she'd guess. And to deal with her father's body.

The thought nearly felled her.

Rob grinned around his last mouthful and then left.

She lifted her hand to her heart and pressed a fist against it, as if that could somehow alleviate the pain.

She had to get out. Escape from Edgars' watchful, probing eyes that would surely notice her distress.

She forced herself to stand straight. She'd try to go again to Goldfern, boldly. And let nothing stop her.

She almost pulled off her cook's apron and hat, and then stopped. She'd be more invisible with them on. The shadow man knew her as a wealthy young woman who mixed in the best circles. He would dismiss a cook out of hand.

Edgars was still lurking in his wine cellar, and she climbed quietly up the back stairs and out into the access lane, pushing the door closed without making a sound.

She felt a little of the pressure lift. For a few moments, she could think of her father and not watch her expression.

She walked first to Chapel Street and looked down the road in the direction of Goldfern to make sure there was no one about in front. The street was empty.

The wind was picking up, and she shivered as she walked back past the kitchen door and along to where the lane met the back alley. She peered around the wall to see the lay of the land. The men who had been arguing earlier were gone, but the rag-and-bone man's cart and pony stood a few houses down, on the left. There was no sign of the man himself.

Gigi decided she wouldn't get a better chance.

She ran the first part of the way, until she was at the cart. The pony nickered as she went by, and she ran a hand along her flank and gave her hindquarters a pat. A little cloud of dust rose up, and Gigi coughed.

The cart was piled high with junk—pieces of wood, old pots and crockery, an old mattress with stuffing oozing out of it at one corner. It made a nice shield, blocking the view of anyone looking down the alley from Aldridge House. Like Edgars.

She looked at Goldfern's back door, and then farther along the alley. There was someone a little way down with his back to her, clearing the lane with a shovel.

She bit her lip, unsure whether to risk being seen.

The shoveler had stopped his work and leaned on his spade, lifting a hand to wipe his brow. He was muscular, on the stocky side. He could be the man who'd followed her the night she'd gone to Dervish's house.

She turned away at the thought, and came face-to-face with a stranger.

Jonathan thanked his luck he'd decided to walk his fury at Georges Bisset off rather than take a cab. If he'd been in a carriage, he wouldn't have seen Madame Levéel as he turned onto Chapel Street. She was looking in the opposite direction, toward the park, and then she scurried down the alley that ran beside Aldridge House.

He ran, uncaring of how his behavior might appear to his neighbors, but by the time he reached the alleyway, she was gone. Not back into the house, he guessed. Her movements had been far too furtive. As if she were checking the coast was clear.

He'd guess she was in the alley behind Aldridge House, where Edgars had caught her the other night. There was some-thing about the lane that ran along the rear of the houses in the street that kept drawing her back. He raced to it and looked right and left.

There was a cart and horse to the right, and no one else in sight. To the left he could hear the murmur of voices just beyond where the narrow alley twisted sharply, obscuring the speakers from view.

Aware time was wasting, he went left, walking as quietly as he could on the rough cobbles.

"An' I said to her, I said, 'Best keep your wits about you, my girl, because the young master's got his eye on you and no mistake.'"

"'E's had 'is eye on a few of 'em over the years. Look where it's got 'em."

"Out on the street with a babe they can't afford, is what."

Jonathan rounded the corner and found two women, ruddy-cheeked and plump, standing in the lane. Each seemed to have come from one of the open doors on opposite sides of the way.

Sir Ingleton's, a few doors down on Chapel Street from Aldridge House, he guessed, and Lord Matherton's from South Street.

"Wha—?" The woman from Sir Ingleton's side gave him a quick look and, with a squawk, dived back behind her door and slammed it shut.

The other stood staring at him.

"You talking about Sir Ingleton's son, Henry?" he surprised himself by asking her.

"We don't mean no 'arm, my lord." But her eyes said different. Said she wasn't sorry about the way they'd been talking.

"Sounds like Henry means some harm, though. Perhaps I should have a word."

"Whatever you think is right, my lord." She crossed her arms over her impressive bosom, all but sneering.

He wondered if he didn't look lordly enough, still had too much the air of the second son about him. Sneering at him seemed to be somewhat of a theme at the moment.

He raised a brow at her, surprising her enough that she let her arms drop to her sides.

"Beg your pardon, my lord," she mumbled, neck and chest red. "Only"—she flicked him a quick look as she edged to her own door—"I'm tired of seeing good girls dragged down. This ain't foreign parts. It's London. But they treat us like we're their har-reem or summat."

"Did a woman come by here, cook's apron on?" he asked before she could take another step.

"No." She answered without thought, then narrowed her eyes. "You ain't chasing your cook down the alley, are you?"

Well, yes he was. But not like she meant. Well, not entirely.

"I'll talk to Henry. I think you'll find he might listen to me. And if he doesn't and the girl gets into trouble, send a note round. I'm Lord Aldridge."

"I know who you are, my lord." She gave a suspicious sniff, then slammed the door on him.

He turned and went back the way he'd come, and as he

rounded the corner, he saw Madame Levéel standing next to the pony, a large flowerpot in each hand, talking to the rag-and-bone man.

When she saw him her eyes went wide, and she turned away, speaking to the old trader for a moment longer before facing him again.

He had missed his opportunity to see what drew her back here time and again, and frustration licked at him like a hungry fire as he approached her.

"My lord." She lowered her eyes, and he noticed a pink stain on her cheeks. "*Au revoir*, Mr. Rice. Thank you for the pots." She gave a final nod to the old man and he doffed his cap to her, but his eyes were on Jonathan, missing nothing.

"I'll carry those for you," Jonathan said, staring straight back at the trader. He took the pots from her, and Mr. Rice looked away before disappearing around the back of his cart. "What are they for?"

"Some herbs and flowers, to brighten the wall outside my room." She still had her eyes averted, and she was walking a step away from him despite the narrow alley, as if to ensure they did not accidentally touch.

Something wild and dangerous rose up in his chest, and as they took the turn left into the alley down the side of Aldridge House, he deliberately began encroaching on the space she'd put between them, until she stopped and pressed herself up against the wall. He stood close enough to feel her breath on his face.

Now, at last, she looked him in the eye again.

"Just what is it you think I'm going to do to you?" He tried to keep his voice calm, but there was an edge he couldn't suppress. "What is it *everyone* thinks I'm going to do?"

"Everyone?" Her body went stiff, still plastered up against the stone wall.

He brushed that away. "You. What do you think I'm going to do? Everyone else can go to the devil."

"Oh." She nodded. "You mean Edgars."

"We'll come back to him. Just answer me."

"It isn't what you're going to do to me." She looked straight at him, body tense as if steeling herself. "I'm not afraid of you. But you're a dangerous complication."

There was so much more to it. It was in her eyes, in her expression, but he thought she was telling the truth.

"Dangerous how?" He waited while she looked away, as if the answer would come to her from Chapel Street.

"I do not want to answer you," she whispered. "I'll regret it if I do."

He leaned closer to her, until his legs were brushing her skirts and the pots he held rested against the wall on either side of her. "Take a chance, madame. Tell me."

She gave a twisted smile. "I've taken more chances these last few weeks than I have ever taken before. I don't need to take another."

They were close enough that all he needed to do was lean forward an inch and their lips would touch. The last time he'd given in to the need to feel her under his hands, he'd lost the opportunity to find the truth. He clutched the pots harder, fighting the urge to set them down and pull her even closer.

"Chances like looking through the papers in my study?" he made himself ask instead.

She closed her eyes. "Yes. Chances like that."

"Who is forcing you to do this? What are they after? I don't keep any important papers lying on my desk. If they thought you could get any privileged information from me, they're mistaken."

Her eyes snapped open. "Forcing me?" She frowned. "What privileged information?"

He suddenly remembered Bisset sneering at him, daring him to call in the Alien Office, as cool as could be. Perhaps it hadn't been a bluff.

"You aren't after information on one of the projects I'm involved in." He meant to ask it as a question, but it came out slowly, a statement of fact.

She shook her head.

"And you're not going to tell me what you were doing?"

She shook her head again.

"If you tell me, I can help you."

She reached up a hand between them, and her fingers hovered, just near his chest, without touching him. "I don't know that you can. That it is wise . . ."

The kitchen door slammed open, caught by the wind, and Jonathan nearly dropped the pots.

She eeled under of the cage of his arms, and when he straightened and turned, she stood demure, eyes downcast, more than an arm stretch away.

"Your lordship?" It was Harry. He looked between them

with no suspicion, just working out what to do, a genuine smile on his face. He stepped forward and tugged the pots out of Jonathan's hands.

"Pots for outside my room," Madame Levéel told him. "If you could go round the side and put them there?"

Harry gave a nod and disappeared around the corner, whistling cheerfully.

"This isn't finished." He would not keep skulking, jumping with guilt whenever someone came near them.

"I know." She fiddled with her apron. "When it *is* finished, I hope you'll find it in you to forgive me."

"Forgive you for what?" he asked, but her lips were drawn tight together, and she was glaring at the kitchen door.

Edgars stood watching them. The look he sent Madame Levéel was shuttered, and it made Jonathan uneasy.

"Your lordship." He gave a little bow without meeting Jonathan's eyes.

"Thank you for carrying the pots for me." Madame Levéel drew herself up and marched to the door, forcing Edgars to step aside to get out of her way.

"I would like to talk to you after dinner tonight, Cook," Jonathan told her, with no give in his tone.

She paused in the doorway and looked back at him. Gave a brief nod, and disappeared amid the fragrant scent of roasting lamb and rosemary.

Edgars didn't follow her, standing, unsure, on the threshold. "You aren't coming in this way, my lord?" he asked in a sort of hushed horror.

"The world won't come to an end if I do, but no, I'll go round the front."

Edgars nodded, relaxing his stiff pose a little, and drew back into the kitchen, closing the door behind him.

Which would make it the second kitchen door slammed in his face today alone. And just think, he could have been sitting in his study, reading reports.

Jonathan threw back his head and laughed.

23

Tonight, when Aldridge called her in after dinner, she would tell him the truth.

Gigi took her carving knife and began to slice the lamb, pink and tender.

Her reasons for not doing so already were good. She had spent the last nine years being trained to say nothing to anyone, and to understand that some secrets should never be told. That only those who asked for their help could be given or sent the information they were seeking; that to give it to anyone else could endanger lives and ruin nations.

But no one could blame her for seeking aid in these circumstances. How could they?

With Dervish gone, she had no way of knowing who to trust, and the time was approaching when the letter would lose its importance because it was not in the right hands and thought lost, and every sacrifice would have been for nothing.

She would not let that happen. Her father deserved more than that.

She laid the slices of lamb in a fan around the tower of potato gratin in the center of the plate. There were minted peas in a beautiful Chinese bowl and honey-glazed carrots roasted with tarragon.

"I can't even think, that smells so nice," Babs said, coming in from outside, a coal bucket in hand.

Rob lifted the tray. "At least you can knock off now, and 'ave some." He tipped his head in her direction. "Mind Babs only has her share, Cook."

Babs was washing at the sink, and Gigi saw the moment when she decided to flick water at Rob.

"If," she said, standing directly in front of Rob, shielding him, "my food gets even one drop of water on it"—she stared Babs down—"the person responsible will have bread for dinner."

Babs ducked her head. "Sorry, Cook."

"All right." She shooed Rob up the stairs and turned back to the table. Mavis was standing at the rear stairs, and the look on her face made Gigi go cold.

"What is it, Mavis?"

"I done a wrong thing." She looked down and twisted her apron like it was a chicken's neck.

"We all do the wrong thing now and then." Gigi walked toward her. The girl's fear was palpable, and she knew that gut-wrenching feeling all too well. She drew Mavis away from the stairs and led her to a chair.

The girl collapsed.

"What is it, Mae?" Babs crouched down beside her, and when she didn't answer, looked up at Gigi, a little frown of worry on her broad, open face. "I'll get Iris."

Gigi nodded. Iris had taken Mavis under her wing from the start. If anyone could get the story out, it was her. Babs rose and disappeared up the stairs, and Gigi poured some tea, loading the cup with sugar.

"I'm sure whatever it is, we can fix it, Mavis. You don't need to worry so." She pressed the cup into Mavis's hands and rubbed her shoulder.

"I broke his lordship's wooden box, the little one on his chest of drawers, while I were putting away his laundry." She shuddered out a sob. "Cracked, it did. Right down the middle, split right open, and now it's s . . . s . . . smashed." She shook, her chest heaving.

"It was an accident, Mavis. Lord Aldridge will understand."

She raised red-rimmed, puffy eyes to Gigi's face. "Mr. Edgars don't. He were angry." She looked toward the rear stairs. "He sent me down while he puts things to rights. But the box can't be put to rights. There's no savin' it."

Babs came down the stairs from the hall with Iris in tow, just as Edgars came down the rear stairs on the opposite side of the kitchen.

He'd worked himself into a high rage, and Gigi thought of Rumplestiltskin again as he stomped down the last few steps.

"You are a clumsy, ham-fisted waster." The finger he pointed at Mavis shook. "Now I have to explain to Lord Aldridge what's happened to his box."

And Lord Aldridge wasn't exactly pleased with him at the moment. Edgars was cornered and, like any wounded animal with no place to go, he was lashing out.

Gigi might have felt some sympathy, as she was partly responsible for his predicament, if the person he'd been lashing out at wasn't the most defenseless person in the house. She put both hands on Mavis's shoulders and drew herself up. "I'll explain to his lordship. It was an accident."

Edgars moved his gaze slowly from Mavis to her, and he dropped his arm. "I am quite capable of doing my own job, Cook. And I'll thank you not to interfere in it." He said each word through clenched teeth.

"If you were interfering with Mavis as you've been interfering with the rest of us all day, you're probably the reason she knocked that box, because I've never known her to be clumsy before." Iris spoke into the dead, cold silence of the room.

Babs gasped audibly at her nerve, and Edgars took a step back, as if he'd been struck.

"That is *enough* of undermining me. Enough cheek out of all of you." He pointed his finger at Mavis again. "You're sacked, and you can thank your friends for that. And Iris, one more bit of cheek from you, and you're out, too."

He tugged hard on his waistcoat and walked past them to the main stairs. "Now excuse me, while I go and explain to his lordship that the antique box he inherited from his mother is smashed beyond repair."

Iris and Babs shuffled out of his way as if he were contagious, and they stood in silence until he was gone.

Gigi knew she must look like the others. Completely shocked.

"Mavis, I'm so sorry," Iris whispered. "I should've kept me mouth shut—"

"No." Gigi sighed. "It was me. Offering to speak to his lordship like Edgars couldn't do the job. I thought I'd be doing him a favor, but he thought I was saying he wasn't up to it."

"What will I do?" Mavis stared down at her hands. "I'll get a beatin', I go back 'ome with no job. No food for me there, anyways." She rocked a little. "What'll I do?" She looked up at them, eyes wide, not expecting an answer. Already defeated. Bracing for that beating, because where did she have to go, but back home?

"*Du calme. Du calme.*" Gigi rubbed her shoulders, thinking furiously. "You're going into a new job. Right now, tonight. You can start tomorrow." Gigi knew there were some risks to what she was about to do, but Mavis had lost her job because of her mistake. Her poor navigation of the belowstairs waters.

"What?" Mavis sat looking at her, agape.

"Go pack your things while I write a note for you to take with you. Your new position is at a house a few doors down, so you'll still be on the same street." She turned to see Iris and Babs staring at her. "Well, go help her. I've got dessert to get ready in ten minutes, and coffee after that." She clapped her hands in impatience. "*Allez!*"

"What house?" Babs asked, her voice hushed.

"Goldfern. Now go." She flicked her fingers at them, then went into her sitting room and pulled out a piece of paper. From the kitchen she heard the soft murmur of voices, and then footsteps up the rear stairs.

She bit down on her nail, thought through what she should say. Eventually she decided on two letters: one for Mr. Greenway, her father's lawyer, and one for Mr. Jones, the care-taker at the house, whom she'd never met.

They had better treat Mavis kindly when she arrived, or they would regret it.

———————

This was what he'd smelled when he'd come through the kitchen, just before he'd caught Madame Levéel in his study. Jonathan stared down at the crème brûlée before him, took up his spoon, and cracked the thin layer of caramelized sugar on top. It made the perfect crunch.

He dipped in his spoon and came up with smooth custard, dotted with tiny vanilla seeds. He put it on his tongue and forced himself not to close his eyes.

He had an audience.

Edgars stood, stiff and vibrating like a tuning fork, and from their uneasy expressions, Rob and Harry didn't know why.

Most likely Madame Levéel again.

For the first time, Jonathan considered that it might come down to either his butler or his cook.

Who would he choose, if it were up to him?

Edgars had nearly fifteen years' service to his family, and having Madame Levéel elsewhere would mean he would no longer be pursuing a servant. No longer have to wonder if she would choose differently, if the power balance between them was different.

But he would no longer eat her food.

He looked down at the crème brûlée.

It would be worth it, to have her.

I hope you can find it in you to forgive me. What had she meant by that?

There was a knock at the front door, and Edgars flinched at the sound. He disappeared out into the hall, and Jonathan took another spoonful of crème brûlée while he still could.

"A message for you, my lord, from Lord Durnham." Edgars returned carrying a silver tray with a note, his mouth a thin, sour line.

Jonathan ripped the note open and frowned at the message. His planned chat with Madame Levéel would have to wait until later.

"I'm going out, Edgars. I won't be back too late, I hope. Please tell Cook I'd still like a word, if she would wait up."

Edgars' lips looked like they were about to disappear. He didn't respond.

"Edgars?" He kept his voice low but didn't try to hide the menace in it.

Edgars' scalding gaze slid away. "Yes, my lord."

If the decision came down to Edgars or Madame Levéel, perhaps it would not be so difficult, after all.

Jonathan scooped up the last of the crème brûlée as he stood. "Be sure to give Cook my highest compliments on the meal."

24

"Now, give the note to Mr. Jones," Gigi told Mavis, who stood shivering and miserable, holding the rough hessian sack with all her worldly possessions in a white-knuckled grip.

Her eyes were dry now, but shock still shook her in tiny, shuddering trembles. She'd had a quick dinner after she'd collected her things, and had hardly eaten anything. Gigi had never seen her less than famished, and it made her burn that Edgars had scared her badly enough to make her lose her appetite.

"If there is any trouble from Jones, you let me know immediately."

"You sure this is all right, Cook?" Her voice was very small.

"I promise you, Mavis." Gigi thought desperately for a way to keep Mavis from talking about her—even as Madame Levéel, the cook—to Mr. Jones. She didn't know Jones, couldn't trust him, and she knew the shadow man would be watching and listening. He wasn't stupid, and he'd work out her disguise quickly enough if he had reason to look in Madame Levéel's direction.

Even if she told Lord Aldridge everything this evening, there was no sense in taking chances. "I've explained in the note that Miss Barrington, the owner of Goldfern, has hired you on my recommendation."

That was a lie; she hadn't explained anything of the sort. She'd addressed the note as herself, as Giselle Barrington, and could only hope Jones didn't question Mavis too much about how his mistress had come to hire her.

She patted Mavis's arm. "Miss Barrington will be returning home soon, and Mr. Jones will need more staff if the house is to be opened up again. It will be more than all right. And if Mr. Jones causes even the slightest problem, you come to me, you hear?" A fierce protectiveness swept over her at the sight of Mavis's thin, pale neck, drooping as if her head was too heavy for her. "You come straight to me."

"Yes, Cook." Mavis hesitated. "But why would Miss Barrington take me on, on your recommendation?"

Gigi gave her a confident smile. "You'll just have to trust me that it's so, Mavis. I promise you it is."

Mavis nodded and clutched her bag tighter.

There was a shuffle behind them. Iris stood in her coat, Mavis's coat in her hand.

"Thank you for walking her there, Iris." She held the note out to Mavis, who took it nervously.

"Right, then." Iris drew in a shaky breath. "Let's go." While she waited for Mavis to join her at the top of the stairs, she looked at Gigi and nodded. She opened the door, and Mavis followed her out without looking back. The door closed behind them with a bang.

"Where are they going?"

Gigi spun and saw Edgars standing at the kitchen table, with Rob and Harry just behind him bringing the empty dishes.

"Iris is taking Mavis to a new job."

Edgars gripped the back of a chair. There was fury in his eyes and high color in his cheeks.

It struck her he might have been planning to hire Mavis back. He'd had time to calm down enough to see that Iris would never forgive him if he sent Mavis packing, and maybe he was here, right now, to show how magnanimous he could be.

She watched him carefully, more and more sure she was right.

And she'd ruined it for him, jumping in with a new job for Mavis straightaway.

Perhaps she should have anticipated he'd change his mind. But she couldn't bear for Mavis to be on the street for even one second, thinking she had nowhere to go and no one to go to.

And if Edgars thought hiring her back after that scene in the kitchen would have wiped the slate clean, he was like the fairy-tale emperor with new clothes. Oblivious to reality.

Rob dropped a tray onto the table with a clatter. "What?"

She looked past Edgars to the two of them. "Mr. Edgars sacked Mavis earlier this evening, just before dinner started."

Harry's mouth fell open.

"I happened to know of someone looking for a maid immediately, so . . ." She shrugged. The less said, the better.

"Mavis?" Harry's voice went low, almost guttural. "You threw Mavis out onto the street?" He looked at Edgars like he was something slippery and brown staining the cobbles.

"Where did you send her?" Rob watched her, sharp-eyed.

"Goldfern House. Just down the road. You can see her whenever you like."

"They'll treat her right?" Rob frowned. "That place is all but shut up."

She gave a twist of her lips. "The owner is returning soon, and when she does, Mavis will definitely be well treated. Until then, I hope so."

"If the owners are coming back, that explains why they need someone in a hurry." Harry relaxed a little.

"But it doesn't explain why she was fired in the first place." Rob crossed his arms over his chest and stared at Edgars.

Edgars said nothing for a moment, watching them with eyes that glittered in the candlelight. He leaned toward Harry and Rob, shoulders hunched, finger jabbing. "I'll remind you both you're answerable to me, not the other way round. Iris has had a warning already. Any cheek, and you're out, too." He was breathing hard, like he'd run up the stairs to the top of the house.

He looked across at Gigi. "You may have weaseled your way in with your fancy references and your connections to other jobs at the drop of a hat, but I'm on to you, madam. You're up to something. I know it. And mark my words, when I find out what it is, not even those big doe eyes and fancy desserts will save you."

Gigi's laugh of disbelief was loud in the sudden silence of the room. "What do you mean by—"

"Save your outrage and your wiles for his lordship." Edgars stalked to the coatrack and took down his coat, shrugging it on with barely restrained violence. "I'm going out."

The door slammed hard behind him, and she slowly turned to face Rob and Harry.

They were staring at the door, not her, both with mouths hanging open.

"Does his lordship want me to go up and see him now?" Gigi asked, suddenly aware of the silence in the house.

Rob started. Then shook his head. "His lordship got an urgent message, had to go out. He asked Mr. Edgars to ask you if you wouldn't mind waiting for him. He didn't think he'd be long."

"First time His Edginess hasn't done what his lordship asked him, that I know of." Harry shifted uncomfortably.

"First time His Edginess has ever had a real threat to the command of his little kingdom." Rob kept his gaze on her, speculative and curious.

Gigi lifted her hands to massage her temples. "And isn't it turning out well?"

———

Lady Holliday, Durnham's widowed sister, was sitting with Lady Durnham in the library when Jonathan was shown in. She looked so like Durnham—beautifully sculpted face with dark hair and hazel eyes—it was striking.

"Durnham will be here in a moment; he's just talking to someone in his study." Lady Durnham rose to greet him and drew him to the little grouping of chairs he'd sat in the day before.

They exchanged pleasantries for all of a minute before Lady Durnham lifted a hand. "I asked some people to watch Lord Dervish's house today. Or rather, to watch anyone watching Lord Dervish's house."

Jonathan had expected this report to come from Durnham, not from his wife, but as it was her people doing the watching, he wasn't sure now why he had. "Did they find anyone?"

"Oh, yes." Lady Durnham gave a slow nod. "A real ramper. Name of Hal Boots." She gave a tilt of her head. "Likes to put the boot in, does Hal. Earned his name honestly."

"I do so love being around you, Charlotte. My vocabulary goes up several notches every time I am."

Jonathan lifted his gaze to Lady Holliday, who was grinning at her sister-in-law with no glimmer of malice, holding a needle with embroidery thread in one hand and a linen handkerchief in the other.

Lady Durnham flicked her an annoyed glance. "As I was saying, Lord Aldridge, they caught wind of Hal Boots and watched him most of the morning. He got up the courage around midday to have a casual word with one of Dervish's staff when they were putting out some rubbish, and after that he went straight off to a building near Whitehall."

"He found out Dervish wasn't even in the country, let alone the house, that he'd been wasting his time for nearly two days, and went off to report and see what to do," Jonathan said, and Lady Durnham gave a nod of agreement.

"My men lost him when he went into the building, so they waited for him to come out again. He was only about fifteen minutes, and he looked tense and his face was flushed when he stepped back onto the street. No doubt the person he went to see didn't like him coming into his place of work to talk. He didn't go back to Dervish's, though. He started walking the streets around it and South Audley, going down the back alleys and then round onto the front streets, keeping a sharp watch out."

"Not that sharp," Jonathan said, "if he didn't spot your men."

Lady Durnham gave him a bright smile. "My men are extremely hard to spot." She leaned back a little, and there was a glint in her eyes he suddenly found very dangerous. "After all, you didn't spot them yourself, and they certainly saw you."

"Saw me do what?" He thought back to the scene outside his kitchen door and waited with heavy dread for her to speak.

"You were looking for someone, and then you encountered one of your staff and carried some pots back for her." She spoke without innuendo, and while he scrabbled to deal with the lack of condemnation he expected, and with his guilty conscience, he saw what she was trying to say.

"Your men know this because this Hal Boots character was in the alley with us?"

He hadn't seen any of them.

He was losing his touch. He hadn't even been out of the army for all that long. Becoming a lord had scrambled his brain.

Or maybe he could lay that charge at Madame Levéel's feet.

"Hal Boots was on the other side of the rag-and-bone man's cart. Hanging around near the back door to Goldfern House, pretending to clear the lane. He went past there at least three times as he walked the neighborhood."

"Maybe he was the man who broke into Goldfern the other night?" Jonathan looked up at her, and she inclined her head, but the move was hesitant.

"Hal Boots may not be the brightest of lights, but he's street savvy. Hanging around the scene of the crime afterward is not his style."

"Unless he was under orders to keep an eye on the place."

"Could be." Lady Durnham watched him intently. "He was spooked when your cook and then you came along. He turned and walked away in the other direction, so you weren't what he was after."

Only, they were. Hal Boots had to be looking for the woman who'd delivered a note to Dervish the night before and then disappeared as if by magic in a back alley. And she'd been standing right in front of him.

A chill of fear brushed over him at the thought of what would have happened if she'd been in that alley this afternoon without Lady Durnham's watchers, without him or the rag-

and-bone man. And if Hal Boots had managed to look past the cook's apron and hat and really see her. Recognize her.

She could be someone caught up in Boots and his master's affairs, or she could have been contacting Dervish for another reason altogether. He didn't think Boots would be particularly gentle with her, either way.

He needed answers.

"You seem worried, Lord Aldridge." Lady Holliday put down her embroidery.

Jonathan tried to tamp down the pent-up energy, the impatience to be off home that gripped him, but it was impossible. He stood. "I think I need to be going."

He strained to hear any sign that Durnham was done with his visitor, and felt more than a spike of annoyance to be summoned so urgently and then made to wait. "If Lord Durnham would like, I can come around later when he's finished his other business, or he can come to me."

Lady Durnham watched him. He had the sense she knew he was keeping something back. "I'm sorry Durnham has kept you so, when it was he who sent round for you. All I can say is that shortly after he sent the note, his current visitor arrived, desperate for a word."

Jonathan shrugged. "I understand. But I have pressing business elsewhere tonight myself—"

"Aldridge, I'm terribly sorry for the wait." Durnham stepped into the room. His eyes moved from Jonathan to his wife. "You weren't going, were you?"

"I was planning to come back again later."

"I'm sorry for keeping you." Durnham walked toward them, and Jonathan could see the worry in his eyes. "My message earlier was to let you know that Mr. Greenway, Barrington's lawyer, is nowhere to be found."

"What does that mean?" Jonathan frowned.

"It means he's gone. His office is shut, and he isn't at home. His servants couldn't say where he was, because he didn't tell them." He stood behind his wife and let his hands drop down to rest on her shoulders. "One of the things the visitor who just left told me is the name and address of Greenway's head clerk."

"You're sending your man round to speak to him?"

Durnham shook his head. "I need him somewhere else. Dervish has left me juggling far more balls than usual, but aside from that, this is part of the Barrington affair, and I don't trust anyone enough. I hoped you would go." As he spoke, a rattle sounded against the windows, and everyone turned in that direction.

"Is that. . . ?" Lady Holliday cocked her head to listen.

"Hail?" Jonathan asked her. "I do believe it is."

25

The sudden click and ting of hail brought Gigi's head up, and she looked at the high windows. She thought of Iris out in it and stood, wanting to do something other than sit and wait and worry.

As she took a step toward the coat rack the kitchen door opened, framing a bedraggled Iris, then slammed shut, loud and hard.

Iris shook herself, letting tiny bits of hail fall in a shower of icy confetti. "Made it in the nick." She shivered as she walked down the steps, and shrugged out of her coat. "I'd already turned into the side lane when it started getting serious." She stood by the fire, arms around her waist.

"They were surprised to see Mavis. Up at the big house." She waited a beat, then turned her head. "But Mrs. Jones seems a decent type; Mr. Jones, too. He read the letter, and looked pretty gob-smacked, I have to say. But there was no questioning it. He took Mavis in, gave her a room. Said how they'd be needing her right enough, if the Barringtons were coming back."

The Barringtons. Plural. Pain stabbed at her, a quick, lethal strike, because her father wasn't coming back. She wound her arms around herself.

Iris rubbed her hands close to the flames. "Think they're a bit worried about it, truth be told. They're old, and they're fine for looking after an empty place. But not a house full o' life."

Gigi said nothing. What could she say to that that wouldn't betray her? That wouldn't give her agony away?

"Mavis look less upset?" she said at last, as the silence stretched out and she found some control.

"Thanks to you." Iris turned, let her back toast a little. "How'd you know about that job, then? How'd you swing it?"

Gigi shook her head. "That's a private matter. The important thing is Mavis is safe and warm and has a new job."

"True enough." Iris turned back again, her body relaxing as it heated up. She gave Gigi another little sidelong look, and there was no mistaking she was still curious. "Babs gone up?"

"Yes. Harry and Rob went out. Edgars, too."

"Who's looking after his lordship, then?" Iris asked, eyebrows raised.

"He's out as well."

"Well, I'll go up." Iris took a step toward the stairs, then pivoted back. "How could he turn on her? He liked her. He took her in."

"He's under strain. Mostly of his own making, but he'd like to blame it on me. Maybe some of it *is* my fault, but he's responsible for his own behavior." Gigi tightened her lips. "He reacted without thinking."

"How can you send someone out to starve without thinking?" Iris asked, her voice soft. "Even if he'd lost his temper, he could have come back during dinner, told her to stay."

"That would have meant he'd have to admit he was wrong. Just changing his mind would be a confession he'd made a mistake."

Iris nodded. "And God forbid His Edginess would ever be less than perfect."

Gigi had never heard her call Edgars His Edginess before. She'd seemed to disapprove of the others saying it.

"If it makes a difference, when I told him I'd got her a new job, he was shocked."

"Maybe he did plan to change his mind?"

Gigi nodded at Iris's half-hopeful look. "Perhaps." She sighed. "He's very unhappy with me."

"Don't you go leaving." Iris took a step toward her, as if to grab hold of her. "Don't let him run you out, too. It's nicer here since you came."

"I . . ." Gigi shook her head. She didn't want to lie, but Iris took her headshake for a denial, and exhaled.

"I don't know how you jigged it, but thank you for fixing Mae up. She didn't deserve what she got tonight, and you set it straight."

Gigi watched her climb the stairs, and wondered how she was going to handle things when it came time to tell the truth.

She dragged the only armchair in the room to the fire and curled up in it, waiting for Aldridge to return.

She must have dozed off, for the bang of the kitchen door slamming open startled her awake. A freezing wind blasted through the kitchen and ripped the warmth out of it like a blanket pulled off in the night.

Her heart thumping in her chest, she stood, half-disoriented, and saw Edgars walking too carefully, too bright-eyed, down the stairs. He placed each foot down as if he were walking across ice, the door open and forgotten behind him. Rain and leaves, a few pieces of newspaper, blew and swirled around him.

"The door," she said, and he looked behind him, shrugged, and kept walking down.

Shivering in the onslaught of cold air, she strode, temper tightening around her like a net, toward the stairs to close the door.

Edgars caught her arm as she moved past him, his grip strong and punishing. "I'm better than you, you miserable Frenchie. Better than you by far." He tried to shake her, but she jerked out of his hold, heart hammering, and ran up the stairs. She slammed the door and turned to face him, breathing hard.

Whether she should have shut herself in or let herself out with Edgars turned drunk and mean she didn't know. But the alternative was the storm raging outside and the shadow man.

Edgars was less of a threat than they were.

"I'll do for you. Send you packing. See if I don't." He waggled a finger at her.

"You'd be fired, and you know it, if you tried to do anything of the sort." She didn't know if this was true, but she believed Edgars thought it might be.

He blew rudely through pursed lips. "Maybe the satisfaction of seeing you gone will be 'nough."

"I doubt you'll think so when you're sober." She walked cautiously down the stairs and gave him a wide berth. "And I think you'd better hope his lordship doesn't need you when he gets back tonight."

"His lordship can kiss my arse. And you'd know about that, wouldn't you?" He gave her a leer. "Given you a nice big kiss there, has he? When you were rolling around outside like animals in heat?"

Edgars stumbled a little as he wound his way to the cellar. "I need a drink, after the walk from th' pub. Nice Bordeaux in here, had my eye on it a while." He said the words staccato, pronouncing them perfectly as he took painfully long to find the key to the door and open it.

He could get fired for drinking the wine. Gigi knew of more than one butler who had been.

She gnawed the inside of her lip as she listened to him fumbling around. She didn't want him on the streets. On her conscience. And she wouldn't be offering *him* a place at Goldfern. That was out of the question.

He stepped back into the kitchen at last, holding a bottle high in one hand. "Got it." But there was something in his face, a sort of panic, that made her think he'd come a little to his senses and was wondering what on earth he was doing.

Behind her, the door slammed open again, the sound making her jump.

Edgars started as well, and she saw the bottle drop from his hand, saw him try to grab it as it fell and smashed at his feet.

He looked up, aghast, and Gigi was grateful for the excuse to turn away from his stricken face, to look at Rob and Harry as they fought the door closed.

"Been waiting the weather out down at a coffeehouse, but we realized there weren't no letting up." Harry turned the key in the lock.

He must have noticed the silence in the room, and, with Rob, looked down at the widening pool of red wine at Edgars' feet.

"Accident?" he said.

"Your sudden arrival startled Mr. Edgars. That door crashes open loud enough to wake the dead." Gigi spoke easily, and went to the sink to get a mop and a dustpan.

"Would you and Rob find all the glass? I think Mr. Edgars needs to change and clean his shoes before the wine soaks into them."

Harry took the dustpan cheerfully enough, but she saw Rob give Edgars a hard stare.

"His lordship waiting for that?" he asked. "Want me to serve him something else?"

There was silence. Edgars had yet to say a word, and Gigi wondered if he thought himself capable, now that he was shocked into a semblance of sobriety.

He lifted a foot, wiggled it to dislodge some glass, and staggered a little. He clutched at the doorframe for balance. "His lordship's not back yet." Then he lifted horror-filled eyes to Gigi. "Is he?"

She shook her head.

Rob's face hardened as Edgars got up the nerve to make for his rooms, each step a squelch of pungent red wine and the odd crunch of glass. He couldn't walk a straight line, and the silence stretched out, painful as the sound of metal scraping on cobblestones. He scrabbled for his door handle, got it open on the third try and slammed himself inside.

"He's plowed," Harry said, with a hush in his voice.

"Top-heavy, and no doubt about it." Rob slid her a look. "Not on his lordship's booze?"

Harry, bending down to delicately pick up a large piece of glass, whipped his head up, eyes wide.

"No." She looked at the wide-open cellar door. Shook her head. "No."

"Or not yet. Had a mind to try the Bordeaux?" Rob lifted a piece of glass with the label on it, stained and wet but still legible.

Gigi shrugged.

"You could point the finger. Get him in a right fix. Or tossed out, even." Rob threw the last piece of glass into the bin, and she started to mop. "'E don't like you. So why don't you?"

She squeezed out the mop, poured the wine and water down the sink, and filled the bucket again. "I don't care for a fight with Mr. Edgars."

"Some would." Rob leaned back against the dresser while she finished up. Harry stood close to the fire, watching them both.

"I'm not some."

"No, Cook. You're not." Rob turned to the stairs up to his room, Harry trailing behind him. "I'm not sure what you are, but you're not the common run o' things, that's for sure."

She stood alone, mop still in her hand, for a long while after he and Harry had gone up.

There wasn't a sound from Edgars' rooms, and she hoped Aldridge didn't need him tonight. She mopped the trail he'd left from the cellar to his room, then closed the cellar-room door.

She wondered where his lordship was.

The dying fire popped, and then the logs collapsed in on themselves.

She shook herself. Wherever he was, it looked like she wasn't going to share her secrets with him tonight.

26

Greenway's clerk, Mr. Unwin, was twitchy. He stood in his tiny hallway, unable to keep still, reminding Jonathan of an enlisted soldier he'd known who'd been caught in a cannon blast. He'd come away without a scratch, but thereafter, on the battlefield or not, he seemed to expect another blast at any time—one that would end his life.

"I don't mean no disrespect, my lord, but Mr. Greenway told me to keep quiet about where he's gone." Unwin rubbed his hands together in an agony of indecision.

Jonathan took out the official letter Durnham had given him and handed it over.

Unwin looked at the Crown seal and his hands shook. "I don't know what to do. Mr. Greenway were really clear. . . ."

"When I came to see Mr. Greenway the other day, I wasn't able to tell him a few things—in the interests of international relations. But it is now felt that it would be more useful to speak to Mr. Greenway frankly, and see if he knows anything that could help us."

Jonathan watched as Unwin smoothed out the paper, as if it would somehow smooth out the tricky situation he was in, and read the short note Durnham had penned. He lifted his head. "Says here to give you my full cooperation, in the name of the king." He rubbed the side of his cheek. "I'd want to keep this letter. Show Mr. Greenway I 'ad no choice."

"Certainly."

At last, Unwin invited him to sit in the small parlor at the front of his neat little house. Jonathan lowered himself onto a surprisingly fashionable sofa with dark green and maroon stripes, and waited for Unwin to settle himself into a large armchair.

"Mr. Greenway closed the office, my lord. Right after you came in to see 'im. I don't know when he actually left. He'd 'ave 'ad to make arrangements, I'm sure."

"Left for where?" Jonathan wondered what instructions Barrington could have given his lawyer for such a quick response.

"To where Sir Barrington was staying, in Stockholm, my lord."

"He went to see Barrington? In Sweden?" Jonathan wished again that he could have told Greenway about Barrington's death when he'd seen him. Could have prevented this wild-goose chase.

Unwin gave a decisive nod.

"But why?"

"They 'ad a sort of system, as Mr. Greenway put it. Sir Barrington would send Mr. Greenway a note every third day. Sometimes, with the post being what it is, it would be delayed a little, or two would come at once. But we're missing three o' them already, my lord, and tomorrow, if nothing comes, it'll be four."

"What was the system for?"

Unwin looked away. "Not my place to say, my lord."

"Let's make it your place for the moment, Mr. Unwin."

Unwin winced. "My understanding—nothing Mr. Greenway told me, mind, but what I worked out for myself—is that Sir Barrington was involved in things. Dangerous things, sometimes. Scared he'd land himself in trouble somewhere, and no one would be able to get him out."

"No one?"

"Well, no one official, was my understanding. That he'd be on 'is own if he got caught with something the Crown would find embarrassing. That he'd 'ave to pretend it was all 'is own doin'. So he'd be stuck."

"And he wanted Mr. Greenway to come to wherever he was and help him?" That would be a sensible precaution, Jonathan thought, his opinion of Barrington climbing even higher. If he were caught with incriminating documentation, it would be very hard for Whitehall to swoop to the rescue without their admitting a part in it.

But Unwin was shaking his head. "No. Not him. Though, o' course, if Mr. Greenway could do something for him, he would. No, it was to get Miss Barrington safe. Mr. Greenway was to drop everything and keep Miss Barrington safe, make sure she wasn't alone somewhere with Sir Barrington in jail or worse, and with no one to turn to."

"And you say three letters were already overdue when I came yesterday?" That would make sense. It was over nine days since Barrington had died.

"Yes. Mr. Greenway was already twitchy about it, but when you came to tell him about the break-in, and someone looking through Sir Barrington's letters, well, that did it." Unwin heaved a sigh. "Like there was a fire under him, it was."

Jonathan recalled Dervish had had to move immediately to catch a boat leaving for Stockholm. If Greenway had moved a little slower, been delayed even slightly, he might have missed it. Might be cooling his heels in Dover right now, waiting for the next boat to leave.

"Thank you, Mr. Unwin. You've done the right thing, and I promise you, there'll be no trouble from Mr. Greenway over this." Jonathan stood, eager to be on his way. If he could reach Dover while Greenway was still there, he could finally do something useful in all this.

If Greenway had missed the boat, he would try to get to Sweden another way, rather than wait the week for the next ship. Pay passage on a fishing vessel, perhaps, or a private boat.

But that would take time. Time Jonathan could use to reach him, if he left without delay.

And if Greenway *had* made the boat with Dervish, he wondered if the two men would meet, get talking and realize they shared the same goals.

Doubtful.

Dervish was as forthcoming as a stone, and Greenway not much better.

He gave Unwin a quick wave as he jogged down the path to the carriage Durnham had loaned him for the journey. He looked up to the driver, huddled in his coat against the rain. "Get me to the nearest coaching inn."

G igi snuck out of the house at dawn. She didn't want to see Edgars and hadn't heard a sound from his bedroom as she'd grabbed the baskets and put on her coat.

It was a relief.

She would prefer him to be up and about, back in control, before she saw him again. Not stumbling hungover into the kitchen after a bad night.

That way led farther down the twisted, antagonistic road they'd begun on, and she wanted off.

This was not her kingdom to fight for. She needed to leave the field of play.

She didn't call Iris to go with her. With Mavis gone, Iris and Babs would have to take on Mavis's jobs. She would manage at the market on her own.

She glanced down the alley toward the back lane, but the thought of trying to retrieve the letter she'd left for Dervish in the early morning dark was suddenly too much for her. She'd tell Aldridge about it when he deigned to make an appearance, and they could retrieve it together. She was tired of taking chances.

The sun was still firmly below the horizon and the streetlamps were on, casting a dirty yellow glow over things. The rain had stopped sometime in the night, though, and the air was cool and clean, with the faint tang of mud.

As she stepped onto Chapel Street she looked left—habit by now—to Goldfern, but there was no one there.

She began walking to South Audley. A man was coming down the street toward her. He stepped into the pool of light from a streetlamp, and she stared at him before his stride took him back into the shadows.

Though she was still in the darkness between lampposts, she knew he had been watching her, too.

He was well dressed. Not a nobleman, she would guess, but someone who worked for one. A lawyer or a banker.

There was something about him—not his looks; nothing about him was familiar—but something in the way he moved, the way he looked at her, that set the hairs on the back of her neck upright, and she gripped the baskets tighter, wishing they could be used as weapons.

She also wished it wasn't five o'clock in the morning, and that she and this stranger weren't the only people on the street.

There was nothing for it, though, but to keep walking toward him. The alternative was to run back home, and she refused to do that.

Gigi increased her pace, her boots thumping a quick beat on the cobbles in time with her racing heart.

She wanted to look away from him, to avert her head, but

that tasted too much like fear to her, revealed too much of her nerves. She deliberately looked toward him as they stepped closer to the next streetlamp, approaching from opposite sides.

He made no pretense about watching her, his lips set in a strange twist, his gaze fixed on her face.

She skirted the edges of the light, pretending to give him space, as a lower-level servant would a gentleman. He did the same, careful to keep his face in shadow, and her fear propelled her higher up the sheer cliff face of terror.

She forced herself to give a polite nod as they passed, baskets held close to her body, but he made no similar response. She sensed his head turn as she moved beyond him, keeping her in sight as she faded completely into the gloom.

She refused to turn her head, looking straight and lengthening her stride. She strained to hear his footsteps continue on, and relaxed her shoulders a little when they did. Only when she reached the corner of Chapel and South Audley did she give herself permission to look back.

She didn't see him where she expected him to be, and her gaze skittered, panicked, up and down the street.

She found him standing only a little farther down from where they'd passed each other, staring at her with his head cocked to one side, as if deliberating with himself.

For a second they both stood completely still. And then he took a step toward her. A deliberate, purposeful step.

Gigi turned in the direction of the market and ran.

27

The coach inn was in chaos. Durnham's coach was forced to stop at least a mile down the road from the big building, and Jonathan leaped out to see if he could find out what was going on from someone in the line of carts, wagons and coaches.

Most didn't know either, but an enterprising stable lad eventually wandered down with news about two coaches caught in gridlock, with panicking horses and furious drivers, not to mention complaining passengers.

Jonathan looked up at Durnham's driver. "Any point finding a different inn?"

The man shook his head. "Next one's a fair distance, but there's no turning round in this lane anyway. We have to go forward."

Jonathan clenched his fists. He wanted to be away, to do what needed doing, so he could get back as fast as possible to Madame Levéel.

He had sensed the capitulation in her nod this afternoon. Yesterday afternoon, he corrected himself. It was now way past midnight. She might still be waiting up for him, he realized. He hoped she was still inclined to take him into her confidence when he did see her.

Two hours of interminable waiting finally deposited him at the inn, and he was able to book passage on a coach to Dover. He wrote a brief note to Edgars, hesitating as he sealed it. He took out another piece of the inn's rough parchment and wrote an equally short note for his cook, begging patience.

He handed both letters to Durnham's driver to deliver on his way home, along with a detailed note to Durnham himself, and felt the weight of his exhaustion tugging at him as he watched the carriage disappear into the night.

The message would be delivered long after dawn, even if Durnham's driver made good time.

The call to Dover sounded behind him, and Jonathan turned and pulled himself into the large, squeaking coach. The chase for Greenway had begun.

The shadow man had found her at last. The thought jolted through Gigi with every slap of her boots on the cobbles as she raced for the market. There would be enough eyes and ears there to make it impossible for her follower to do anything to her.

It could be another watcher he had sent out for her, but she didn't think so.

This was him.

She looked over her shoulder again and saw he was gaining, although he wasn't running at full tilt like she was.

As if it were beneath him. As if her capture was inevitable.

That, more than anything, told her she was looking not at an underling, but at the man himself.

Anger at his arrogance added an edge to her fear.

Or perhaps he'd seen which house she'd stepped out of. Knew even if he failed to run her to ground here, he could always find her later.

Her feet stumbled at that thought, but she steadied herself. He *couldn't* have seen her come out the side lane. He'd only turned onto Chapel once she was already walking down the street.

Though even if he hadn't seen where she'd come out, he would know that if he watched Chapel Street long enough, he'd find her eventually.

He couldn't even be certain who she was. She'd worn her cook's apron and cap deliberately, and he hadn't seen her in anything close to a full light.

Something about her—her walk or looks—must have struck him as familiar, and he was taking his time stalking her, curious rather than hot on the trail.

She had no doubt that would change when he finally saw her clearly. If he'd been telling the truth to her father, he'd been introduced to her, or at the very least had watched her at embassy functions.

She, on the other hand, had had too many new acquaintances in Stockholm to juggle in her head, and she had no hope of remembering him.

The lights and sound of the market hit her as she turned the last corner to the square, panting with exertion. The wooden barrows and tables were jauntily lit by lanterns and the smell of baking bread filled the air.

She forced herself down to a steady walk and made her way straight into the thick of the crowd, in case he asked around about a woman running.

Once safe in the arms of the market-goers, shielded and protected, she relaxed a little. She edged to a stall selling fish, tried to angle herself so she could see if he came into the market, but there were too many people.

"Fresh fish! Fresh fish!" The shout near her ear made Gigi cry out and drop one of her baskets, and it broke with a loud snap under the boots of a large laborer walking past, hefting a crate of fruit.

He gave her a filthy look as he kicked the basket back toward her and disappeared into the crowd.

Gigi picked up the broken wicker with shaking hands, and then turned indignantly to the fishmonger who'd startled her. He avoided her eye, busying himself with stacking the boxes of fish before him.

"We make home deliveries," he told her at last.

She opened her mouth to say she wouldn't need a home delivery if he hadn't caused her to drop her basket, but then snapped it shut. She'd been wondering how to get home.

And it hadn't escaped her that she had to do the shopping,

shadow man or no shadow man. Her relationship with Edgars was too unstable for her to risk coming back empty-handed. He might take it as the last straw of disrespect and fire her, the consequences with Lord Aldridge be damned.

If she had her shopping delivered, she could sneak into the back alley at the top of South Audley without her purchases slowing her down, and get to Aldridge House without using the main roads.

"I should think you *would* deliver," she told the stallholder, handing him her broken basket to throw into his rubbish bin. "And I expect your best price." She chose her fish and gave the address, then began to move from stall to stall, keeping watch, cautious as a mouse.

She saw her man once, standing with his back to her, watching the lane they'd both used to come to the market.

She would have to choose another way out, but that wouldn't be difficult. And he couldn't watch them all.

With every moment that passed, the buzz of panic in her ears grew louder. It seemed harder to choose produce, as if the quality and size of the chicken would decide her fate, or the gleam and color of the apples was the difference between life and death.

Snow White, she thought, as she pointed irrationally away from the dark red apples on one side of the cart and chose the rosy pink and green ones instead.

Only she wouldn't be sleeping until a kiss woke her, unless Lord Aldridge's kiss could bring back the dead.

And now she was putting Aldridge into the role of handsome prince. She hunched her shoulders in disgust.

No one could save her from this other than herself.

The market was getting emptier, as cooks and servants headed home to make breakfast, starting the day before their lords and ladies arose from bed. She'd have to leave before she lost the shielding crowds.

She did a careful check to see if the shadow man stood where she had last seen him, but he had gone, and she forced herself not to swing around wildly to make sure he wasn't right behind her.

Instead, she turned calmly in the direction she'd chosen and began walking toward the exit, letting her gaze sweep the crowd as if she were searching for someone.

She saw him at last from the corner of her eye, standing out from the others in the market because of his still watchfulness. He hadn't seen her, and she slipped between a footman carrying half a lamb wrapped in brown paper and a group of women chatting loudly as they made for one of the far lanes.

The sun had yet to rise, and she used the darkness to her advantage, keeping the footman between her and the shadow man.

When they reached the lane she increased her speed, dodging around the women and running to the corner, then turning right, in the opposite direction of the one she needed to get back to Aldridge House.

She kept up her pace, working her way back to Chapel by a circuitous route as the sun rose at last, checking behind her at every corner.

She really was a little mouse, just as she'd told Aldridge.

But she was alive, and the letter was still safe in the pocket of her petticoat. Now that she'd made her decision to trust Aldridge, she couldn't wait to spill her secrets to him and be rid of it. If the shadow man was going to get her, she wanted the letter in the right hands, at least.

It was still early, but Edgars would expect her back by now. Long before now, truth be told. And he would have a mean temper and a pounding head on top of it, if she were any judge.

She stopped at the corner of Curzon Street and South Audley, looking down the street. All she'd need was to slip onto South Street, which ran parallel to Chapel, and then access the back lane from there. If the shadow man were watching anywhere on Chapel Street, he wouldn't see her return to Aldridge House.

There was a sound of female voices behind her, and she turned to look.

Two women, one plump and trying to juggle three baskets, the other sturdy enough but not as rounded as her companion, were stepping out of a small bakery, the only shop open on the narrow street at this hour. Gigi was surprised when the sturdy one raised her hand in greeting.

She waited for them, trying to think where she could know them from.

"Thanks for waiting, love; thought it were you standing there. It's time we 'ad a chat." The sturdy woman set down her baskets and studied her. "'Specially when I heard it said at market t'other day you be the new French cook at Aldridge

House. Could 'ardly believe me ears. I'm Mrs. Thakery. I'm to the back o' you and down a little way, facing South Street. Cook for Lord Matherton." She nodded to her companion. "This be Mrs. Lambert. Works three doors down from you on Chapel, at the Ingleton place."

"I'm very pleased to meet you. I am Madame Levéel."

"Madame Levéel, is it?" Mrs. Thakery gave her a hard, disbelieving look, and Gigi stared back in surprise.

This woman couldn't recognize her; she'd never seen her before.

To cover the moment of sharp silence Gigi turned to Mrs. Lambert. "May I help you carry your extra basket?" The older woman lifted her head with a jerk, then smiled.

"Much obliged."

Gigi took it from her and waited for Mrs. Thakery to pick up hers. She'd stopped staring and was rubbing her hands to get the circulation going in her fingers before she picked up her heavy load again.

"Tell me, Madame Levéel, you take after your mother, do you, in your looks?" Mrs. Thakery spoke conversationally as they walked toward South Street from the bottom end of South Audley. The sun was high enough now to illuminate Mrs. Thakery's face clearly. Her lips were set in a twist, and her brows were arched.

"I do." Gigi hefted Mrs. Lambert's basket.

"Knew a Frenchwoman who looked very like your mother would have looked, then. Years ago, this was. I worked for her in her kitchen as a maid. Not like most ladies, she was. Came down into the kitchen all the time. Knew her way around an oven, did my lady." Mrs. Thakery didn't so much as glance her way. "Did me a big favor. Got me the job as cook for Lord Matherton, truth be told."

"Is that so?" Gigi's throat tightened.

"Heard you got a job for someone, yourself. That little wisp of a girl Iris was trying to feed up. Over at Goldfern House she is, now." Mrs. Thakery set her baskets down, and they stopped and waited for her to rub her hands again.

"Where did you hear that?" The tension in her wound a little tighter. She had hoped there would be no outside talk about Mavis's move down the road, but Mrs. Jones, the housekeeper at Goldfern, could be a gossip. It seemed that she was.

"News travels fast down the back lane," Mrs. Thakery answered, and something in her eyes gave Gigi a little comfort. This woman did not mean her harm. "Speaking of back lanes, did Lord Aldridge find you yesterday?"

"Lord Aldridge?" She couldn't think what the woman was talking about, until she recalled the way Aldridge had appeared out of nowhere at the rag-and-bone man's cart. She'd been so startled, felt so guilty for her subterfuge, it hadn't occurred to her to ask him what he was doing back there. "He was looking for me?"

"Oh, aye." Mrs. Lambert spoke for the first time, chewing on the words like a particularly tasty morsel. "Came round the corner while me and Mrs. Thakery were having a little chat in the back lane. Were in a mighty hurry to find you, he was."

Gigi breathed in sharply. Why had Aldridge been looking for her?

She supposed it no longer mattered. She would have to face him after breakfast this morning and tell him the truth. "He found me."

"Well." Mrs. Thakery slid her a speculative glance. "That's all right then." She looked up ahead, and Gigi saw a man stumbling down the road toward them. "Would you say Lord Aldridge is a man who keeps his promises?"

Gigi stopped short. "Why do you ask?" She tried to keep her tone even as she squinted in the growing light to see if it was the shadow man or not.

"Made a promise to me, yesterday. To sort out a little problem he heard Mrs. Lambert and me discussing. Just wondered if his word is good."

"I hope so," Gigi said. "I'm counting on him myself."

Mrs. Thakery's gaze never left the man coming toward them.

"I hope so, too." Mrs. Lambert's voice was low and nervous. She was staring ahead as well.

Mrs. Thakery bumped her basket to Mrs. Lambert's in a gesture that spoke of solidarity.

"Would the man coming down the street be the problem Lord Aldridge promised help with?" They'd moved forward enough that the sun wasn't completely in her eyes anymore, and she had a good view of him. He wasn't the man who'd followed her. He was younger, wearing evening dress and barely able to walk in a straight line.

"Yes. Sir Ingleton's son." Mrs. Thakery kept walking forward, but there was a heaviness to her tread that hadn't been there before.

"Well, I doubt Lord Aldridge has had a chance to do anything yet," Gigi said. "Let's turn down South Street, shall we, walk you to your door? Mrs. Lambert and I can take a side alley to the back lane. Avoid any unpleasantness."

It was what she'd planned to do anyway, but having Ingleton stumbling about, sure to cross paths with herself and Mrs. Lambert if they carried on past South Street, was a convenient excuse.

Mrs. Lambert relaxed. "Quite right, m'dear. Much more sensible."

They turned down South, and for the first time since she'd seen the shadow man that morning, Gigi felt safe.

28

There was a strange carriage waiting out on Chapel Street. Gigi caught sight of it as she came down the side alley to the kitchen door. She stopped and stared at it for a moment, dread sinking through her. She'd be in trouble if Aldridge needed to go out early, and her not in the kitchen to make his breakfast.

Ah well, it was only seven in the morning, and if he wanted such an early start, he should have told her sooner.

She pulled open the door and had taken three steps down into the kitchen before she registered the crowd of people below her. She stopped and stared at them.

"What's wrong? Has something happened?" She caught the gaze of a slim, foxy-looking man with ginger whiskers and a brown jacket, and then noticed Iris, standing white-lipped and wide-eyed beside the fire, away from the rest of them.

"Who are you?" The man with the brown coat had a

deeper voice than she would have guessed, from the look of him. He was of medium height, and while his coat and trousers weren't expensive, they fit him well and were neatly pressed. His brown eyes didn't leave her face.

"That's Madame Levéel." Edgars shouldered past a group that Gigi had finally sorted into Rob, Harry, Babs and two strangers. "That's the thief."

She looked at Edgars with astonishment. "What on earth are you talking about?"

"She's no thief and you know it." Iris took a farther step away from the crowd, as if they were tainted. "*You're* the one with something to answer for, going through her things."

Gigi gaped. "You went through my private belongings?" She caught Edgars' eye and he glared back at her before dropping his gaze.

"My name is Gilbert. I'm a senior constable from the Queen Square Public Office." The man in the brown coat stepped forward. "Mr. Edgars called my colleagues and me in early this morning. Claims the jewelry in your trunks is stolen." He gestured with his hand, and for the first time she saw her mother's jewelry laid out on the kitchen table, the black velvet pouches she used to store it piled to one side.

"That jewelry is my mother's, which I inherited on her death." She spoke clearly, slowly, though her heart was racing. She looked at Edgars again, trying to make sense of it. "Why would you do this?"

When Edgars wouldn't answer or look at her, she turned to Rob. "Where is Lord Aldridge? What does he have to say about what Edgars has done?" Her gaze went back to the pile of pearls, diamonds and gold on the table, and she had to force herself to remain in place, even though everything in her wanted to scoop it up and hold it close to her. It was a tangible link to her mother, and how *dare* Edgars touch it? Use it against her.

Gilbert looked sharply at Edgars. "A good question. Where is Lord Aldridge?"

"Off on important business for the Crown." Edgars' words were short.

"He sent a note. It was delivered just after you left for market, Cook." Babs spoke up for the first time. "I were clearing the fireplace in the library when the note came, and I heard a little of what was said. There were a note for you, too."

Everyone looked at Edgars. He shuffled back, as if the weight of their gazes were pushing at him. "Where Lord Aldridge is has nothing to do with whether Madame Levéel is a thief or not."

"From whom do you imagine I stole the jewelry, Mr. Edgars?" Gigi asked coldly. "You know it isn't from Lord Aldridge."

"Why would he know that?" Gilbert asked, standing so he could watch her and Edgars easily.

"Because he would know what jewelry Lord Aldridge has in this house, if any, and if he's been pawing through my mother's jewelry, he knows it isn't the same." She could barely speak around the ice-cold stone that seemed to be stuck in her throat. When she'd taken on the role of servant, she hadn't realized her privacy would be so inconsequential, that a single finger pointed in her direction would be taken so seriously.

"Well?" Gilbert asked Edgars.

He looked away. "No." He cleared his throat. "The jewelry isn't from this house."

One of Gilbert's men shifted a little nervously. "Eh? That's why we're 'ere. Thought the theft was of his lordship's property."

"Yes." Gilbert dragged the word out. "I'm afraid you haven't been very clear, Mr. Edgars."

"It's 'cause of last night, isn't it?" There was a rough edge to Rob's voice. "She weren't going to say nothing, Edgars. She wouldn't even give you up to me 'n' 'Arry, and we were right there! She would never have dropped you in it with his lordship."

"Last night?" Gigi frowned—and then she understood. She fumbled behind her on the steps and sat down, because her legs wouldn't hold her up any longer. "You . . ." She couldn't finish her sentence. Edgars had thought she would use what had happened last night—the things he'd said and done—to have him dismissed. He must have greeted the news this morning that Aldridge was away as a stay of execution. And he'd seized on the opportunity to get rid of her before she could get rid of him. Before he became powerless to stop her.

When Aldridge came back, Edgars could have made up whatever story he liked. He was panicked enough, terrified enough, to have lied about it later. If he'd had to say anything at all.

Aldridge might simply have accepted that she'd moved on.

The thought of that hurt, but she had to face it. Despite the intensity there seemed to be between them, she was only his cook, after all.

She put her head in her hands. "I'm not a thief. The jewelry is mine. Mr. Edgars is mistaken."

She really *was* the Goose Girl of London Town. The princess betrayed by her maid. Or the youngest son in "Puss in Boots," turned out by his brothers. She'd been in fear of the danger outside, but had forgotten there was danger within as well.

She hadn't liked Edgars, but she had never wished him harm.

He wished her in a jail cell. In a prison, or on the hulks.

She couldn't find a better description of harm than that.

She felt a touch on her shoulder and lifted her head to see that Iris had come to stand beside her. She curled her fingers around Iris's hand for a brief moment.

Edgars made a noise, almost a cry, of despair. She raised her eyes to his but he was looking at Iris. Then he turned to her, and she saw hot, furious hate. "Take her away."

Gilbert's men didn't move.

"Take her away!" His shout into the tense silence made everyone jump.

Gilbert went stony-faced, and Gigi saw a man with power about to lose his temper. Edgars was trying to manipulate him, challenge him, and neither suited Gilbert's image of himself.

Fear dribbled icy rivulets down her neck. This would not go well for anyone.

"I'll admit that the quality and amount of jewelry Madame Levéel has in her possession is more than I'd expect a cook to own, but the items are not reported stolen, as far as I'm aware." Gilbert tugged at his waistcoat. "I'll take her in, because something don't smell right, but I'll not put her before the magistrate until Lord Aldridge comes to speak to me. I'm not sending her to prison. And I'll hand her back to him if he can vouch for her."

Edgars breathed in sharply through his nose.

Not what he wanted to hear. The explanations, the lies he would have to tell to talk himself out of this, were growing.

Gigi clenched her jaw to stop herself from arguing with Gilbert. Or telling him who she really was.

Nothing she said now would be taken seriously. She'd taken on the role of invisible cook, and now she was finding out just how invisible her disguise had rendered her.

She was only grateful that Edgars apparently hadn't found the hidden compartment in her clothes trunk that contained the money with which she and her father had been traveling. He would never have believed she'd have taken a job as cook if he'd seen the amount.

Gilbert began to place the jewelry back in the velvet pouches, and she bit her lip to stop herself from urging him to be careful.

"May I have the letter Lord Aldridge sent me?" She held out her hand to Edgars.

"Babs was mistaken. There was no letter for you." He gave a crooked smile. "And you could be in the station a while, I fear. Lord Aldridge had to go down to Dover."

"That'll be days." Gilbert's man shot a quick look at his boss. Reluctance was in every rough line of him.

"Then it'll be days," Gilbert snapped, straightening up with the jewelry bags.

"Where are you taking her?" Iris asked, and her hand clamped down hard on Gigi's shoulder.

"Queen Square." Gilbert sounded like a man at the end of his patience. "The station cell. She'll be safe enough there."

"I'll send Lord Aldridge round soon as he comes in." Iris stared at Edgars as she spoke.

"See that you do." Gilbert stared at Edgars as well. He motioned to his men, and they stepped toward her with grim purpose.

Gigi stared at them dumbly.

"You need to go with them." Rob came to her rescue, stepping forward and holding his hand out to her.

She took it and he pulled her to her feet.

"I don't understand what you mean to do," she said to them.

One looked away, but the constable who'd spoken earlier gave her a look that said he didn't think he should be there at all. "Long as you don't plan to run or nothing, we don't mean to do anything."

She gave a nod and stepped aside, and he went ahead of her, then gestured for her to follow him, and the other fell in behind.

They'd opened the carriage door, and she was about to step in when a gleaming carriage with a flamboyant crest pulled up.

Georges Bisset leaped out. "*Ma chère!* Where are you going? I could not come yesterday after that horrible man spoke with me. The duke had a very important dinner party last night. But I come as soon as I can this morning. *Viens.* I take you back safe with me." He walked toward her, his arms open wide, and Gigi couldn't help the sob that escaped her.

She had been doing all right until that moment, but the sight of Georges, of the possibility of an end to the nightmare, broke her.

Her step forward was brought up short as Gilbert grabbed the collar of her coat and yanked her back, and then shoved her behind him. "No, you don't." He sent a narrow-eyed glare at Georges. "Who are you?"

"Georges Bisset." Georges flicked his eyes from Gilbert to his men, and then back to Gigi. A red flush began to creep up his neck and stain his cheeks. "He did it. *Mon Dieu!* I told him to go ahead with his silly Alien Office, and he did. They are taking you away? Gigi, you need to speak up, *ma petite.* This is not worth it, whatever favor you do for these government people. Tell them who you are!"

"Alien Office?" Gigi blinked. "Who threatened to call the Alien Office?"

"That *imbécile.*" Georges gestured wildly behind him at Aldridge House. "That *idiot,* Aldridge."

"Let me get this straight." Gilbert was staring at her a lot more coolly than he had done before. "Lord Aldridge had cause to threaten Madame Levéel with the Alien Office?"

"No. That is why I told him to go ahead. There was no cause. I knew he would look like the *idiot* that he is if he did it." He paused. "If you are not from the Alien Office, who are you?" He stepped closer to Gilbert, and for the first time, Gilbert seemed to realize how big Georges was. How angry.

"Gilbert, senior constable, Queen Square Public Office."

"What? You are a *gendarme?*" Georges spat the word like it was an abomination on his tongue. "What business do you have with my Gigi?"

"She's been accused of theft." Gilbert lifted the pouches and then smirked as Georges stared at him dumbly. "Smith, Peterson, get her in." He spared only a moment to hand the small bags to Smith. Then he turned back to Georges.

"You do well to keep your eyes on me and your hands free. Because no one takes my *trésor* off to prison. She's never stolen so much as a bonbon in her life." Georges came in even closer, and Gigi could see Gilbert's hands forming into fists.

"Georges." She spoke sharply, cutting through the growing threat of violence like one of Georges's knives. "You can help me better if you aren't arrested yourself. Ask your duke for help. Please. I'm sure he knows how to sort this out quickly. Aldridge had nothing to do with this. He isn't even here. They say they'll release me to him as soon as he comes back."

Georges drew in a shuddering breath, teetering on the balls of his feet, his massive hands clenched in front of him. "What is it they say you stole?"

"My mother's jewelry." Her voice broke as she said it.

"They say . . ." He was speechless, and there must have been something in his face, because Gilbert scrambled into the carriage.

He hit the roof of the cab with his fist so hard to signal the driver, he must have damaged his knuckles.

Gigi caught a single glimpse of Georges, eyes closed, feet apart, massive arms held away from his solid body, and the carriage jerked and then sped down the street. There was a roar of fury, and then Gigi heard the thunder of Georges's footsteps as he gave chase.

"Duke?" Gilbert asked her, and there was a slight wobble to his voice. He cleared his throat.

"His employer." Gigi leaned out the window, craning her neck to see Georges. "The Duke of Wittaker."

The carriage made a sharp turn at South Audley, and, too late, Gigi noticed the man standing on the corner.

Their eyes met with a clash that stole her breath.

The shadow man.

Instinct and blind fear had her pulling her head in, grabbing the fabric of her dress with both fists.

It was hard to breathe, but she forced herself to keep it even. To lean back against the seat of the coach.

"What is it?" Gilbert's sharp eyes missed nothing.

She hesitated a moment. The truth wouldn't help her. Gilbert would only make note of what she had to say; she didn't expect any real action. But could the truth really hurt? "There is a man who wants to kill me. I just saw him standing on the corner of the road."

Gilbert half stood and leaned out of the window, then pulled himself back in. "The one in the black coat?"

She nodded.

"Why does he want to kill you?"

"I saw him do something. He wants to make certain I don't give him away." She would not mention the letter, or Gilbert might take it into his head to search her for it.

"What did you see him do?" Gilbert spoke seriously, but she wasn't sure if he was humoring her or not.

"I saw him kill my father."

Gilbert went still, and she heard Peterson suck in a breath. "I haven't heard of any Frenchmen being murdered in the area." Skepticism leached into his tone.

"My father is English. And the murder happened in Stockholm, not London, nearly two weeks ago. That man has chased me across the North Sea."

There was silence in the coach. The cries and calls from the street and the rumble of the wheels on the cobbles seemed a hundred miles away.

Peterson, the one who'd so far shown her kindness, was frowning at Gilbert. "You sure about taking her in, sir?"

"Yes." He flicked at something on the knee of his trousers.

"I haven't done anything wrong." Gigi kept her composure.

"Seems some people believe otherwise, miss." Gilbert watched her with his brown, foxy eyes. "And just by looking at you, I can tell there's something off. You ain't what you seem. And this story about a man wanting to kill you . . ."

He shrugged. "I don't know how to take you, and that's the truth."

Gigi closed her eyes and leaned her head back. It seemed no one knew how to take her. She'd thought posing as a cook would be the easiest thing in the world for her, but she'd been wrong.

She only hoped the shadow man didn't find out who was with her in the coach and where she was going.

Because if he was someone in the Foreign Office, he'd be able to get to her if he was desperate enough to risk exposing his real name and occupation. She'd be neatly trapped and at his mercy, sitting in a cell.

29

He must stop letting his father and brother's frugal habits influence him, and get a carriage of his own. Jonathan stepped down from the coach and the ground continued to vibrate under him for a moment.

The roads were terrible, pitted and scarred by the rains. While having his own carriage wouldn't change that, it would mean his bones would be shaken and rattled about in private comfort, rather than public discomfort.

It was already midmorning, and there would be at least an hour's wait while the coachman changed the horses and grabbed a bite. Time enough for Jonathan to eat a meal as well, and inquire whether Greenway had come this way.

He followed his fellow passengers into the dark-paneled main room of the inn, set out with tables around a large fireplace. The fire was well stoked and most of the travelers began to congregate near its warmth after the drafty, cold journey.

The innkeeper stepped forward, and Jonathan intercepted him before he could get caught up with his guests.

"If you don't mind sparing a moment?"

The innkeeper gave him a quick look that took in his clothes, his boots and the sovereign in his hand. "Certainly, my lord. How can I help?" He palmed the coin smoothly.

"I'm trying to catch up with someone. I have an urgent message for them, and I know they left for Dover either yesterday or the day before." He watched the innkeeper's polite face and sighed inwardly. How could he expect the man to remember someone who might have come through two days ago? He plowed on. "His name's Greenway, and he's a lawyer. Dark red hair. Thin. Tall."

"Ah. Yes, I remember the gentleman. Wrote a letter for me to send for him. Recall it, because the letter was addressed to the place he was going. He said in case the post traveled faster than he did, he would give the people he was going to some advance warning."

"Which day was this?" The hope that it was yesterday, that Greenway had missed the boat and was waiting in Dover, gripped him hard.

"Day before yesterday. Two smart types came through that day. Eyeing each other with much suspicion, I think. One a nob . . . er, a lord, like you, my lord, the other this lawyer fellow you're asking about."

Dervish. Greenway had managed to catch up with Dervish. Not that either would know who the other was. Although when they got to Stockholm, that would change quickly enough, when they both found themselves searching for Giselle Barrington.

"I hope that was helpful?" The innkeeper tipped his head.

"Thank you. It was." He could go home, Jonathan thought. There was almost no chance Greenway hadn't caught that boat, since he was traveling through at the same time as Dervish. A trip to Dover would be a waste of time.

Something in him relaxed a little at the thought. He didn't know why he was so uneasy at leaving Madame Levéel before they'd spoken about her secret, but he was. He was relieved to turn back.

He walked out into the yard to find a coach home.

There were two cells in Queen Square. One for men, and one for women.

The women's cell was at the far end of the passage, and each step she took toward it shoved another double blade into Gigi's gut. Fear and rage. Rage and fear. She couldn't have said which was stronger.

She didn't look at the male prisoners as she passed their cell, and while she knew by their tone and gestures the things they called to her were probably very bad, she didn't hear any of it.

She had come quietly, with the logical thought that when Aldridge returned, she would get out. A scene and a struggle would simply prove Edgars' point.

But now that she was here, walking step by terrible step toward the wall of narrow steel bars, she didn't feel logical anymore.

She wanted to shout, to scream. To fight out of Peterson's

grip on her arm and run for the door. If the shadow man came for her here, there would truly be no escape.

"Easy." Peterson spoke very quietly. "I know it's a bad sight, but you've played it right. And I'll keep an eye. I promise. No harm'll come to you."

She drew in a shuddering breath. For one step, then two, it could have gone either way; then she paused and gave a tiny nod of her head.

"Good girl." Peterson didn't look at her, and his voice was still pitched for her ears only. "I know a spiteful git when I see one. You'll be having the last laugh, come the end of this."

He was trying to calm her, but she wanted to give a harsh, bitter laugh, because he couldn't guarantee how this would end. But if she did anything, said anything, it would end in her crying—and she would not allow that.

They stopped by the door, and Gigi saw there were three women inside. One had on a deep purple dress with a low neckline, made even more revealing because the shoulder had been ripped from its seams and the slick fabric gaped open, revealing most of the woman's voluptuous breast.

Her light brown hair had fallen from its dressing and there was a smudge on her cheek.

The two other women were in far drabber clothing, muted browns and grays, but worn with an eye to revealing as much flesh as possible. One had taken a pair of scissors to bodice and hem, without bothering to neaten the raw edge, and long threads floated like a haphazard fringe.

"Well, hello there, love." The one in purple lifted an eyebrow and jutted out a hip as Peterson unlocked the door. "Come to see us again? And you brought us a friend."

The other two laughed, a little too long and loud.

"Come now, let us out, there's a love. We could make it worth your while." Purple Dress clicked her tongue at him in a way so unconscious, Gigi was sure it was the way she hailed her customers on the street.

She hadn't wanted the bars around her, but now she was also nervous about whom she would be locked up with.

She hesitated before she stepped inside.

"We don't bite. Well, we do, but only people we don't like, ain't that right, girls?" Purple Dress chuckled, and Gigi gripped a bar on the door, resisting the pressure of Peterson's hand between her shoulder blades, propelling her in.

Eventually, she let go and stumbled forward a step.

The shove Peterson had given her felt like a betrayal, and she kept her face averted from him, taking in the reality of her cell.

She heard the solid thunk of the lock engaging, and then Peterson walked away. When he passed the men's cell the shouts and hoots rose like a wave on the beach, and she could see a few arms shoved through the bars as if to grab him. He ignored them and they subsided as he stepped back into the station's front section, closing the door behind him.

"Soooo." One of the women in brown began to circle her. "What we got here? A lady? What did ya do, then? Show some ankle or summat?" She sniggered.

Gigi ignored her, walked to the long bench bolted to the back wall, and sat down. She wondered how they'd been able to peg her as a lady just by looking at her. She was still in her cook's apron and hat.

"I know all the shakes round these parts, and she ain't one. 'Less you're horning in on our patch while we're in 'ere?" The second woman in brown stepped closer, and there was a feral, aggressive quality to her.

"Mebbe she's what the fancy call a soiled dove," the first woman in brown said. "You fall a little, hmm? Get caught with the backside of your skirts a bit green?"

It was so like the accusation Edgars had made, Gigi raised her head and stared the woman down. "How do you know I'm a lady?"

"Spend me time looking for a likely mark, don't I? Bit o' pocket picking saves me 'aving to troll the streets looking for a gentleman friend." The woman snorted. "You got lady written all over you."

"Now then. Be friendly." Purple Dress sat down next to her, and Gigi could smell pungent, cheap lavender water mixed with the musky scent of sweat. She saw with a jolt that the smudge on the woman's cheek wasn't dirt, but a bruise. "We might as well get on. We'll be seeing a lot of each other in the near future." She gave a cheeky wink.

Gigi looked at her, unsure whether she was being serious or not. But the bruise changed things, somehow. Made her far less frightening. And despite the fact that someone had obviously attacked her, ripped her clothes and hit her across the face, she wasn't in the least cowed or broken.

"You're right. I'm sorry. My name is Gigi." She somehow

found a genuine smile, and after a beat, Purple Dress smiled back.

"Gigi." Both Purple Dress's eyebrows rose this time as she repeated the name, mimicking her French accent.

An accent Gigi realized had become an unconscious habit. One she'd have to force herself to break later.

"Now, that's a name I wouldn't mind using from time to time. Me real name's Gertrude, although me clients mostly know me as Delilah." She gave a throaty chuckle. "But Gigi, now there's a name that has a little something extra."

Gigi stared at her and then laughed. "You are most welcome to use it whenever you like."

"Ooh la la." Gertrude grinned. "You can teach me, Violet and Bess here a few Frenchie sayings, mebbe. Some o' the soldiers wot are looking for companionship, well, a bit of Fransays might just bring back good memories of those foreign ports while they were off fighting Old Boney."

"All well and good, Gertie, but what's she in for?" Violet spoke up, a little petulantly. "I still say she don't look like a shake."

"Wot you up to then? Bit of a con?" Bess rubbed her shoulder as she spoke, and Gigi noticed a bruise where her neck met her collarbone. Dark, ugly purple marks in the shape of a man's fingers.

Gigi wondered why these women were in jail, when they were the ones who had clearly been abused.

Bess noticed her looking and dropped her hand as if the bruise had burned her. "Never seen the mark o' a man's hands on a woman before?"

She shook her head.

Bess sneered. "Lucky you, then."

She couldn't reply to that. Her father was dead and she didn't feel lucky at all, yet in her life as Giselle Barrington, she was far, far luckier than Babs, Mavis and Iris. And a hundred times luckier than these three women in the cell.

"Who did that to you?"

"Mr. Gilbert." Bess stared back when she lifted her gaze in disbelief. "Just because he treated you better, what with your fancy clothes, don't mean he can't get nasty. I'd like to know why he did nick ya. What'd you do?"

She didn't want to talk about it. It was too complicated. Too risky.

"Come on, won't you trust us wit' the truth, darlin'?" Gertrude fiddled with her ripped sleeve. "We can't work out where you fit."

Gigi rested her elbows on her knees and lowered her head into her hands. "You aren't the first person to say that to me today." She rubbed her face. "It's what got me into trouble in the first place."

"They locked you up for not fitting in?" Violet scoffed.

Gigi shrugged. "I pretended to be a cook for a while."

"Slumming it, eh? Fine lady like you, must 'ave been right hard." Gertrude cocked her head to one side.

Gigi shook her head. It hadn't felt hard at all. Perhaps if she hadn't needed to search for Dervish and hide from the shadow man, behavior that had brought her to Edgars' attention, she'd have gotten away with it.

"Wot? Why you shaking your 'ead?"

Gigi leaned back against the cold exposed brick of the wall and crossed her arms over her stomach. "I didn't find it hard. I enjoyed it. Except for the bit where it put me at the mercy of a man who . . . didn't like me."

"Found that out the hard way, did ya?" Violet slid next to Gertrude on the bench. "Got no rights in service. They c'n starve ya, beat ya, tup ya, then throw you out."

Gigi didn't ask her if that was what had happened to her; she could hear it in the bitter edge of the words.

"I didn't even think about it. I've never been under anyone's control like that before, and I couldn't conceive of it."

"Must be nice in fancyland." Violet tugged at the neckline of her bodice.

"Why'd you do it, then? Put yourself under someone's thumb?" Bess sat as well, and Gigi shifted down a bit so they could all fit on the bench.

"I needed to hide from someone." She shivered as the cold of the wall seeped into her back, and leaned away from it.

Bess gave her a nod. "You do become invisible in service."

"Not invisible enough." She snorted. "Or too invisible. I'm not sure which. That a man can point a finger, with absolutely no proof, and be taken seriously . . ." She gripped her hands together. "I'm going to do something about it when I'm out of here."

"If you want the blighter dead, I've got connections." Violet was looking at her with flat eyes. Slowly, she drew a finger across her throat.

Gigi gaped at her. "Er. Thank you. I was thinking more of hiring a lawyer for women in service who are arrested."

Gertrude grimaced.

"You don't think that will help?" Gigi asked.

"What'll a lawyer do? Help the nobs and the law, more like. Not any woman who gets fingered."

Gigi frowned. "I'll pay them to help the women."

Gertrude patted her knee. "You really are away with the fairies, ain't ya? No lawyer's ever going to help a poor woman against a nob or a magistrate, no matter what they done to her, no matter what you pay 'em."

Gigi forced her rising frustration down. "I'll make sure they do."

Violet sent her a pitying look. "Good luck with that, love."

She chose to take it seriously. "Thank you."

"So, what's your fancy moniker, when you ain't pretending to be a cook?" Bess was back to rubbing her shoulder again.

Gigi knew she shouldn't say, but somehow this felt like the end. The end of her hiding. The end of the line.

"Miss Giselle Barrington of Goldfern House on Chapel Street. Well," she hunched her shoulders. "I'll live there again after I've managed to dodge the assassin who's after me and get out of jail."

"You lead an interesting life, for a lady of quality," Gertrude said. Then she started laughing. A delighted, full-throated shout of a laugh, and after a beat, Bess and Violet joined in.

A moment later, Gigi did, too.

30

Gigi lifted her head when the shouting started up.

They'd been given a spare meal at midday of bread and cheese, and a jug of water, and as the day drew on, even the men calmed down.

She was sitting on the floor, leaning back against the wall.

Bess was lying on the bench with Gertrude at her feet, and Violet was propped against the wall opposite Gigi.

There'd been the occasional sound of voices from the front since she'd been locked in, but this was a sustained argument, and something in the cadence made her think of Georges.

The voices got louder still, and, feeling eyes on her, she shifted her gaze from the door at the end of the passage to find Violet watching her.

"Friend of yours?"

"It might be."

There was a thump on the door, and Gigi wondered with a

sinking sense of doom if a butcher's knife was now embedded in the thick wood.

Georges would not have come unarmed. And he was very good at throwing knives.

He'd once pinned his sous-chef's hat to the door—after the man had burned his roux for the third day in a row—while the sous-chef was wearing it. She still remembered the silence that had descended on the kitchen at the sight of Georges's thick chopping knife holding up Rene's white hat dead center as Rene crumpled, shaking, to his knees.

The door rattled as if someone was trying to pull it from its hinges. Bess slowly sat up, Gertrude straightened, and all four of them stared down the narrow passageway to watch the entrance.

The door slammed open so suddenly, Gigi flinched.

Georges was struggling against Peterson and Smith, with Gilbert behind him, pushing them all forward.

There was indeed a knife buried in the door.

Gigi rested her forehead against her knees for a moment in exasperation before she pulled herself to her feet.

"Gigi!" Georges's roar cut through even the shouting that had started up in the men's cell.

"Georges, *du calme!*" Her shout snapped the air like a whipcrack and the men stopped fighting and turned her way. Even the male prisoners went quiet.

In the silence Georges coughed, and Gigi was alarmed at the color of his face, the way he was struggling for breath. He had worked himself up into an apoplexy. For the moment, he could do nothing but suck air into his lungs.

"This . . . person feels rather strongly you should not be here, Madame Levéel." Gilbert's hair was standing wild around his face, and he had a dark bruise on his jaw. Gigi looked from it to the bruise on Bess's shoulder and felt the first glimmer of satisfaction.

"Monsieur Bisset is very fond of me. He is an old family friend and can easily confirm the jewelry in my trunk belonged to my mother. No doubt he was a little forceful in conveying this information, but he is like a second father to me and is clearly distressed that I have been imprisoned on nothing more than the word of a disaffected employee."

There was another silence, and Gigi realized she had spoken the King's English in that little speech. There had been no trace of a French accent at all.

For the first time, Gilbert looked uncertain of himself. "Who are you?"

Gigi crossed her arms under her breasts and leaned against the bars. "Will telling you get me out any quicker? Or will you still insist on seeing Lord Aldridge first?"

Georges jerked his arm from Smith's meaty paw. "Bah. They are truly *gendarmes*! They are not interested in truth, in justice. They know Aldridge hasn't known you more than a week, yet *he* must release you. Not the man who has known you since you were a child."

Gilbert went quite white. It was the remark about the *gendarmes*, Gigi was sure. There could surely be no greater insult than to be compared with the police of France.

"Throw him out of the station." He turned to his men and

Georges. "You are lucky I don't charge you with assault and disturbance of the peace."

"I do not go. If you hold Gigi here, I will stay with her. Georges Bisset does not abandon his friends." Georges planted his feet in a way that made it clear it would take considerable force to shift him.

"Unless you arrest him, we can't throw him in the men's cells." Peterson took a firmer hold on Georges's arm. He leaned closer to Gilbert, and Gigi was sure she caught the Duke of Wittaker's name in the hurried whisper.

"He wants to be with his friend, put him with his friend, then. No one can fault us for that. We're just following the man's request." Gilbert smiled a small, tight smile.

Peterson looked uncertain, but Georges gave a curt nod and moved forward toward her. "*Merci*. This is exactly what I wish."

"Georges. What good will both of us being here do?" Gigi stuck a hand out between the bars and touched the side of his face. "Then we both have to wait for Aldridge."

Georges gave a little shake of his head. "Trust me, *ma petite*. Georges has his ways." There was a diabolical gleam in his eye.

She moved back as Peterson opened the door, and Georges stepped inside. He rubbed his hands together gleefully, dominating the cell with his size and personality. "Why don't we 'ave a story while we wait, eh?" He looked at Gertrude, Violet and Bess and gave a low bow. "*Enchanté, mesdames*. Did you know our Gigi has stories from all around the world? I have missed your stories, *ma petite*."

She saw Gilbert's face as he turned away, and hoped Georges did have a plan. Because Gilbert's dislike of Georges seemed to have climbed into the rarefied air of hate.

She lowered herself onto the floor again and leaned her head back. "I can tell you the story of the *stallu*. The shadow man."

Jonathan had given Durnham's address to the cab driver, but as the hansom shuddered and swayed through the streets of Mayfair, he regretted the impulse to report in straightaway.

He wanted to get home.

He was exhausted, hungry and in need of a bath. Like the old days in the army, when he'd have given anything for a quiet, warm bedroom, hot water and a decent meal.

He closed his eyes, unable to summon the energy to call to the driver and change the destination to Aldridge House.

When the coach rocked to a stop, he dragged himself out onto the street and, from the look on the driver's face, paid him far too much.

He didn't ask for change. He couldn't remember how much he'd handed over.

He knocked and then leaned against the wall until the door was opened.

Durnham's butler took a moment to recognize him. Given how sharp-eyed he seemed to be, and how recently Jonathan had been there, Jonathan decided he must truly look as bad as he felt.

He was escorted in and shown to the library, and stood, swaying a little, while he worked out who was in the room.

It was Lady Durnham and Lady Holliday again, sitting in the same place as before, sipping tea.

Next to Lady Durnham on the sofa was a pile of what looked like ledgers and books of account, and when she saw him, she closed those that were open and set them all on the floor beside her chair.

"Lord Aldridge. You look done in. Come and have some tea and cake." Lady Durnham's face lifted to his in concern.

Jonathan was afraid if he sat down, he wouldn't be able to get up again, but he risked it anyway. The tray had cake, sandwiches and tiny petits fours that looked like they would be worth disgracing himself for.

"You haven't slept." Lady Holliday leaned forward and poured him some tea.

"No, I haven't. Is Durnham around?" He relished the sweet, strong tea and realized he'd finished his cup in three gulps. Lady Holliday poured him some more.

"My husband's out." Lady Durnham handed him a plate piled with food. "But there is something my watchers came to tell me this morning that may be of interest to you."

"The ones keeping an eye on Dervish's place?"

She shook her head. "We switched their focus to Goldfern. Hal Boots stopped watching Dervish's house when he found out Dervish was away, and since he seemed so interested in Goldfern, I had the lads take up position there instead."

Jonathan's mouth was full of bun, so he nodded for her to continue.

"Firstly, it seems your butler dismissed one of your maids last night, and someone gave her a new job at Goldfern."

"What?" Jonathan swallowed the last of his bun down the wrong way and thumped himself on the chest to get his breath back. "Who did he dismiss?"

"Someone called Mavis. The question is, who gave her the job at Goldfern?" Lady Durnham tapped her foot. "I thought you might have arranged it with Goldfern's caretaker?" She gave him a quick look, and he shook his head.

"Oh. Well, the girl isn't saying—not that she'd have cause to tell my boys. They were lucky to get what they did out of her, pretending to collect the ash bins. I wonder who it was, then?" She took a sip of tea, then looked across at him again and leaned forward. "But that isn't the exciting bit."

"It isn't?" What on earth had been happening at Aldridge House? He'd only been gone a day.

"Indeed." Lady Durnham watched him now, and there was something in her face that made Jonathan sure this was about Madame Levéel. Not only that, he was sure Durnham had discussed Madame Levéel with his wife, discussed his unease at Jonathan's relationship with his cook.

"Your butler has been a busy man. As well as dismissing the scullery maid, he called round the constables from the Queen Square station and accused your cook of theft."

Jonathan thumped the plate back onto the table, petits fours forgotten. "What did he say she'd stolen?"

"He went through her trunks while she was out and found some rather good jewelry there. He was certain it couldn't be hers, and called the officers. According to one of your other maids, who is spitting mad at the arrest, which is why my lads got so much out of her, the constable said nothing like it had been reported stolen, but he took your cook in anyway. He'll only release her to you."

Jonathan rubbed both hands over his cheeks, then shoved his fingers into his hair. From the way Lady Holliday looked at him when he finally dropped his arms, he guessed his hair was standing on end. "What the devil is Edgars up to?"

Lady Durnham leaned back in her chair, arms crossed, and shrugged. "I suppose you'll have to go home and find out."

He stood. "I came to tell Durnham that Greenway took the same boat as Dervish. He and Barrington had put a warning system in place for Miss Barrington's safety in case Barrington was ever arrested. It went into effect when Barrington was killed, and all it took was the news of the break-in at Goldfern to send Greenway haring off. He's gone to find Miss Barrington and bring her home."

"But he doesn't know where she is, specifically?" Lady Holliday asked.

Jonathan shook his head. "All he's got is the Barringtons' last address, same as Dervish."

"Daniel is usually the calmest, steadiest person I know." Lady Holliday was looking into the distance, her hand fisted tight around a white handkerchief. "This case has him shaken up. If Miss Barrington is dead, he'll feel he's failed a good friend."

Watching her, Jonathan had a quick flash of insight.

Lady Holliday and Dervish.

Well, well, well.

She tilted her head up to look at him, and there was quiet desperation in her eyes.

"There's still the mystery of who at Goldfern hired Mavis." Lady Durnham played her fingers over her lips.

"It could have been the caretaker at Goldfern House, Jones, or his wife. They probably know my staff—our houses are close enough to each other. They may have taken pity on Mavis."

Lady Durnham sighed. "That makes sense. A very practical explanation."

"Speaking of practical, it sounds as if I have some domestic issues to deal with." Jonathan gave a bow of farewell. "Like getting my cook out of jail."

31

"And the little girl, all alone in the deep, cold wood, knew that the *stallu* needed a shadow to jump to, or he could never get close enough to her to kill her. So she put the small carving of a mouse her grandfather had given her upon the snow-covered ground. She shone her lantern so that the carving's shadow was the only one touching the shadow of the tall old tree where the *stallu* was hiding.

"And thinking she was a silly little girl, and forgetting that she had outwitted him so far, tricking him into leaving the village and following her out into the wood, the *stallu* slipped from the tree shadow to the mouse shadow. And just as he did, the little girl moved the lantern again so that the mouse shadow was by itself in the small clearing, surrounded by light.

"The *stallu* was trapped. He couldn't jump to anything else. Now the little girl had to move quickly—faster than she'd ever moved before—to give the *stallu* no time to attack. She shot out her hand and grabbed the mouse, snatching it up and holding it close to her chest. Its shadow disappeared, leaving the *stallu* with no shadow to cling to, surrounded by lamplight. With a shriek of rage and disappointment, the *stallu* vanished into nothing. And the little girl, lamp in one hand, small mouse carving in the other, began her long walk home." Gigi's voice was husky by the end of the tale.

There was a long moment of silence.

"Is that an old fireside tale from Lapland?" Gertrude asked at last.

Gigi shook her head, finding it hard to speak again. "There are tales of *stallu* in Lapland—that's where I learned of them—but no. This story is one I made up."

"So a *stallu* is someone evil who can use the shadows, become the shadows, and attack you?" Violet tightened her hold on her knees.

"Yes, he can use the shadows, slip between them and take on another shape." Gigi could bear the cold floor no longer and stood up, rubbing at her arms. She realized the men must have been listening in their cell, too, because only now that the tale was over could she hear them moving and murmuring to each other again.

She gripped the bars of the door with her hands and accepted that she might have to spend the night here. At least she had good company.

"When do you get out?" She released the bars and turned to Gertrude. "Or are you here for the night, too?"

Gertrude shook her head. "We been in nearly a full day—

since yesterday evening. They'll let us out at shift change, round six o'clock."

"'Cause keeping us off the street for a day is a blow against crime." Violet's sarcasm was so bitter, Gigi could almost taste it. "We lose a day's earnings, and a starving whore's so much better for society than one who's made enough for a crust of bread. Our kids are alone while we're in here, and we have less money to feed 'em with. It's a fine day's work all round."

"How do they catch you?"

She shrugged. "Hailing to clients or when we're negotiating terms. Once caught me busy up against an alley wall. Gent's John Thomas was already docked, right and proper. Does he get nicked? No. Only me. Didn't get paid that time, neither."

"They do it once a day, at dusk, when we first come out. When people are still around to see 'em. Makes it look like they're cleaning up the streets." Bess spoke quietly. "But it's just for form. We were the unlucky ones yesterday. Tonight it'll be someone else."

Unlike Violet's, her voice contained no bitterness—only resignation.

From behind the door at the end of the passage Gigi heard the sound of voices, and Georges stood up, anticipation in every line of him.

She leaned closer to him and lowered her voice. "What was your plan? I was so busy telling the story, I didn't ask you."

Georges turned his face to hers, looking like the very devil himself, delightedly watching the world come to a bad end. "I took so long getting here because I had to find the duke. He was still at his club, playing cards. Right through the night he played, and into the morning. But I hunted him down, and impressed upon him the urgency and importance of the situation, and he agreed to go home, bathe, change and eat a light repast, and then come here to get you out."

"But why did you stay, then? You didn't need to get yourself locked in here with me."

Georges shook his head. "Though I impressed upon him the severity of the situation, the English nobility . . ." He puffed out a breath. "They are sometimes like the eels, no? They wiggle out of their responsibilities, unless it is clear the alternative is much more unpleasant. The duke, he will not stir himself unless his own comfort is compromised—he is far too lazy. But with the best chef he has ever had locked up, and the prospect of no good lunch or dinner, or any food at all of my standard until this matter is taken care of . . ." He smirked. "Well, then. I think I can safely say we can expect the duke at any *moment*."

Gertrude chuckled. An earthy, sexy chuckle that clung stubbornly to a few tattered scraps of innocence and happier days. "Monsieur Bee-say, you are a devil. The kind of devil a girl would be lucky to have on her side."

Georges smiled back and gave a deep bow. "*Merci, madame.*"

A key scraped in the lock and the door opened. Gigi moved back a little, watching along with everyone else as Peterson and then Gilbert stepped through. Someone was behind them, but until they were a few steps into the passage, she didn't see who it was.

The shadow man. The dark, compact stranger who had followed her through the market this morning.

The sight of him froze her. She moved her lips with difficulty. "Georges, please tell me that is not the duke."

"That is not the duke." He frowned, then seemed to notice her fear. "This isn't—?"

"The *stallu* himself."

"You know this gent, Madame Levéel?" Gilbert was watching her with his sharp, clever eyes again, the broken light from the far window catching the red in his bushy sideburns. "Seems very keen to get you out o' here and take you into his care."

"He's the man who was standing on the corner as you drove me out of Chapel Street." She took another step away from the bars. "The man who is trying to kill me."

"Yes, I thought I recognized him." Gilbert turned sideways. "You were wearing a black coat earlier, but you're the same man." He tapped just under his left eye. "Never forget a face, me."

Gigi finally saw the shadow man properly for the first time. Well-made, clean-cut features, a pleasant face. Hiding in the shadow of earnest decency.

"How did you find me here?" Gigi asked.

"I'm afraid Lord Aldridge's butler doesn't like you very much." The shadow man's lips quirked at the edges. "He was only too happy to talk about how you got your comeuppance."

"Get his name and his office, Mr. Gilbert." Gigi forced herself to retreat no further. She would not cower back. "There are sure to be men in Whitehall who will be very pleased with you if you do."

"Come now, Gilbert. Are you going to be bossed about by a suspected spy?" The shadow man clicked his tongue. "Manipulated by a pretty face?" Some of his ugliness leaked out from beneath the shadow cloak. His countenance had a twist to it, as if he were struggling to control his temper.

Gilbert was a hard man to read. He was touchy. She couldn't be sure if he'd rise to the shadow man's taunts or turn against him for trying such an obvious ploy.

"*If* I let you take her, it will only be on receipt of your name and office." He crossed his arms. "And you'll give me those details even if I don't let you take her." Gilbert's voice had turned decidedly cool.

"You're insolent, Gilbert, and out of your league." The shadow man drew himself up and stepped into Gilbert's space.

Gigi shivered at the ugly rage she saw in his face. Gilbert seemed to shrink back, and the shadow man sent her a sidelong look of triumph. "Hand her over now, or you will be lucky to work on the street watch."

Gigi forced herself to hold his gaze, and then Georges pushed forward in front of her. "You will have to go through me to get to her." There was no give in his tone. She stepped to the side and saw the shadow man recoil at the sight of him.

"Who are you?"

"I am Georges Bisset." He spoke as if no further explanation were necessary.

The shadow man turned away from them, his face tight. "You're being played by a couple of Frenchies, Gilbert. I'm with the Foreign Office, and I am perfectly within my rights to demand you hand them over."

"Both of them?" Gilbert had straightened again, and his tone was sly. "What's the Foreign Office charge against Monsieur Bisset? You never mentioned him when you came in."

The shadow man struggled to stay calm. "I didn't know he was here then. But all right. Just the woman will do for now." He narrowed his eyes at Georges. "What do you have him in for?"

"Oh, Monsieur Bisset isn't a prisoner. He requested to wait with Madame Levéel until she is released. Seems quite concerned for her welfare."

"Not a . . ." The shadow man took a nervous step back.

"That's right. He's within his rights to follow you out of here if you take his friend, and I don't think you'd be easily rid of him." Gilbert seemed to be enjoying himself, pitting two men he clearly did not like against each other. "Now, before we go any further, your name and office, please, sir."

The shadow man hesitated, then shrugged. "John Miller, Department of Foreign Trade."

"Well now, that was easy wasn't it?" Gilbert jerked his head at Peterson. "Run down to the Department of Foreign Trade and ask after a John Miller. Be sure to get a physical description."

For a moment, in the space of the blink of an eye, she saw the shadow man's face blanch.

"You calling me a liar?" Miller, if that was his name—and Gigi doubted it—leaned into Gilbert again.

And just like that, she could see he was desperate. He reeked of it.

Coming here, openly trying to pry her from Gilbert's grasp, was a desperate act. Even if he never gave his true name, his face had been seen. If he did manage to bully Gilbert into giving her to him, Gilbert would remember him. Remember everything if her body was found somewhere. And he hadn't even factored in Georges.

That would have come as a nasty shock.

Georges was someone who would cause a fuss about his taking her, demand a search, hunt him down in whatever department he occupied in the Foreign Office, under whatever name, and point the finger.

She wondered why he was taking the chance.

Either it was critical that there be no delay in getting the letter, or the shadow man's cohorts did not accept failure.

By coming into the station he'd put his career in jeopardy, and if he were caught, he'd hang. She could only imagine they'd threatened him with a painful and more immediate death if he did not succeed.

Whether it was the French, or some faction of the Russian court, they would make him wish he was dead before they killed him—and if he hadn't thought of that before he took on their dirty work, he must surely be thinking of it now.

Peterson gave a nod and left the room, and Miller looked after him. Gigi couldn't see his face.

"Just good procedure; I'm sure you understand." Gilbert spoke gravely, stroking his left sideburn with one finger.

Miller rallied, gave a cool smile. "Well, while he checks it, perhaps you can release the woman to me and get the paperwork sorted."

He would grab her and run, the moment she was within his reach. She could see it in the way he began to ready himself for a fight, tensing, his expression going still and flat, his arms loosening.

A commotion from the front office froze Gilbert's reply, and they all turned.

"Where is my chef?"

The man at the end of the passage was tall, elegantly dressed and slouched against the doorframe. He looked in his early thirties, and there was a dissolute charm and slightly seedy handsomeness to him that he wore with careless arrogance. He had dark circles under his eyes, and when he walked forward, Gigi got the sense he was not quite sober.

"Now *that*," said Georges, "is the duke."

32

As Jonathan's coach drove swiftly toward Queen Square Public Office, he cursed Edgars.

She'd been willing to tell him her secrets yesterday morning, he was sure of it. The way she'd nodded to him in the kitchen doorway had spoken of a decision made, no matter the consequences.

The thought that she had been so close to trusting him, only to have her come to harm under his own roof . . .

Damn Edgars!

The coach pulled up outside the building and he told the driver to wait, not knowing how long he'd be inside. He pushed through the door hard, and it took him until he was halfway across the main reception area to realize everyone's attention was on an elegantly dressed man propped up in a doorway at the back of the room.

The man had his back turned, looking down a passageway, but Jonathan knew him immediately.

The Duke of Wittaker.

When they'd had their shouting match in the duke's kitchen, Georges Bisset had promised to take Madame Levéel back to Wittaker's mansion. And here Wittaker was—the duke had stirred himself to fetch her personally.

With a sinking dread that slowed every new step he took, he thought of the threat he'd made to Bisset that day, about calling the Alien Office to investigate, and wondered if Bisset thought he was behind this arrest.

If the burly cook had convinced Madame Levéel that he was, he might never see her again.

"You've locked my chef up!" Wittaker's voice rose to a shout. "On what charge, sir?"

There was a murmur of response, and Wittaker took a step deeper into the room.

A clerk jerked in surprise to see Jonathan standing right beside him. "Can I help you, my lord?"

"I'm here to fetch my cook. I'm told you're holding her here."

"What?" The man seemed so taken back, Jonathan focused on him more sharply.

"I was told the senior constable would only release her to me. I'm Lord Aldridge."

"She must cook a real treat." The clerk leered.

"I beg your pardon?" Jonathan checked his step forward and turned back to stare at the man.

"No offense." The clerk scrambled back behind his desk. "Just . . . you're the fourth gentleman come for her since Mr.

Gilbert brung her in. There's a tug o' war going on in there over her now."

Jonathan turned his attention back to the passageway, and stepped through.

It was very crowded.

A cell full of men was immediately to his right, and they were pressed up hard against the bars, straining to see as much as possible. At the far end of the passage, Wittaker stood with two other men. Just beyond them was a smaller cell and he could see Bisset standing up against the cell door, along with Madame Levéel.

She looked past Wittaker and saw him, and he held her gaze. There was relief in her eyes, and resentment, and a hot, well-stoked anger.

That shaken-bottle-of-champagne feeling came over him again.

"Lord Aldridge." She called out his name so her words cut through the commotion, and for a moment, there was absolute silence as everyone turned to him.

Wittaker started in first. "I say, Aldridge, you having your cook arrested has caused me all sorts of inconvenience. I was about to take Harriford for his yearly allowance when Bisset interrupted me to come down and get her. What's going on? According to my chef she's an angel in the kitchen, and we're taking her with us. So your loss. Ha-ha."

Jonathan opened his mouth to reply and then stopped. And stared at one of the other two men.

He knew him. He'd seen him only a few days ago, and he'd felt an instant dislike for him.

Frobisher! The man whose rumor about Giselle Barrington had sent Dervish off to Stockholm.

"What on earth are *you* doing here?" He didn't think he mistook the way Frobisher pushed back against the cold stone wall at the sight of him, or the wild-eyed look he'd been giving Wittaker before he noticed Jonathan.

"You know this man?" the final man in the room asked.

"Who are you?" Jonathan got the impression of someone quick and alert, before his gaze strayed back to Madame Levéel. She tightened her grip on the bars.

"Gilbert. Senior constable, Queen Square Public Office."

Jonathan didn't like the way he spoke; a sharp sliver of contempt scraped the edge of his words raw. When Jonathan swung back to him, Gilbert held his gaze with a cocky aggressiveness that held only the slimmest thread of nerves.

Jonathan was tired, and his coating of polite manners had been rubbed almost through. Under the gold plate were all manner of reactions no one here would like.

He had not fought and killed in Spain, become one of the most decorated officers in his regiment, by being polite.

"I don't know why you arrested my cook—particularly as I understand there was no crime, or evidence of a crime—but I would like her out of this cell immediately," he said coldly.

"First you want her in, now you want her out?" Wittaker asked him, and despite his drunken rambling earlier, Jonathan could see the gleam of wicked intelligence in his eye. It didn't surprise him.

Wittaker was no one's fool, and Jonathan had long suspected that at least half the time he only pretended to be drunk.

"I never wanted her in." He looked back at Madame Levéel and reached out to hold the same bars as she, his fingers closing around the cold metal just above hers. His gaze never left her face. "I never wanted you in. I promise, I had no idea about this until I came home."

She gave a tiny nod and then looked past him to Frobisher, eyeing the Foreign Office man like a feral dog off its leash. "Who is that?" she asked.

He turned, and as he did so he realized Frobisher had been edging away from them all toward the door. As their eyes met, Frobisher shoved Wittaker out of the way and ran.

"Get him!" Madame Levéel's call was urgent.

Instinctively he took up the chase, back, for a moment, in the steep mountains of Spain. But he only got three steps when he realized he didn't care about Frobisher. The man could run all he liked, shove dukes out the way, and ruin his career. It was nothing to Jonathan. The only important thing here was to get Madame Levéel out of that cell.

He brought himself up short and turned back.

Everyone was staring at him. He noticed Gilbert had lost his sneer.

"No hiding that you're a military man, Aldridge." Wittaker straightened his coat and righted himself from the shove. "Why did you stop? You could have had him, man."

"Yes." Jonathan looked back at Madame Levéel. "He wasn't important."

"He *was* important." Her hands were fists at her side, her eyes flashing. "You need to get him! He'll go to ground now." She stamped her foot. Actually stamped it. When he didn't move, she closed her eyes and took a deep breath. "You couldn't know. But . . . you should have stopped him."

She turned to Gilbert, and now her eyes were narrow, her voice clipped. "You said you'd release me to Lord Aldridge. Well, there he is."

No one in the room could mistake her bitterness, or her resentment at having her freedom dependent on someone else.

Bisset had been quiet until now, standing a step back and watching them all. He stepped forward and put a hand on Madame Levéel's shoulder. "When these *imbéciles* let you out, you will come home safe with me."

"You'd be most welcome," Wittaker said magnanimously, as if his chef had asked his opinion on the matter.

She didn't say anything for a moment. She patted Bisset's hand absently and gave Wittaker a nod. "Thank you both. I will need to get my things from Lord Aldridge's, and I need to speak to him privately. Perhaps it would be best for me to stay with you for a day or two, while that *stallu* is still on the loose."

"*Stallu?*" Gilbert frowned.

"The man who pushed His Grace aside to run off. The man who pretended his name was Miller." Madame Levéel glared at him. "The man to whom you were going to hand me over." Her tone was heavy with recrimination.

"That was the *stallu?*" A wo6man in a rough-cut gown

stepped forward, coming to Jonathan's attention for the first time.

"Would someone tell me what a *stallu* is?" Gilbert's voice was whip-sharp.

"A bogeyman from Lapland. Everyone knows that," one of the prisoners from the men's cell called out. There was the sound of muted sniggering.

"Frobisher gave his name as Miller?" Jonathan asked, trying to work through the ramifications. If Frobisher was on official Foreign Office business, if he had a legal right to take Madame Levéel into custody, why had he run?

"Whoever he is, he wants to kill my Gigi. That's enough reason to keep her close." Bisset put his arm around her.

Kill her?

Jonathan thought of the way she'd behaved since he'd met her, of her fear when she walked alone, of the risks she'd taken to get away from the man watching Dervish's house, and wondered what the hell Frobisher was up to. "If she feels safer with you and wishes to leave me after we've spoken, I will bring her around personally. You have my word." Jonathan was simply grateful she would speak to him at all.

Gilbert stepped forward with a key and then hesitated, leaving it just short of the lock. "I may have erred a time or two in today's business, madam, but there's one thing I know I'm right on: you're not who you seem."

"And that's a crime, is it?" One of the other women in the cell sneered, pushing a loose purple sleeve back up her shoulder. "No one can have anything private, is that right?"

"You don't keep much private as a matter of course, Gertie." Gilbert shot her a look of pure dislike, and she bared her teeth in a dangerous smile.

"Frobisher knows I'm in London now." Madame Levéel gave a shrug. "Let me out, let Gertrude, Bess and Violet out, too—I know it's time for you to release them, anyway—and I'll tell you."

Gilbert hesitated another moment, and Jonathan put a hand on his arm. He said nothing; anger at the way Gilbert was toying with them clamped his throat too tight.

Gilbert looked up at him, his face annoyed, until their gazes clashed. Then he staggered back, snatching his arm away, and fumbled in his hurry to get the lock open.

"No hiding it at all," Wittaker murmured.

The door swung open and Madame Levéel stepped out, with Bisset and three prostitutes right behind her.

"Well, go on. Tell 'im." The one with the purple dress looked decidedly smug. Like she was about to see Gilbert receive a nasty shock, Jonathan thought.

"You were right, Mr. Gilbert." Madame Levéel suddenly spoke English with the crystal-clear tones of a young lady of the ton. "I'm not really a French cook, although that's what I've been pretending to be for the last week. My name is Giselle Barrington."

33

To her surprise, Lord Aldridge looked stunned. Curiously, she caught a flash of surprise on the duke's face as well.

"You—" Aldridge seemed unable to speak. "*You* are Miss Barrington?"

She gave a nod. "You may remember my parents, Lord Aldridge, as my house is just a few doors down from yours. Goldfern."

He didn't look intrigued; he didn't look surprised. He looked furious. She frowned.

"You . . ." He pointed a finger at her, then lifted his hands as if he would like to put them around her neck.

"I think a private talk with Aldridge is not a good idea, eh?" Georges drew her closer to him. "We go straight 'ome, *mon seigneur*," he told Wittaker, giving the order easily.

A flash of amusement crossed Wittaker's face, accompanied by not a little measure of curiosity. "You all right, Aldridge?" he asked.

Lord Aldridge looked at his raised hands and then shoved his fingers into hair that already looked wild, as though he'd been pulling on it for some time.

He ignored Wittaker, he ignored everyone else. He looked only at her. "Why?" It was the first coherent word he'd managed.

She thought of the kisses they'd shared, of the way they seemed to spark off each other, and knew her fears regarding what he'd think about it when her true identity was revealed had been fully justified.

He must feel betrayed by her—trapped or fooled.

"I don't think Lord Aldridge intends me any harm, Georges. Let me go with him and get my things, and then he can bring me over to you. He deserves an explanation. And I have something I need to give him."

Wittaker looked even more interested. He hesitated with his lips pursed and then turned to Aldridge. "If we don't have her back in two hours, old chap, I'm afraid we'll come looking for her." He played the word-slurring insouciant well, but there was something much harder, much sharper in his eyes as he clapped Aldridge on the shoulder.

Aldridge shrugged him off, and Gigi saw a tense, suppressed violence in the action. Aldridge played a different role than Wittaker, putting on a milder, more polite and sensible persona, but, like Wittaker's, it was only a thin disguise.

There was a sleek strength and a frighteningly focused determination under the calm, gentlemanly facade.

It should have made her nervous to leave with him, but it didn't.

Gertrude, Violet and Bess watched the byplay with enjoyment, but Gilbert was tugging his waistcoat with a nervous hand, his eyes flitting between the two noblemen as if suddenly aware he was confined in a small space with two dangerous animals.

He edged past them all and flourished an arm toward the front office. "As you all seem to have plenty to do . . ."

"Go well, Gigi." Gertrude leaned over and gave her a smacking kiss on the cheek. "And good luck with that *stallu*, love."

Bess gave her a small smile and Violet a brief nod, and they walked past Gilbert with their heads high and a slight sway to their walk.

"Don't let me catch you again," Gilbert said to their backs.

Gertrude looked over her shoulder at him. "It'll be a pleasure to keep clear of ya." She flounced the last few steps and disappeared into the front office.

Gigi followed after them and turned at the door. "I believe you have a number of things belonging to me, Mr. Gilbert?"

He flushed and moved past her, took out a key, and walked to a small office. While she stood waiting for him, Georges came to stand very close. Wittaker leaned against the doorway to the back cells, watchful. His presence caused the whole station to quieten.

Not often that a real duke came to Queen Square.

"I can come with you to Aldridge House," Georges murmured, but Gigi took one look at Aldridge, standing tense and apart from everyone, and shook her head.

"Aldridge and I need to talk privately." She took the velvet bags Gilbert held out to her, and tipped them onto a nearby table. Then she went through them one by one.

"You think there'll be any missing?" Gilbert spoke through clenched teeth.

She shrugged and continued with her check until she was satisfied she had every piece. Then she gathered the ribbon handles in one hand and looked up. Aldridge was watching her, his face unreadable. She held out her free hand to him and he stepped up to her and crooked his elbow.

She slipped her arm through.

It should have felt safe and normal. Instead, it felt as if she were about to plunge herself into a raging rapid, to be tumbled and thrown about.

"Two hours, Aldridge." Wittaker had dropped his drunken-aristocrat facade entirely.

Aldridge slowed a step, but that was the only acknowledgment he gave Wittaker's threat. He led her out of the station and put her into the waiting cab without a word. While he called up to the driver, she tried to find some calm, to stop her heart racing like a mail coach trying to catch the last boat.

Aldridge swung up into the cab and sat opposite her.

She could see he was still struggling to contain his reaction to her true identity.

"I am sorry." She clasped her hands together on her lap. "I understand you must be angry with me. The way we dealt with each other . . . I know it would not have been the same if you'd known who I was. I have no excuse for allowing you to kiss me, and all I can say is that it puts no obligation upon you at all."

He stared at her, for one long beat after another, until she was squirming, her cheeks hot. "You're trying to set my mind at rest about the *proprieties?*"

He sounded not only angry but disgusted. And why would he not? She'd set herself outside polite society with what she'd done. She'd accepted it at the time, but the reality of it was harder than she'd anticipated.

He pinched the bridge of his nose and drew in a deep breath. "How did you come to be in my house?"

"Georges." She frowned. "Why aren't you asking me *why* again? I never answered you."

"Because I know some of the why." He propped a shoulder against the wall of the cab as it bounced over loose cobbles. "But if you'd like a why, why were you risking yourself every day, watching Goldfern?"

She ignored that. "How do you know some of the why? Who are you?"

"A person who could have helped you right from the start if you'd told me the truth."

The accusation in his voice burned her deep, and she reared up against it like a horse in battle. "I don't know how much you know of my business, but how *could* I have told you the truth? I had no idea who to go to, who had been my father's contact."

"Why didn't you approach Wittaker himself?"

He was near the edge of his temper. She could see it in the way his nostrils flared.

She rubbed her arms. "I have something important to hand over, although perhaps you know that, too?" She couldn't keep the sarcasm from her voice. "Georges thought Wittaker might throw it in the fire, because he is angry at the Crown over some tax dispute. I couldn't take that chance."

He tapped on his knee with long, blunt fingers. "I can understand your not wanting to hand over a letter from the tsar, which opens the way for a secret treaty between England and Russia, to someone who might throw it into the fire."

She wasn't even surprised anymore that he knew so much. She lifted her skirt and drew the letter from the secret pocket in her petticoat, then held it out to him. "My father died for this letter. I couldn't take the easy route and give it to just anyone."

"No." He took it without looking at it, his eyes on her, bracing his other hand on the side of the coach as it shuddered over the rough road. Slowly, he slid the parchment into the inner pocket of his jacket.

She felt no great relief, no lessening of the grief that sat on her heart like a stone, at giving up her burden.

Sadness and a sense of loss came over her, mixing with her exhaustion. She wondered how much he must dislike her.

"I really am sorry for hiding in your house. I needed a place to get my bearings, to work out what to do next. I was still very . . . upset . . . about my father's murder. It seemed the perfect solution."

She cast her eyes down to her lap to avoid the bright blue

gaze that seemed to burn through her. Her skin was too tight all of a sudden, too confining.

"Two others and myself have been working night and day to discover whether you're alive and well. One of us, Lord Dervish, rushed off to Sweden because we'd heard you might still be there. Except the whole time, you've been under my own roof, taking risk after risk with your life." Those bright eyes were snapping with temper.

She blinked. And in that down-up movement of her eyelids the anger she'd been fighting all day sprang fully to hot, leaping life, pushing aside her guilt, her sense of loss, her self-pity.

She gave a deliberately laconic shrug and leaned back against the cracked leather of the seat. "Well, accept my apologies, Lord Aldridge, for not informing you. I didn't know you were involved with my father's sideline. I didn't have a single name, thanks to being kept continually in the dark. I knew the value of what I carried with me, and I also knew that the man who killed my father worked for the Foreign Office. I couldn't trust anyone I didn't know, and I didn't know anyone except Georges."

She took a deep breath. Blew it out. "I was trying to find a man who corresponded with my father, a man my father trusted, and after I met Dervish that morning at Aldridge House, I thought it might be him. That's what I was looking for that day in your office. A note from him, to see if his handwriting matched that in the letters to my father."

His hand curled into a fist and he knocked it on his upper

thigh. If he was thinking of what had happened between them in that study, she couldn't tell from his expression.

"Searching desks, running about at night—you were hardly lying low, though, were you?"

"How else could I find the man who killed my father and bring him down?"

He sucked in a breath. "You could have ended up dead, like your father." His words were harsh, and she flinched.

"I didn't, though. And now we know who he is, even if we weren't able to hold him." Anger made her rash, the sarcasm dripping from her words like cream over a hot tart.

He said nothing, giving her a long, cool look, and she stared straight back, crossing her arms under her breasts.

The coach turned a sharp corner and she had to grab hold of the strap hanging from the roof to keep from sliding off the bench.

"I thought your mother the most beautiful, wonderful woman alive." His change in conversation was so abrupt, she couldn't speak for a moment.

"I know," she said eventually.

It was his turn to be surprised. "You do?"

"I was there that day at tea, Lord Aldridge." She didn't know how the smile came to her lips, given the charged, angry air between them, but it did. "The clear good taste you showed that day has worked very much in your favor with me."

34

Now that he knew who she was, he realized she was Adèle Barrington come back to life. An almost perfect replica of that warm, sleek beauty and elegance.

It was the eyes that had misled him.

Where Adèle Barrington's had been a deep, soulful brown, her daughter had inherited her father's light hazel-green. The contrast with her dark lashes, her dark, elegant sweep of hair, and the warm cream of her skin was breathtaking. It had certainly been taking his breath since he'd met her only a week ago.

It was taking his breath now.

While she glared at him defiantly, and insultingly assured him she wouldn't hold him to his earlier behavior. As if he were worrying about that.

The kiss in the study, the way he'd leaned into her by the wall at the kitchen door. The way they had watched each other, felt the sparks. She thought he'd done that as a dalliance with a servant. That he would never have touched her if he'd known she was a woman of his own class.

She was wrong.

But now wasn't the time and place to say so.

The cab came to a stop, and Jonathan opened the door reluctantly onto the real world. He helped her out into the gloom of the street, half lit by the light shining from his hallway.

Edgars opened up before they reached the top step, holding the door and standing to one side so they could enter.

There was an uncomfortable silence while Miss Barrington looked at Edgars, and he avoided looking at her.

Edgars took his coat in what could have been an automatic movement, but when he turned from hanging it, he pointedly avoided Miss Barrington's gaze again.

After a moment, Jonathan slipped her coat off her shoulders himself, and enjoyed the feel of her under his hands, the sound of her murmur of thanks.

Edgars' eyes lifted to his face, and they stared at each other.

"We didn't expect your return until tomorrow, my lord, so I'm afraid I've given the staff the night off. I'm the only one here." Edgars cleared his throat.

"We'll be going back out shortly, so it doesn't matter," Jonathan said curtly.

"I'll go down and get my luggage. With so many people having gone through my things, I may need a little time to sort it all out." She spoke quietly, but there was a razor-sharp edge to her words and she was looking pointedly at Edgars.

"Take the time you need, but it will be better to move quickly, if you can." Jonathan's lips quirked. "I believed Wittaker's threat of coming for you in two hours."

She gave a tiny smile in return. "I believed it, too."

She turned and walked across to the servants' stair. Something twisted inside him at how she knew the way, the confidence in her step as she negotiated his home.

She knew so much more of him than he did of her.

Edgars was twitchy, his eyes finally on Miss Barrington now that her back was turned. "I need to speak with you, my lord."

"I think that would be a good idea." He walked into his library.

Edgars followed a pace or two behind, and when they had both stepped into the room, he looked back to the hall as if he expected Miss Barrington would try to listen in.

"What have you got to say, Edgars?" Jonathan suddenly regretted how short the journey home had been. He hadn't managed to discover what had happened between Giselle Barrington and Edgars, why his butler was behaving the way he was.

"That woman, my lord." Edgars looked out toward the passage again and lowered his voice. "She's a French spy! I knew she were up to something, I *knew* it."

"And who told you she was a spy?" Jonathan had a cold feeling in his gut.

"Fellow came round from the Foreign Office just after Gilbert took her away this morning." Edgars gave a sniff. "Hiding under our roof the whole time, she was. Carrying on her sinister deeds."

"Edgars." He controlled his voice with effort. "The man who came round this morning is a traitor and a liar looking for Miss Barrington—Madame Levéel—so he can murder her, just as he murdered her father."

Edgars opened his mouth to speak, but he only managed a croak. He tried again. "He—he told me to tell you. To explain . . . what she was."

"She's been hiding here from him, and this morning he at last tracked her down. If you see him, tell me immediately. He's extremely dangerous and, since his identity was revealed earlier today, extremely desperate."

"He'll kill her?" Edgars' face was gray.

"Not straightaway." Jonathan rubbed the bridge of his nose. "He'll want to know where she's put an important document he's planning to steal, first." He shuddered at the thought of the chances she'd taken since the night her father died.

"My . . . lord?" Edgars turned again in the direction of the hall, his whole body trembling. "I let him in. Not half an hour ago. I . . . he's downstairs."

She stepped into the kitchen, which was silent and dark except for the fire in the grate. After the gloom and cold outside, it made the large open space almost cozy.

She would miss this place.

She knew only too well she wouldn't have the same run of things in the kitchen at Goldfern. When she sent for Pierre, who was probably going mad with worry for her at the count-ess's, he would let her do a little, but it would be his kitchen, no doubt about that.

She reached for a lantern on the mantelpiece and lit it with a taper, then gathered herself to face whatever mess Edgars and Gilbert had wrought in her rooms.

Her door wasn't even fully shut, and she pushed it open with a quick, hard shove of anger.

Her trunks were closed and piled carefully against the wall, and the sight released her rage.

Iris had done this. Maybe Babs, too. And Rob and Harry to move them neatly to the side.

She set the lantern on her small writing table, fighting the tears that suddenly burned against her tired eyes.

What would they think of her subterfuge?

"I was about to go through your luggage, but fortunately you arrived before I had to put myself to the effort." The thin, cold slide of a blade against her throat accompanied the words whispered in her ear from behind.

And then she felt the hard, ungiving pressure of a pistol in her back.

Just like he'd done with her father.

"You do love the shadows, don't you?" She was ashamed that her voice wavered slightly.

"You've led me a merry chase, *bitch*." He breathed hard, standing so close she could feel the movement of his chest against her shoulder. He rubbed a finger along the dip between her shoulder and her neck, and she couldn't help the shiver that racked her. She thought back to Violet, running a decisive finger across her throat.

"You finally have the sense to be scared, I see. It's about time." He went quiet, and she had the feeling he was listening.

For Aldridge and Edgars.

She went cold. "Edgars . . ."

"A very helpful man. Very eager to believe the worst about you." He laughed, a hot blast in her ear. "I'm not sure how long he can hold Aldridge, so you have until the count of five to give me the document." He pressed the knife hard against her skin, and she felt the searing pain as it cut her.

"I don't have it."

"One . . ."

"You think I've had it all this time? I've been in London for over a week! I gave it up days ago."

"I don't believe you. Why else would you still be in hiding, then?" He gave her a little shake. "Two . . ."

"Because I was trying to catch you," she hissed as he increased the pressure even more, and she felt the warm trickle of blood. "While you thought there was a chance I was still hiding with the document, you'd take chances. Take risks to see if you could still get it."

He lifted the knife and spun her around to face him.

"I would have heard if you'd handed it over."

She forced a dry smile. "I was there that night in the garden at Tessin Palace. You didn't see me, but I watched you kill my father."

She could see he hadn't known that by the way he flinched.

"I couldn't see your face in the darkness, but I heard your voice, and I knew you were British." She forced herself not to lift a hand to her neck. "So everyone who was there was under suspicion, until this afternoon, when you revealed yourself at Queen Square."

She straightened as she prepared to lie. To convince him there was no easy escape. "None of the diplomatic staff who were in Sweden at the time were told anything, because the powers that be I approached in London thought it the easiest way to smoke you out." She took a step back. "And they were right."

"I thought you'd found the body after I left," he said quietly, almost to himself. "I've been trying to work out how I didn't pass you on the way in to the ballroom."

Then he went still as they heard the thundering sound of someone racing down the stairs.

35

Jonathan ran through Edgars, knocking him aside. When he reached the door he took a precious second to pull out the knife in his boot, and he noticed Edgars had fallen badly and hit his head against the desk. He was moaning, though, so the little bastard wasn't dead.

He took the stairs three at a time and jumped the last five, landing in the gloom of the kitchen with every sense alert.

He felt the familiar fizz of excitement and nerves in his blood he'd had in Spain at the start of every battle.

But this time, there was also a debilitating fear.

"I was hoping your butler could keep you occupied for longer," Frobisher spoke from the shadowed doorway to the left, and when he moved into the weak firelight, Jonathan saw he had Giselle Barrington clamped to his chest.

"He thought I still had the document," Miss Barrington said calmly, and he finally saw the deep cut across her throat, the rivulets of blood.

His fear snapped to rage and he held himself very, very still.

"It almost doesn't matter." Frobisher edged toward the stairs up to the back door, dragging Miss Barrington with him. "Wittaker and the whole of Queen Square Station know my name. I'm ruined anyway. But the letter would have meant I wouldn't have to keep looking over my shoulder for the rest of my life."

Jonathan weighed the knife in his hand, and Frobisher stopped his awkward sideways movement.

He propped the hand holding the pistol onto Miss Barrington's shoulder. "No time to reload, so if I shoot, I'll have to be very sure of stopping you." He seemed to consider the odds. "If you lift that knife arm or step a foot closer, I'll risk it. Or . . ." He turned the pistol so it was resting against Miss Barrington's temple. "Now *that* will be a sure thing."

They froze in a silent standoff. A loud pop and crack from the fireplace made Frobisher jerk the gun barrel, and it seemed to bring him back to himself. "Throw the knife across the room, and when I get to the kitchen door, I'll let Miss Barrington go."

Jonathan hesitated. One quick, well-aimed throw would be all it would take. If he could get a clear target.

"Let me put it this way. If you don't throw the knife into that far corner there, I will shoot Miss Barrington when I get to the door. Believe me, I've dreamed of killing her for some time now. It would be no hardship."

Jonathan threw the knife without a second thought. It

clattered and skittered across the floor, coming to rest some-where in the shadows.

He would have to use his hands.

"If you shoot her, you'll have used your bullet. And then I'll come after you." Jonathan thought he saw a movement behind Frobisher, and realized he was looking at the servants' stairs on the opposite side of the kitchen. Resisting the urge to stare harder, he kept his gaze on Frobisher's face. Waiting for the moment when he lowered the gun.

"It'll be worth the risk to know she's dead, and you had to watch her die." Frobisher shuffled toward the stairs to the kitchen door again, and the gun barrel dipped down.

Jonathan was gathering himself to leap, when a frying pan came down from above Frobisher's head and smacked him full force.

Frobisher went down, conscious but dazed, and Miss Bar-rington lunged for the kitchen table, flicked open what looked like a bundle of linen and pulled a wicked-looking fillet knife out of it.

Iris stood with the pan held two-handed in her grasp, ready to strike again, and Jonathan belatedly realized that Frobisher had dropped the pistol and that it had slid almost to his feet. He picked it up, then pointed it straight at Frobisher's heart.

"I were too sick at heart to go out with the others," Iris said, her voice hushed. "I heard voices down here and came to see what was what."

"I told you you were a Valkyrie," Miss Barrington said. She sat down on a chair and winced as she lifted a hand to the cut across her throat. "And I congratulate you on choosing exactly the right person to fall in battle."

———————

As he walked to his club, Jonathan felt as if he were in the limbo of a soldier waiting for the call to arms. All was ready, everything prepared—but until the enemy entered the field, there was nothing to be done but wait.

He gave a half grin at what Giselle Barrington would think of being compared to an enemy army.

She'd probably enjoy it.

She was a force to be reckoned with. She had proved that in everything she'd done.

He couldn't count the number of times he'd looked down toward Goldfern and forced himself not to walk in that direction, unsure whether he'd have the self-control not to knock.

He didn't know what he would do if that knock were answered.

Everything he wanted to say would be in poor taste, given that she was mourning her father and recovering from a knife attack.

And so he waited. Wanting desperately to engage, to clash, to fight for his place in her life. But while she remained behind those massive double doors in her massive house, waiting was all he could do.

He turned the corner, and as a hoot of raucous laughter sounded from the entrance of his club, Jonathan slowed his steps.

Henry Ingleton and three friends stepped out, loud, brash and cocky. He felt a surge of pure anticipation.

The smell of violence about to erupt always had the tangy, hot scent of metal to him, the sweat of horses and men, and the crushed green of bushes and grass trampled underfoot. It was so clear, he could almost feel he was drawing it into his lungs on this cold London street.

He'd made a promise to two women, and realized with a sense of shame that he hadn't done anything about it. Almost five days had passed since he'd come across Lord Matherton's and Sir Ingleton's cooks talking about the danger Henry posed to one of the maids.

He hoped it wasn't too late.

"Ingleton." He tried to keep his voice level, but one of Ingleton's friends eyed him more cautiously than was normal on meeting a fellow club member. He must not be hiding his hunger for a confrontation well enough.

Ingleton swung his way, perfectly sober but, by the looks of it, in high spirits.

Ah, youth.

Jonathan smiled, and Ingleton's step faltered. He lost some of the smug amusement on his face.

"What is it?"

"A friendly warning." Jonathan kept the smile on his face, and Ingleton blinked.

"I have it on good authority that you're a lech, Ingleton. You prey on the staff in your father's house—women who can't fight back against you without fearing at the least the loss of their jobs. I can't understand how abusing your power with women who have none of their own could possibly be stimulating—but then, I'm not a bully who obviously can't get women any other way but by coercion and force." He spoke almost pleasantly, keeping himself loose and ready.

Ingleton was white around the lips, his eyes bulging. "Who—?" He swallowed. "How dare—?"

"I'll be happy to talk to your father about this, the next time I see him at the club. And I won't keep my voice down. I'm happy to speak to any number of society ladies about it, too. Lady Durnham and her sister-in-law, Lady Holliday, spring readily to mind. They're sure to pass on the information to the mamas of the ton. No one likes a husband who diddles the staff. Especially when the staff aren't willing."

He cocked his head. "I'm sure your mother will hear about it, too, eventually. Although perhaps she knows already? Or suspects? If so, more shame on her."

He was hoping Ingleton would be rash enough to strike out, and he wasn't disappointed. But it was a poor attempt, sloppy and ridiculously off.

He stepped to the side to avoid it, and realized with disappointment that he couldn't justify hitting back.

It would be too uneven a match.

Something in his face must have registered, because Ingleton dropped his arm, breathing heavily.

"I would love to thrash you." Jonathan could hear the leashed wolf in his voice; it was almost a croon. "Give me one more excuse and I will."

Ingleton staggered back.

"I have a number of sources regarding your behavior, and I will hear if you so much as look incorrectly at your maids again."

He didn't bother keeping his voice low, and Ingleton's eyes went wildly to his friends and back.

"I understand you're responsible for one maid being fired because she was carrying your child, and I want to hear from my sources that you've provided for her. I give you until tomorrow afternoon to see to it. And it had better be a generous provision."

Ingleton stared at him.

"You can go." He crossed his arms over his chest and watched Ingleton stagger back to his group.

Bringing down Ingleton didn't quite make up for being outdone by his maid in dealing with Frobisher, but it helped a little.

"Do I want to know what that was about?" Durnham murmured from behind him, and Jonathan looked over his shoulder with a slow grin.

"Probably not."

He waited for Durnham to reach him on the pavement, and they both watched Ingleton as he walked away.

"What's the news on Frobisher?" Jonathan asked.

Durnham sighed. "He'll hang. There is no doubt about it. But he won't say who his paymasters are. Maybe we'll get an execution-day confession."

"Why won't he talk?"

"Spite, I think. Because we won't lessen the sentence." Durnham hunched his shoulders against the evening air and held out a letter. "This came from Dervish with the evening post. He and Greenway were tying up some loose ends for Barrington in Stockholm and arranging for his body to be transported home. They'll take the next available boat back to England."

"Does Miss Barrington know?"

Durnham lifted his brows. "I'm not sure. Greenway may have written to her." He paused. "How does the land lie between you? When you thought she was your cook . . ."

Jonathan said nothing, and after a moment, Durnham gave a sigh and patted him on the shoulder.

"Come to dinner tomorrow night. My wife has invited your former cook as well. If she doesn't already know it, you can tell her the news yourself."

36

She had accepted the invitation to dinner at Lord and Lady Durnham's with some reluctance.

She still felt like a mouse, one that wanted to hide in its little house a bit longer and gather its courage. And then she laughed at herself for even thinking of massive Goldfern as a mouse hole.

And here she was at this dinner, anyway.

She was *le chat botté*, Puss in Boots, although boots were not fashionable at dinner parties, so she was wearing very pretty satin slippers instead.

It was a small affair. The Durnhams and their close family, as well as Lord Aldridge and the Duke of Wittaker.

They were all strangers to her, really. Even the Durnhams, who had been so kind to her over the last few days since Frobisher had been brought down.

Mrs. Jones had carefully dressed her knife wound and then draped a choker of pearls over it, so that it was almost invisible, but she kept lifting a hand to it and then forcing it back down to her side.

Lord Aldridge moved easily through the small group, greeting everyone with his quick smile and innate charm. She liked watching him; it created the same tension and excitement in her that she always had at the start of a new trip with her father.

He was an adventure come to life.

Even though the facade of a society gentleman was troweled on thick tonight, there was still a hint of the savage beneath, the man who could burst into deadly, immediate action, who could fly down stairs as if he had wings.

Lady Howe, Lady Durnham's former guardian, placed a hand on his arm and engaged him in conversation, and Gigi moved her gaze to Wittaker. He was playing the sober nobleman tonight, in tune with the mood of the gathering—the drunk, sardonic duke was nowhere to be seen.

She didn't think this more conservative behavior was his true self, either.

He noticed her watching him, and turned her way. She had the sense he'd known she was looking since the moment she'd focused on him. He moved across the room to her, and they stood where Gigi had positioned herself, slightly apart from everyone else.

He glanced down at her throat. "Neck all right?"

"It is." She resisted the urge to raise her hand to it again.

"I would like to speak frankly with you, Miss Barrington." Wittaker gave her a sidelong look. "I have to admit I know

the nature of the letter you carried, due to various commit-
tees I sit on, and I'm curious: why didn't you ask Georges to
give it to me?"

"I did." She paused and saw she had his full attention now.
"Georges said you were fighting the Crown over some taxes,
and he thought you might throw it in the fire, just for spite."

He turned fully to face her, looking genuinely shocked.
"Did he?"

"You were playing the drunk and dissolute rake a little too
well, as it turns out. You even had Georges convinced you
were nothing but a wastrel, and it takes a fine skill to get past
Georges." She gave him a smile as his mouth gaped. "It would
have saved a great deal of trouble, pain and suffering if you
hadn't been so good at your act, but *c'est la vie*." She gave a
very French shrug.

Her eyes strayed inevitably to Lord Aldridge and as she
watched, he gave Lady Howe a bow and walked over to join
them.

"Miss Barrington." Lord Aldridge bowed. "You look a little
at sea, Wittaker."

Gigi tried not to smile but a small one leaked out, until she
realized the two men were staring at each other, sharing a
long, cool look that she could not decipher.

Then at last Wittaker swung his gaze to her, looking at her
from under lashes almost as long as hers. There was that wry
amusement again. "I'm thoroughly put in my place. I didn't
know your father, but in knowing you, I begin to see why he
was so respected."

It was her turn to be surprised, but before she could answer, he gave a smart bow and moved off.

She kept her gaze on him to avoid looking at Lord Aldridge for a moment longer. She liked watching him from afar, but close up, it gave her the sense of journeying in an out-of-control carriage over rough road. Thrilling, but inherently dangerous.

"He's right, you know. You've done your father proud. We didn't think you were even alive—but you not only were alive, you made it to England, with the letter safe, and were able to hide yourself and smoke out a traitor." He reached out a hand as if to touch her and then dropped it. "You are a most unusual woman, Miss Barrington."

Her breath caught and at last she turned to face him. She had been told too often in the last few days that she was different, but this time, she didn't mind. "Thank you. It will be hard to settle into this life at first, I think. I'm used to traveling to wild places and meeting all manner of interesting people."

"It sounds like being in the army." Aldridge's lips twisted up in a smile. "It is hard at first, getting used to a more conventional life. But there are ways to make up for it. Other excitements to be had."

"Like acting as an agent for the Crown?" She was teasing him, but the jerk of his shoulders told her she'd hit a mark.

She quirked a brow. "Don't worry, I won't be applying. I'll leave the skulduggery to you. I have another project to tackle, and the three opinions I've had on the matter so far tell me I'll have my work cut out for me."

"We've had a letter from Lord Dervish that you may be interested in." He changed the topic abruptly, keeping his voice low.

"Yes?"

"Durnham's message that you are here in London, safe, and the letter is in the right hands, reached him. He and Greenway had just returned from Lapland, and they were dealing with your father's affairs in Stockholm. Arranging for his body to be brought back, and they're bringing someone with them. Pierre Durand."

Her breath caught. "Pierre? That is wonderful."

"Who is he?"

"My chef." She gave him a smile. "Much better than I in the kitchen. Georges used to be his sous-chef. I am, too, when he lets me in the kitchen."

Aldridge gave a short laugh. "Doesn't seem fair Goldfern will have two master chefs, when I haven't had a decent meal in five days." There was something in his face, a yearning that she hadn't seen before. She didn't think it was to do with the food.

"You've been very quiet, sequestered in your house."

"I told you once before, my lord. I am the little mouse." She laid on the French accent again to make him smile. "I curl up in my house for a bit, to get my courage up."

"Courage for what? Frobisher is caught." He frowned, but the lost look was gone, and she liked it better that way.

"To face the world without my father, without my old life. The loss of all the traveling, the adventures . . ." She blushed, her mind flashing up the image of them in his study, kissing.

He leaned back against the wall. "You told me you wouldn't hold me accountable for my behavior toward you in my house." It was so close to what she was thinking, she had to look away in case he could somehow read her thoughts.

"Yes, I did."

The bell rang for dinner, a soft, deep chime that had everyone heading for the dining room.

"I wanted to ask you if you would. Please. Hold me accountable."

She drew in a sharp breath. Excitement pricked at the back of her neck and along her arms, and she smiled as he held out his arm to escort her in to dinner.

"You never know, Lord Aldridge. Maybe I will."

AUTHOR'S NOTE

In April 1812, Russia, England and Sweden signed secret agreements against France. Russia was in an alliance with France at that time, but relations between the two countries had deteriorated since 1810. Sir Edward Thornton was the British diplomat in Sweden who brokered the agreements between the three countries. However, while the secret deal making is quite true, everything that happens in this book regarding how those deals came to be is purely my imagination at work.

BANQUET OF LIES

MICHELLE DIENER

Giselle Barrington is a young woman whose experience of life is far outside that of most of her peers. Well-traveled and well-educated, and unstifled by the rules and unspoken taboos of the British aristocracy, she has lived an adventurous and fulfilling life with her father, an independently wealthy and knighted folklorist.

Because of Giselle's father's unusual occupation, which takes him to corners of the world that no Englishman would normally travel, he has accepted the role of secret courier for the British government at the behest of personal friends of his who work at high levels for the Crown.

When he is forced out into the open by a traitor in Stockholm, and dies rather than reveal Giselle to his killers, Giselle is determined not only to complete the mission her father committed them to—to deliver an important diplomatic document in London—but also to bring his killer to justice. She has never seen the man's face, but she knows he is an Englishman, and that no one in the British Foreign Office can be trusted.

Using her intelligence and experience, she flees to London and gets in touch with the only person she can trust in the city: the man who used to work as a sous-chef in her family's kitchens in London, the now celebrated master chef Georges Bisset. With his help, she finds herself only a few doors down from her own family home—a place where she is sure her father's killer will come looking for her—pretending to be a French cook for Lord Aldridge. She vaguely remembers Aldridge from her childhood and she knows her parents liked him and his family. That's enough to make her feel safe, for the moment.

But, of course, she isn't just pretending to be a cook, she actually has to be one, and she slowly learns the position is not simply about making excellent food. It comes with responsibilities and political strings in the belowstairs world of the servant pecking order. In this environment, Giselle makes more than a few mistakes, unwittingly creating an enemy who will almost be her undoing, with all her energy and focus on the man who killed her father and who is searching the streets of London for her.

But although Giselle does not navigate the belowstairs waters as nimbly as she cooks or puts clues together, her honesty and genuinely good heart win her allies too. She also begins to realize that the consequences of her subterfuge will have far-reaching effects. She interacts more and more with her new employer, Jonathan Aldridge, and as his fascination with her grows, she becomes uncomfortably aware that anything that happens between them as servant and master will be seen very differently when Aldridge discovers that they are actually social equals.

When both the enemy outside the walls of her safe house and the one inside gain the upper hand, and Giselle is at the mercy of a system skewed very much against women with no wealth or station behind them, she begins to fully realize how gilded and lucky her life as a member of the upper class is.

Topics and Questions for Discussion

1. The book opens in Stockholm, with the tense and devastating murder of Giselle's father. What do we learn about Giselle's relationship with her father from the subtle messages Eric Barrington sends to her as he plays mind games with his soon-to-be killer?

2. What do we learn about Giselle herself when she meets with Georges Bisset for the first time? She is the daughter of Georges's former boss, but does this come across? Is this the meeting of friends? Mentor and student? Or something else altogether?

3. Recall your first impression of Edgars. What is the first thing he tries to do when he meets Giselle, and is this consistent with his

character throughout the book? Do you sense a duality in him, that he is fighting two sides of his nature?

4. What side of Giselle is revealed by her first meeting with Edgars? Until this point in the story, she has been under threat and devastated by grief. Does the way she handles him show the reader a new aspect of her personality? In a good or a bad way?

5. What kind of work environment does Giselle step into when she starts working for Aldridge, and how do the decisions she, Edgars and Iris make throughout the book change this?

6. What is your first impression of Aldridge? How do you think he is changed by the events in the book and do you think—his relationship with Gigi aside—he is more comfortable in his own skin by the end of the book?

7. There are numerous examples of female friendship in the novel. Gigi's friendship with Iris, Iris's relationships with Mavis and Babs and the short but intense friendship Gigi forms with the prostitutes in her cell at Queen Square Public Office— even the relationship between Mrs. Thakery and Mrs. Lambert, the cooks from down the road, and the short interaction they have with Gigi. How do these relationships move the novel forward, and enrich the characters' lives?

8. The discussions Gigi has with the prostitutes in the cell at Queen Square reconfirm what she has just learned, that she is almost invisible in the eyes of society in the role she has taken on. What impact does this have on her, and how do these scenes enrich the novel?

9. What are your thoughts on Aldridge's fascination with Gigi? Did your opinion about his motives toward her change through the novel?

10. How justified is Gigi in fearing the consequences of her actions with Aldridge when he later discovers the truth about her? Did you think Aldridge would react the way he did when he learned who she really was, and why do you think his reaction was so strong?

11. Consider the two villains in *Banquet of Lies*. Would you give them equal status, or do you think Edgars is the more understandable and sympathetic of the two? Or the worst?

12. Discuss the fairy-tale analogies that run through the book. Did this enrich the novel for you? Did you find the analogies appropriate?

13. Discuss the food in the book and the role it plays, both as a means to divide some of the characters and set them against each other (Edgars and Gigi), or bring them together (Aldridge and Gigi), or even open them to new friendships and experiences (Babs, Iris, Mavis, Rob and Harry).

14. Although the reader never discovers the details of Dervish's relationship with Gigi's parents, the food he eats obviously evokes strong memories of them for him, and a difficult time in his own life. Do you sometimes experience food in the same way, as a means to travel either geographically or to a certain moment in time, much like music?

15. Throughout *Banquet of Lies* a number of people refer to the Duke of Wittaker, and the reader slowly builds up an image of him and what he is like. How is this subverted at the end of the book?

Enhance Your Book Club

1. If you want to make some of the dishes Gigi serves up in *Banquet of Lies* at your book club, go to the author's website and you'll find them here: http://www.michellediener.com/books/banquet-of-lies/recipes-from-banquet-of-lies/.

2. For more Regency recipes, you can go here: http://www.janeausten.co.uk/online-magazine/regency-recipes/. *The Cookbook of Unknown Ladies* is another gem, handwritten and filled with recipes from the early 1700s through the mid-nineteenth century: http://lostcookbook.wordpress.com/tag/regency-cookery/.

3. The author did a great deal of research into chefs of the Regency period, including the history and recipes of the most famous chef of that time, Antonin Carême. This three-and-a-half-minute snippet shows British chef Heston Blumenthal making one of Antonin Carême's favorite recipes, cock's testicles, which was the inspiration for the threat Georges makes to Jonathan Aldridge when he comes to speak to him about Gigi: http://www.youtube.com/watch?v=mZCkW23Y8hQ.

4. For a virtual look at Tessin Palace in Stockholm, where *Banquet of Lies* opens, you can download this beautiful brochure of the palace and its gardens: http://www.lansstyrelsen.se/stockholm/SiteCollectionDocuments/Sv/publikationer/2012/tessinska-palatset-engelska-2.tr-2012.pdf.